Now and Then

Hart's Ridge

Kay Bratt

Now and Then

A Hart's Ridge Novel

Books by Kay Bratt

Hart's Ridge Series
Hart's Ridge

Lucy in the Sky

In My Life

Borrowed Time

Instant Karma

Nobody Told Me

Hello Goodbye

Starting Over

Blackbird

Hello Little Girl

So This is Christmas

Every Little Thing

Now and Then

Tell Me Why

By the Sea trilogy
True to Me

No Place too Far

Into the Blue

The Tales of the Scavenger's Daughters series
The Palest Ink

The Scavenger's Daughters

Tangled Vines

Bitter Winds

Red Skies

Life of Willow duology

Somewhere Beautiful

Where I Belong

Standalone Novels

Wish Me Home

Dancing with the Sun

Silent Tears; A Journey of Hope in a Chinese Orphanage

Chasing China; A Daughter's Quest for Truth

A Thread Unbroken

Train to Nowhere

The Bridge

Caroline, Adrift

The Wishing Tree series

The Wishing Tree

Wish You Were Here

Wishful Thinking

A Wish in the Wind

Dragonfly Cove Dog Park series

Pick of the Litter

Collar Me Crazy

Copyright © 2025 by Kay Bratt

All rights reserved. This book or any portion thereof may not be reproduced or used in any manner whatsoever without the express written permission of the publisher except for the use of brief quotations in a book review.

Printed in the United States of America

First Printing, 2025

Red Thread Publishing Group

Hartwell, GA 30643

www.kaybratt.com

Cover Design by Elizabeth Mackey Graphic Design

Disclaimer

This book is a fictional dramatization that includes one incident inspired by a real event. Facts to support that incident were drawn from a variety of sources, including published materials and interviews, then altered to fit into the fictional story. Otherwise, this book contains fictionalized scenes, composite and representative characters and dialogue, and time compression, all modified for dramatic and narrative purposes. The views and opinions expressed in the book are those of the fictional characters only and do not necessarily reflect or represent the views and opinions held by individuals on which any of the characters are based.

Chapter One

Janelle Tiffin sat in her kitchen, the dull hum of her old laptop the only sound that filled the quiet room. The smell of the bologna sandwich, its edges slightly crispy from the toaster, mingled with the faint scent of dog shampoo lingering in the air from her grooming business just outside. Her fingers hovered over the keyboard, but she didn't type anything. She just stared at the screen. The Facebook feed was an endless scroll of what could have been, snapshots of people living their best lives—friends and family enjoying dinners, vacations, birthdays, and celebrations.

Her eyes landed on a photo posted by her brother, Samuel. There were pictures of his two granddaughters, Alice and Lennon, smiling wide in a park, their faces full of innocence and joy. She felt the familiar pang in her chest, the emptiness that seemed to widen every time she saw her family moving forward without her.

Without Clem.

It had been nearly ten years since her husband had been locked away, convicted of murder and aggravated assault, a crime he swore he didn't commit. A crime that took away her mother's life and nearly killed her niece. But no one cared what Clem had said—what they cared about was the child's testimony, how she said the assailant looked like her Uncle Clem. That was all it took for the town to condemn and the justice system to fail him.

Janelle's thumb hovered over the mouse, the cursor blinking next to the words "like" and "comment" under Samuel's post. But she didn't click anything. Her heart just wasn't in it anymore. The world had moved on from her, and she had nothing left to contribute. The dog grooming business she ran in her backyard shop barely kept the bills paid, and it was hard not to see the way the town looked at her—like she was a leper, a woman whose husband was a murderer, tainting everything she touched.

Her friends had all disappeared, one by one. The ones who had been close, the ones who had promised to always stand by her—none of them had stuck around. Eventually they'd either turned their backs on her, or, worse, told her to "face the truth" and stop waiting for Clem.

They had no idea what it was like to watch someone you loved be thrown into the darkness of a prison cell for a crime they didn't commit, and then be forced to live with the cloud of a town's hatred.

Her fingers absentmindedly picked at the crust of her sandwich as her eyes drifted back to the screen. The next post was from her nephew, Sam. She clicked on his profile, staring at the photos of him with his wife, Taylor, and their kids at the farm. The older girl was the spitting image of Sam. Hard to tell who the baby was going to look like yet.

They all looked so happy. Why wouldn't they be? They had everything—a family, a booming business with a side rescue, a life that looked so full and bright.

Everything she'd once had.

Something new, too. Graystone Investigations, she noticed. Sam's wife had a career in law enforcement and now they'd opened a detective agency. So that's where they had landed, in a world that seemed so far removed from hers, yet ironic in nature.

Janelle couldn't help but wonder: Why couldn't they have done it back when she needed help? When Clem was first arrested, when she tried to get someone, anyone, to look at the evidence that had been overlooked, when she fought against a town that refused to see anything other than what they wanted to believe—where was Sam then?

Well, she supposed he hadn't yet met Taylor Gray back then. Was probably still in the military, working himself up into the life he had now.

But now, she didn't know how to ask for help. She had no right to. Her nephew looked happy with his life. She wasn't about to drag him into her mess. She hadn't even seen him since he was a teenager.

Still, there was something about Taylor's page that caught her attention. The warmth in the photos, the way the family seemed so tight-knit—it made her ache with longing. She wished she had that. She wished she had someone to turn to.

Janelle clicked on the next post in her feed. A news article. She almost scrolled past it—until a photo caught her eye.

She froze. Her heart skipped a beat. The mugshot attached to the article was grainy, but the face—God, the face—was evil. Someone named Ed Mannopi had been convicted of molesting his three daughters. She stared at the photograph of the man, trying to shake the tingle crawling up her spine.

He looked so much like Clem.

Her hands shook as she clicked on the article. Ed Mannopi had been sentenced for his crimes that took place in the next county over. It was a small town not far from hers, a place she'd driven through many times over the years, but never thought twice about.

What if?

The thought hit her like a bolt of lightning. The chances were slim, she knew that. But could it be? She fully believed that Clem's conviction was a mistake, a rush to judgment based on a child's misidentification.

What if this Ed Mannopi had been in the area when her mother was killed? Her niece beaten and traumatized.

Janelle rubbed her temples, trying to fight off the waves of doubt crashing over her. *Maybe I'm just desperate,* she thought. *Maybe I am delusional like everyone says I am.*

But she couldn't ignore the pull. The thought that there might be something here.

She sat back in her chair, her eyes shifting to the framed photo of Clem on the wall. It was from years ago, the two of them at Dollywood for their anniversary, smiling like they had all the time in the world. Clem had always been so certain of their future. The future they were supposed to have, rocking on the front porch, traveling together in retirement.

Instead, Clem was locked away, and Janelle was alone.

He'd even told her to move on, to start living her life without him. But she couldn't.

Didn't even want to.

Not without her Clem.

Her finger hovered over the message button on Sam's Facebook page. What would he think hearing from his old aunt, out of the blue?

She didn't know what to say, or if he would even help her. But for the first time in a long time, she felt a glimmer of hope.

With a deep breath, she clicked the message icon.

"Sam, I need your help."

Chapter Two

Andy Warhol once said that the idea of waiting for something makes it more exciting. Taylor wasn't sure about that, but she was happy to have arrived in Indiana. After a long day of traveling, with Lennon pretty much being a great car rider other than a few bumpy moments, Sam eased to a stop in front of Janelle's small, modest house in Kokomo. The porch light flickered softly in the evening gloom, illuminating shadows across the overgrown yard. The lawn looked as though it had been recently mowed, but the driveway was choked with weeds. The house itself, a once-cheerful shade of pale yellow, had faded with age and neglect, its peeling paint reflecting the toll of years spent alone.

Taylor felt a pang of sympathy for Sam's Aunt Janelle, imagining the isolation she must have experienced in this crumbling home. It was as though time had stopped for Janelle, the world moving on around her while she stayed stuck in this small, forgotten place.

Sam's face was unreadable as he surveyed the house through the front windshield.

"So, this is it, huh? Our first big case as Graystone Investigations," he said, his voice trying to sound light, though Taylor could hear the hint of uncertainty there. It wasn't that Sam wasn't confident in her abilities—he was—but Taylor could tell he was carrying the pain of family history into this one. "I mean, the case has been closed for almost ten years. The little girl identified my uncle as the attacker. It's pretty cut and dried, right? I just don't want you to get your hopes up that we can do anything more than what my aunt has already tried to do."

Taylor exhaled softly, her gaze turning toward him. She ran a hand through her hair, trying to shake the unease. "Not everything is what it seems. You always tell me that. Let's at least hear her out before we make up our minds." She paused, her eyes softening as she glanced at the house again. "After all, she's your family, and it was your grandmother who was murdered."

"I guess it won't hurt to hear her out. I don't remember much about the case, since I was away, but, now that I'm older, I'd like to know the details firsthand."

They'd spent the day before combing through everything they could find online about the case. Nothing stood out to Taylor that the wrong man had been convicted, but reading articles and rumors on the internet was different than hearing what really happened.

As Sam opened his door and climbed out, she kept her eyes on him. He unbuckled Lennon from her car seat with practiced ease, securing their one-and-a-half-year-old daughter snugly in the baby papoose around his chest. Lennon stirred slightly but didn't wake. Taylor found herself watching Sam for a moment longer, her heart catching in her chest.

He's so good with her, Taylor thought. It never ceased to amaze her how effortlessly Sam had embraced fatherhood. It was like it came naturally to him, as if he'd always been meant to be a father. She had never once doubted his ability to love and care for their daughter, but it still caught her off guard sometimes, how he seemed to embody fatherhood so effortlessly.

It was one of the reasons she had fallen for him in the first place. Watching how he was with Alice. And now with their baby, she'd definitely chosen the right life partner.

He turned to her, the baby carrier securely fastened. "Ready?"

Taylor snapped out of her thoughts, straightening in her seat and grabbing the diaper bag. "Yeah," she said, pushing a smile onto her lips. "Let's do this."

They walked toward the porch. The old wood creaked underfoot, the smell of fresh-cut grass mixing with the faint scent of dog shampoo that lingered in the air. Taylor's heart ached for Janelle. She could only imagine the loneliness that had settled in these walls over the years, the loneliness that seemed to hang in the air like the dust she saw floating through the light from the porch.

How long had Janelle been waiting for someone to listen to her?

The door opened just as they reached the top of the porch steps. Janelle's face was tight, her expression anxious, but she managed a small, nervous smile. Her hands, which had been wringing at the edges of her shirt, now stilled at her sides.

"Sam," she said, stepping forward to pull him into a tight hug.

"Aunt Janelle. Nice to see you again," Sam said warmly, patting her back before pulling away.

Janelle broke away from Sam and looked at Taylor, her expression full of uncertainty. "And this must be Taylor," she said, extending her hand. "Thank you so much for coming."

Taylor took it, offering a firm handshake. "Yes, nice to meet you."

Janelle smiled faintly at Lennon's head, her eyes lingering

on the baby. Then she glanced nervously toward the house behind her, as though searching for reassurance from the walls themselves. "Well, come in, come in. I've got coffee on."

Taylor nodded as she followed Janelle inside. The warmth of the house hit her immediately, the contrast between the chilly night air and the cozy interior stark. As they moved toward the small kitchen table, Taylor noticed a sense of exhaustion in the air, the kind that only time and struggle could breed.

"How's your dad doing, Sam?" Janelle asked.

She bustled around the counter, gathering cups and saucers, pouring drinks with a practiced but slightly erratic hand. Her movements seemed hurried, as though she was trying to fill the silence with action. Yet there was a steadiness to her—a woman used to holding things together on her own. Taylor wondered how long Janelle had been holding everything in, waiting for someone to listen, to believe.

"He's fine," Sam said. "He's too fidgety to retire, so I have him supervising my mechanic shop now. I hired two guys to do the dirty work, but Dad likes to be involved. He also likes it that I'm stepping away from the garage to try something else."

"That's good," she replied. "I'll admit, I was surprised to see that you are doing investigations. I know your dad passed a lot of skills down to you that have come in handy."

"He sure did. Had me putting in my own carburetor and changing tires when I was thirteen," Sam laughed. "Oh, and calling what we're doing investigations right now might be a stretch. So far, it's been mostly people wanting to see what their spouses are up to when they aren't around, and a few lost pet cases. But everyone has to start somewhere."

Taylor nodded in approval. She knew it wouldn't be easy leaving the department and branching out on her own, but she had high hopes they'd done the right thing. Only time would tell.

Finally, Janelle sat down across from Sam and Taylor, her hands trembling slightly as she held her mug. "I—I'm not sure where to begin," she said, her eyes flickering between Sam and Taylor, then down at the table. "I guess we should talk about your fee first. I have to admit, our savings is gone, and I'm nickel-and-diming just to get by. But I could perhaps take out another loan?"

Sam gave her a reassuring smile, trying to put her at ease. "Don't worry about that right now. Just take your time and tell us exactly what happened. Why do you think Clem didn't do it?"

Janelle's eyes seemed to dim for a moment as she took a steadying breath. "Well, let's go back to the night my mother was killed." She took another breath, the words sitting heavily in the room. "My niece, little Amy—I don't think you've met her, Sam—was staying with my mom that night and was beaten unconscious. When she woke, she walked over to the neighbor's and knocked on their door. I'll never forget the phone call I got. Amy beaten badly and my mother—your grandmother, Sam—well, she was ... gone."

Her voice cracked on the last word, but she quickly composed herself. "The police were certain it was Clem. They said that Amy's statement made it clear—she said the assailant looked like him. But I know my husband. Clem would never hurt a child, never. Not only that, but he was with me during the projected time span of the attack. I know that for a fact because I stayed up late doing a puzzle, then I had a hard time sleeping. I was still tossing and turning in the wee hours of the night when the event happened."

"What time do they think it happened?" Taylor asked.

"Between two-thirty and five in the morning. But Clem got home at two-thirty after being out drinking with friends. Even a neighbor testified to that, having seen his headlights pulling in."

Out drinking with friends and just got home at the beginning of the projected time of the attack wasn't a very good alibi, Taylor thought.

"Mom's house is an hour from here. He could not have done it, then got back here by three in the morning, all cleaned up without a speck of blood anywhere on him or his truck."

"Amy later recanted, right?" Taylor asked.

"Yes," Janelle said. "She was so young when it happened. So traumatized. She eventually said that she'd only told the neighbor that the assailant *reminded* her of her Uncle Clem, because that was the only man she could think to compare him to with his size and hair color."

Sam nodded, his eyes soft with understanding. "And you think there was something wrong with the investigation? Something they missed?"

Janelle looked up at him, her eyes fierce. "Yes, I do. They had tunnel vision from the very beginning. Just as soon as Amy said Clem's name, they didn't even look at anyone else. Just Clem. I gave them his alibi. I gave them everything I could find that might help. I even made a list of criminals in the area—people who might have had a reason to do something like this—but they didn't want to hear it. They were so focused on Clem."

"Dad said the DNA found on Alma was inconclusive for a match," Sam said.

Janelle nodded. "That's right. So that shows it wasn't his, right? We filed for an appeal immediately, but it was denied. The judge ruled that, because the jury convicted Clem without the DNA originally, it's likely he would have been convicted even if it didn't match."

"No, that's not the way it works," Taylor said. "If it's inconclusive, it still could be your husband's."

"It's not," Janelle said confidently.

Now and Then

Taylor took a sip of her coffee, her eyes narrowing as she watched Janelle closely. The woman's pain was palpable, ten years of heartache spent fighting alone hanging in the air. What was it like for Sam to grow up with this history? He'd never even mentioned it until his aunt had reached out. She glanced at Sam, who sat quietly, his jaw set with determination. When she'd asked him about why he'd never mentioned it, he'd shrugged it off, saying he didn't think much about it after Clem was convicted. Having a convicted murderer in the family wasn't something he liked people to know.

How strange it must have been for him to carry that secret silently for so long.

Janelle continued, her voice growing steadier. "After Clem was convicted, everyone I knew— all of my friends—they started drifting away. One by one, they told me to face the truth—that Clem had done it. I just couldn't believe it. I know him, and he's a good man. I know he didn't do this." She paused, her gaze drifting toward the window as if searching for something outside. After a long moment, she turned back to Sam and Taylor. "And then, just a few days ago, I saw a picture online of a man named Ed Mannopi. I swear to God, Sam, he looks just like Clem. He lived in the next county over and was convicted of molesting his three daughters."

Taylor cringed internally.

"—when I saw that mugshot, I just—I just couldn't shake it."

Sam leaned forward, his expression intent. "Aunt Janelle, I'm sorry, but—"

Janelle hesitated, her fingers gripping the edge of her coffee cup. "I know it's a long shot, Sam. I know it sounds crazy. But when I looked at his picture, it felt like a sign. I don't believe in coincidences. I just—something in my gut tells me that Clem didn't do it, and maybe Ed Mannopi is the one who really did."

She took a shaky breath, her eyes welling with unshed tears. "I know it's crazy. But I need someone to believe me. I need someone to finally find out the truth."

Taylor exchanged a glance with Sam. What would be the odds that his aunt would come across the photo of the murderer her husband was doing time for? It sounded impossible. Too good to be true.

Sam gave her a small nod, then turned back to Janelle. "We'll take a closer look, Janelle."

Janelle's eyes brightened, a flicker of hope sparking within them.

He smiled gently. "But let's not get ahead of ourselves. First, we'll start investigating as if the case is brand new. Interview everyone we can find, talk to Clem and, unfortunately, also Amy. Then we'll dig into this Ed Mannopi guy and see what we can uncover. If there's anything there that shows any connection whatsoever to what happened to my grandmother and Amy, we'll find it."

Janelle nodded, her shoulders relaxing slightly. "Thank you, Sam. Thank you both. I—I don't know what to say."

Taylor reached over and placed a hand on Janelle's. "You don't have to say anything. We're in this together now but, please, don't get your hopes up too much. We don't want you to be too shattered if this turns out to be nothing.

As Janelle looked between them, a tear slipped down her cheek. This time, it was not from sorrow. Despite Taylor's warning, Janelle was going to allow the first tear of hope she'd felt in ten years.

The small Airbnb cottage felt like a cozy retreat from the long, exhausting day. After putting Lennon to bed in the tiny extra bedroom, Sam and Taylor climbed into bed, both of them still dressed in their travel clothes. Taylor kicked off her shoes and propped herself up against the headboard, grabbing the bag of Doritos they'd picked up from the convenience store earlier. She opened it with a satisfying crinkle and took a handful, tossing the chips into her mouth.

Sam, already cracking open a can of Dr. Pepper, leaned back against the pillows beside her. They sat in silence for a few moments, the only sound the soft crunching of chips and the occasional fizz from Sam's soda can.

Taylor's phone sounded off and she picked it up, reading the text message. It was from Lucy, and included a dozen photos of Bea, short for Bianca Catherine Vanzo, the newest addition to the Gray family tree.

Lucy and Jorge were head over heels with their new daughter, and who wouldn't be? She'd arrived looking like a masterpiece, and a mini of her father. Dark hair, eyes, and a deliciously kissed skin color, a stranger would never guess that her mother was their fair Lucy.

Bea was only two months old and already the queen of the household. According to her sister, even Johnny was enamored. They were all hoping to meet her at Christmas time.

Thankfully, Lucy was doing well in her new life, and Taylor believed that starting over somewhere, with the solid support from Jorge, was the key. In Uruguay, Lucy was far away from all the mistakes she'd made, and judgment from those who knew her. She'd made a new friend, a girl named Catalina from the farmer's market. Lucy called her Cat, and, when Jorge locked himself away to finish a painting, the girl was a lifeline to keep Lucy from being too lonely.

Not that Jorge did that often, but, with all the renovations they were doing, they still needed to keep funds coming in, so he hadn't stepped away from his work completely.

Taylor scrolled to one of the photos in which Lucy was holding Bea up to her face and they were smiling at each other. She zoomed in, focusing on her sister's eyes, analyzing every square inch of her face.

Yes, Lucy looked happier and more at peace than Taylor had ever seen her.

In their last phone call, they were talking about deep things like the perils of raising daughters, then Lucy had lightened the mood by saying the most important advice she needed to pass on was for Bea to be very, very careful with whatever she decided to do to her eyebrows.

Taylor smiled to herself. They could always depend on Lucy to come up with something off the wall, or funny, or just totally inappropriate. Taylor missed her more than she'd thought possible.

Finally, Sam broke the silence, his voice low but curious. "So, how does this work? Getting the information from the police files? As private investigators, will we be able to get all the files from the Kokomo Police Department?"

Taylor took a sip of her own soda before responding, her fingers tapping absentmindedly on the bedspread. "Maybe not. That always depends on the situation," she began. "If we were working for the defense or for an interested party like an insurance company who hired us, then usually yes, we'd have access to everything through what's called demand for discovery. That's how defense attorneys and other parties get access to all the evidence the police collected in a case." She paused, considering. "But it's a bit trickier for us. We're not part of the legal team or law enforcement."

Sam raised an eyebrow, intrigued. "So, what does that mean?"

Taylor leaned back, settling into the bed, and shrugged. "It means we don't always get everything. If we're lucky, they'll be nice and hand it over. But even if they don't, sometimes we PI's get access to more evidence and information than the police themselves have. Since we're not sworn officers or court members, we can do things they can't."

Sam's eyes lit up with interest. "Like what?"

Taylor smiled slightly. "Well, for one thing, we don't have the same rules they do. We can go places, ask things, and do things that law enforcement can't. For example, we don't have to advise someone they need an attorney when we talk to them, like the cops have to with Miranda Rights. We can listen in on conversations without needing a warrant and take statements from people who might not want to be identified—whether because they're afraid of repercussions, or because they're involved in criminal activities themselves."

Sam nodded, looking impressed. "So, like ... we could dig through the garbage without a warrant like they do on TV?"

Taylor laughed, though it was a bit grim. "Yep. It's a nasty job, but it's legal. We're just regular citizens, so we don't need the same permissions as law enforcement."

Sam grinned. "That's amazing. Maybe we'll find something the original detectives missed."

Taylor smiled, her eyes flicking toward the darkened window. "It might come in handy. But it's not that we're more privileged than law enforcement, Sam. We just aren't bound by the same rules. We can do a lot more legwork, too, because we don't have the same caseload as the police. Those guys are overloaded most of the time, with way too many cases to juggle."

Sam gave a half-nod, processing this information. "So we have more time, huh?"

"Exactly." Taylor set her drink on the nightstand and wiped her hands on her lap, her thoughts turning back to the case. "And that's why we have to take our time with this. If we start digging and find nothing of value in the next couple of weeks, we'll have to walk away. Janelle can't have her hopes built up too much and we can't afford to let this drag on any longer than it has to."

Sam looked over at her, his expression soft. "Yeah. And if we don't find anything after three weeks, we'll head back. Alice will be fine with Anna, but we'll need to get back to the farm. I know it's been nice to get away, but we can't ignore doing our part for too long. First, I think we go talk to Amy."

Taylor nodded in agreement, though she could tell he was thinking the same thing she was. "It's hard to disturb her, though. She's what, fifteen now? From what Janelle says, she's moved on and is doing okay. We don't want to drag her back into all of this if we don't have to."

Sam grimaced. "Yeah, but we don't have much choice. Janelle said she'll talk to Amy's mom, approach it carefully, and see what she can do. If Amy's willing to talk, then we'll have to be ready. If she's not, we move on next and interview Clem."

"First we go to the police department, see what we can get from there." Taylor leaned back against the pillows, sighing heavily. "We've got three weeks. That's what we have to work with. If nothing shakes loose by then, we go back to the farm and focus on smaller cases again until something else comes up."

Sam stretched out next to her, a slight sigh escaping his lips. "Deal. It's hard not to get invested though. Janelle's been fighting this for ten years. She's trusting us with something huge. I just hope we can help her find the answers she's been waiting for."

"I do too," Taylor murmured. "But I also hope we're not chasing shadows." She looked over at Sam, his face serious but determined, and smiled softly. "Either way, we'll give it our all, for your grandmother. And Amy."

Sam took a deep breath and nodded. "Yeah. We will."

They sat in the quiet for a while longer, unanswered questions about the case hanging in the air, but, for a moment, Taylor allowed herself the comfort of knowing they were in this together. Sam made a much easier partner to work with than Shane had.

Cuter, too.

Chapter Three

Anna's shoes squeaked slightly against the waxed linoleum of Hart's Ridge Community Hospital as she made her way through the narrow corridor toward the ER staff room. Four months into her new job as a registered nurse, and the newness hadn't worn off yet. Every shift still came with a mix of anticipation and anxiety—and a weighty, quiet pride.

This was her second act.

Long gone were the manicured afternoons at the tennis club, the forced smiles over country club luncheons, and the tight, painful way she used to hold herself just to keep her world from cracking open. Pete had taken so much from her. Years of her life spent convincing herself that his belittling was love. That his affair was somehow her fault.

Country Club Anna Chambers was never real. That Anna was a fragile shell, molded and maintained by a strict husband who had used physical and mental abuse to keep her in line.

Anna Gray had been buried deep within Anna Chambers for more than a decade, but thankfully she was back. Her life was so much freer and more peaceful, now that she could be herself. Completely herself. Not as someone's wife. Or someone's trophy.

As a nurse. A damn good one, too, if she could say so herself.

With her summer fling that had started in Mexico, with a younger man named Hazard, of all things, her confidence was back. Or at least on its way back.

It had been fun with Hazard and just what she'd needed to feel wanted again, to laugh and be carefree, always entertained by his antics, but real life didn't involve a tryst with a man at least ten years her junior. One who wanted more attention than she had available. Her kids and her career had to come first. Her romantic life was put back on hold.

She clocked in and dropped her bag in the break room, tying her blonde hair up into a quick knot before heading to the nurses' station. Her badge clipped neatly to her scrub top. Her stethoscope looped around her neck. She was already thinking about NICU—her long-term goal. The thought of working with those fragile, tiny beings stirred something maternal and fierce inside her.

"NICU, huh? I heard that's your goal," said Liza, one of the other ER nurses, as she handed Anna a warm coffee. "God help you if you land in Pediatrics first."

Anna raised a brow. "That bad?"

"Worse. And don't make me talk about holidays. They're the worst of the worst. I was here last New Year's Eve. Half the ER was kids, their parents claiming they couldn't keep anything down. We gave 'em water, and, if they held it down for an hour, we sent 'em home. You could see the disappointment on some of the parents' faces. If they did get admitted, suddenly the parents had more important things to do than stay by their kids' sides."

"Maybe they had other kids at home? Or jobs?" Anna offered, though her stomach already turned at the thought. She would never leave her child in a hospital without her.

"I hear that all the time," Liza replied, her voice low and tight. "But there's a difference between juggling life and disappearing. Some of those admitted get no calls. No visits. Not even answering the phone when we try. Some of those kids were here for weeks. No one came. And it's worse in NICU, because you do everything you can to keep them alive and sometimes have to watch them go home with parents who you know won't give them the same care you did."

Another nurse, Carina, joined them. She was dressed in office casual, not scrubs.

"I don't do bedside anymore, but let me be devil's advocate," she said, clearly having caught the tail end of the conversation. "As the Maternity Care Manager now, I talk to these mothers on the phone every day. Most are amazing. They sleep in recliners and cry over feeding charts. But the others? If I had to face them in person, my facial expressions would get me fired."

Anna let out a soft laugh. "Guess I'll have to start Botox again because my face is not good at keeping my opinions to myself."

Inside, her stomach twisted. Because if there was one thing she knew she'd gotten right in this life, it was being a mother. And the thought of women treating their own children like burdens made her jaw tighten.

An image of Lucy with her new baby girl came to mind. From what they could tell, she was being a good mother to the infant. It seemed that marrying Jorge had really changed Lucy into a different person.

Anna was cautiously optimistic that it would stick this time. Lucy was like a chameleon, always turning into whatever someone needed her to be in the moment. Only time would tell if this transformation was real.

Carina leaned forward. "There was one baby boy ... I'll never forget him. He was tough. Going through withdrawal, inconsolable. I took care of him every shift I could, and, over time, I figured him out. His cries, his needs, his patterns. We connected. He was in longer than usual, waiting for placement. The day before he was supposed to leave, I brought a little outfit. Just something that said, 'You mattered.'"

Her voice cracked slightly. "When I came back, they said a 'church volunteer' had picked him up early. Two-hour drive to a foster family who'd never even visited. Someone who had no idea what sort of things consoled him the best."

Anna swallowed hard. "That's ..."

"Heartbreaking," Carina finished. "And that's one story. Out of many."

Anna opened her tablet, blinking away the image of a child passed off like lost luggage. She pulled her first chart.

Kelsey Marshall.

The name sent a quiet chill down her back.

She stared at it for a moment. Pete had burned through a string of girlfriends since the first affair she'd caught him in. Kelsey ... that name had come up recently in court when they were adjusting the custody agreement again—more drama from a man who couldn't stand not being the center of attention any longer. Could it be the same Kelsey?

The year of birth listed on the chart fit. Pete liked them young.

She pushed open the exam room door.

"Good morning. I'm Anna. I'll be your nurse today."

Kelsey looked up from her phone. Even pale and gown-clad, her cheekbones were sharp, her lashes thick.

"Hi," she said, offering a smile that didn't reach her eyes. "Kelsey."

Anna busied herself with the vitals, trying not to stare.

"Any pain? Nausea?"

"Nope. Just feeling foggy and my chest hurts. I can't get rid of this cough either."

"Any history of smoking? COPD? Asthma?"

Kelsey shook her head no.

Anna noted Kelsey's pulse, oxygen levels, temperature. Everything was within range. However, she did have a fever.

Probably just the flu.

"I'll be back with your labs as soon as I can."

She stepped into the hallway and pulled out her phone. A few quick taps, and she found it—a photo from a school pickup Pete had attended with Kelsey on his arm. Big smile. Hand on her lower back. Same woman.

She blinked at the screen, then locked it.

Of course.

She walked back toward the nurses' station slowly, her chest tight with the ghosts of old memories. Pete's cutting remarks. His control. The cold fights behind closed doors. How small she'd felt for so long.

No one else knew the full extent of it. Maybe no one ever would. If she ever had to speak some of it aloud, she would feel like an accomplice in the things he made her do, rather than a victim. It was better off buried.

"You okay?" Liza asked, coming up beside her.

Anna startled slightly. "Yeah. Just ... distracted."

"First year is like that. It gets better."

Anna nodded, then forced herself to focus.

She would get through it. Kelsey was her patient. She wasn't the enemy. And chances were, she hadn't seen Pete's true colors yet.

Poor girl.

She didn't know what was coming.

Chapter Four

People bury the truth because it's dangerous, and Taylor had to agree, sometimes it is. But not as dangerous as living without it. She and Sam walked through the front doors of the Kokomo Police Department, the sound of their footsteps echoing in the small lobby. The receptionist, a middle-aged woman with a stern expression, barely looked up from her desk as they approached.

"What can I do for you?" she asked, her voice flat.

Sam cleared his throat, stepping forward. "We're here to speak with someone about the case of Alma Jennings. We've been hired to investigate a possible wrongful conviction of Clem Tiffin for her murder."

The woman's eyes flickered with suspicion, but she didn't raise her gaze. Her fingers tapped the edge of the desk, her attention still on the paperwork in front of her. "That case was closed a long time ago. Appeal denied. There's nothing more to be done."

Taylor took a step closer, trying to soften her tone. "We're just looking for the case files. We believe there may be new information that wasn't fully investigated at the time. Clem's wife has hired us to do another investigation."

The receptionist didn't respond immediately. Her fingers tapped the desk rhythmically, her brow furrowing slightly as she considered them. Finally, she sighed, picked up the phone, and dialed a number, giving them a reluctant shrug. "Wait a minute. I got this."

She hung up the phone, and a young detective stepped out from a nearby office. He was in his early thirties, with short-cropped hair and an aura of quiet confidence. "I'm Detective Harrison," he introduced himself. "I don't normally handle this type of request, but I'd like to help. I didn't think the investigation was thorough, to be honest." His voice dropped low as if not wanting to be overheard. "From what I've seen, the previous detective was ... focused on one angle and didn't really dig into other possibilities."

Taylor exchanged a glance with Sam. This was unexpected, but the detective's willingness to help felt like a lifeline.

"I'll meet you at the coffee shop down the street in an hour," Detective Harrison continued, glancing toward the front desk to ensure they were not being overheard. "You can go through the files, but I'll warn you, some of it's hard to stomach."

Sam and Taylor nodded, grateful for the detective's help. They didn't fully understand why he would risk his position by suggesting the case had been mishandled, but they didn't question it. Not now.

An hour later, they met Detective Harrison at a corner table in the busier-than-usual Big Ben coffee shop. Harrison had already ordered, his cup of coffee steaming in front of him, his fingers tapping nervously on the table as if he couldn't sit still. Taylor went to the counter and ordered Mountain Top Mochas for herself and Sam before joining them at the table.

"So, what do you think?" Sam asked, settling into the seat across from Harrison.

They'd agreed not to mention Ed Mannopi to him. The idea that Janelle had randomly seen a photo of him and thought he was the real killer, when so far there was no connection, was too absurd to share professionally. She and Sam didn't even believe it could be that easy—and wouldn't risk sounding like raving lunatics.

Harrison took a deep breath, glancing around the coffee shop before speaking. "There's a lot of stuff here. Too much to go over all at once, but I'll give you the gist. There's one thing that always bothered me about the case: the lack of follow-up after Amy's statement. Everything was based on what she said—she claimed the assailant looked like her uncle Clem, but that's all it was. Absolutely no physical evidence to tie him to the crime. I'm going to need you to file a friendly subpoena. Just as a CYA, you know."

She nodded. That was fair.

Taylor opened the file in front of her, her fingers trembling slightly as she began flipping through the pages. The first few were routine reports about the scene—the horrific discovery at the home of Alma Jennings and her granddaughter, six-year-old Amy Simpson. The words jumped off the page in raw, unrelenting detail, painting a gruesome picture of what had happened on the early morning hours in June.

The scene was horrific. Clem Tiffin's mother-in-law, 63-year-old Alma Jennings, had been found on the living room couch, her body beaten so savagely that her nose, jaw, collarbone, and skull had all been fractured. The report noted that the cause of death had been determined as strangulation.

Amy, who had been sleeping in her grandmother's bed, was

awakened by the noise of the attack. Her voice echoed in Taylor's head as she read the report: "I got out of bed and I went to the kitchen and I looked and I seen that there was a strange guy in the kitchen, but it scared me, so I ran back to the bedroom."

Taylor's stomach twisted as she read those words. This little girl, barely six years old, had witnessed a nightmare unfolding right before her eyes.

The interview continued.

Amy's statement was chilling. She had hidden under the covers, pretending to be asleep when the intruder eventually entered her room, struck her in the face, and knocked her unconscious. The report detailed how the child was strangled and beaten. She had suffered a small cut to her throat, but, miraculously, she survived. There were also graphic descriptions of her injuries—enough to make Taylor's chest tighten with horror as she read.

Amy had regained consciousness at around 7 a.m., and the man was gone, her grandmother slain. She'd managed to call a neighbor, leaving a heart-wrenching message on their answering machine: "I'm sorry to tell you this, but my grandma died, and I need somebody to get my mom for me. I'm all alone. Somebody killed my grandma. Now, please, would you get a hold of me as soon as you can? Bye."

Tears welled up in Taylor's eyes as she read the message, the horror of it settling like a stone in her stomach. How had this child survived such unimaginable trauma?

When no one called or came, Amy had made her way to the neighbor's house, knocking on Shelly Sexton's door. Sexton came and told the battered, bloodied child to wait on the porch while she finished cooking breakfast for her kids, finally driving her home about an hour later, and called the police from there.

Now and Then

Taylor's pulse hammered with anger. What kind of woman leaves a traumatized, bleeding child waiting on her porch?

The report noted that this hour-long delay was significant, marking the time when authorities began piecing together the timeline that would later lead them to Clem.

She flipped to the next page, revealing the photos from the crime scene. Her breath caught in her throat as she saw the images of Alma Jennings's body, the brutal violence too much to fully comprehend. Without thinking, she quickly slid the photos to the side, covering them with her hand to shield Sam's view. She was accustomed to crime scenes, but she didn't want it in his head.

"Don't look at these, Sam," she said softly, trying to keep the tremor out of her voice. Sam, noticing her distress, gave a nod and a subtle, quiet understanding.

He had no idea how bad it had been. How graphic. How heartbreaking.

Taylor closed the folder and sat back, overwhelmed by the horror of what she had just read—the images she had seen. "How could they not have seen the possibility that someone else was responsible?" she asked, her voice trembling.

Detective Harrison sighed, his expression somber. "They were too focused on Clem. Amy's statement was enough to convict him in their eyes. They didn't look at other suspects. Not really. They didn't look at the details, the timeline, or even the possibility that someone else could have done this."

Sam clenched his jaw, his eyes dark with anger. "What a nightmare."

"We need to keep digging," Taylor said, her voice firm. "We need to find something—anything—that links someone else to this. For Janelle's sake, and for Clem's."

She thought of Ed Mannopi for a split second. If not him, then who?

Detective Harrison gave a small nod, his eyes scanning the room nervously. "I'll see what I can do. But you two need to be careful. Some of the people involved in this case are still around, and they won't be happy if you start asking questions."

Taylor looked at Sam, her heart heavy. The truth was buried deep. Ten years was a long time for wrongs to be righted, but it wasn't impossible. Look at what had happened with her mother. All she knew at this moment is there was no turning back now.

Chapter Five

At the Kokomo Beach Family Aquatic Center, the sound of footsteps was a light shuffle on the asphalt of the parking lot. Taylor and Sam had decided to take a break from the investigation, knowing that a few hours away from the case would do them all some good—especially Janelle. She'd let on that her depression had been so consuming lately that even the simplest outings felt like monumental tasks, but, today, they were determined to get her out of the house. After some cajoling and gentle persuasion, along with the argument that they were waiting on the detective to get back to them, they'd convinced her to come along.

The aquatic center was a sprawling, lively place—perfect for families looking to unwind for an affordable price. It featured a large outdoor pool with water slides, a lazy river, and a giant play structure that sprayed water in every direction. The sound of children laughing and the gentle splashing of water filled the air, and the sight of families enjoying their day was a welcome distraction from the heaviness they had been carrying.

After paying and getting their hands stamped, they put their belongings into a locker, dressed down for the water, and met outside the locker rooms.

"Ladies," Sam said, smiling at them both, then looking to his little girl. "The three of you are a lovely sight." He took Lennon from Taylor and beckoned them toward the lazy river.

Janelle, in her flowered swimsuit and a large hat, looked ready to bolt when she got a look at the crowd of people milling about all around her. When they'd picked her up that morning, her first question was whether they had checked out Ed Mannopi yet. She was like a dog with a bone.

Sam had done a bit of research on Mannopi the night before, and the man was indeed a sick criminal, but he'd found nothing linking him to Kokomo, or the crime. They weren't done checking him out, but he wasn't any sort of prime suspect for them.

"Come on, Janelle," Taylor said, pulling at her hand. "Just a few minutes in the water. You'll see. It'll feel good."

Janelle hesitated, looking at the waves of the pool as though the water might pull her under. But when she glanced at little Lennon, now settled into Sam's arms, her expression softened. Lennon was like a magnet, and Janelle couldn't help but smile every time she gurgled or reached for her.

Sam knew he had his aunt then, and he grinned as he carried Lennon toward the shallow end, his large frame making the small baby seem even tinier in his arms. "The lazy river's calling our name," he teased. "Lennon's first float. It'll be a family affair. Come on, y'all."

Taylor was right on his heels. She didn't want Lennon more than a reach away from her while on the water.

Janelle's lips twitched, a small smile breaking through her guarded expression. She followed them reluctantly, though Taylor noticed she was moving just a bit faster than she had earlier.

Sam handed Lennon over to Taylor and he grabbed three tubes, then threw them into the entrance where the water lazily flowed around a circular path, allowing people to float peacefully.

The sun had started to warm up, and the water's coolness was a welcome relief from the heat.

Sam helped Janelle settle into her tube, then Taylor handed Lennon back off to Sam so she could squeeze into her own. Lennon was quickly back in Taylor's arms and then the three of them pushed off, along their way. For a moment, they simply floated in the current, letting the water carry them as they soaked in the sun and relaxed in the calm.

"We used to come here with my brother's family," Janelle said, breaking the comfortable silence. Her voice had a wistful quality to it, like she was lost in the memory. "We'd all meet here for the summer. My kids, his kids, just ... laughing, playing in the water. I remember that feeling of ... togetherness. The natural comfortableness you only have with family."

Taylor glanced at her. She could see Janelle's mind wandering, remembering better times before the tragedy that had torn them apart. "I bet those were some good memories."

Janelle nodded, her gaze faraway. "After everything happened, though ... it was like the family just split right down the middle. My brother and his wife stopped talking to me. And my kids—well, I gave them everything I had left, but I was so focused on Clem, on trying to save him. I couldn't be there for them the way they needed me to be."

Sam reached out to Taylor for Lennon and held her in his arms as they gently drifted along the river. Looking over at Janelle with empathy, he said, "That must have been tough. Trying to carry all of that alone."

Janelle shrugged, as though she could let it go with a simple gesture, but Taylor could see the struggle in her eyes. "I just wanted to make sure Clem was okay. I'm all he has left."

"I know, Aunt Janelle," Sam said softly, his hand brushing against the side of the tube. "But you've done everything you can for him. And now, maybe it's time to take a step back and focus on the people who are still here. You and your kids. Your family."

"He means if we can't find anything to help his case," Taylor added, sending Sam a quick scolding look. "But whatever happens, Janelle, you're not alone in this. We're all in it together."

For the first time in what felt like too long, Janelle visibly allowed herself to relax a little, her shoulders loosening and her body floating more comfortably in the tube. She met Taylor's gaze, the smallest hint of gratitude in her expression. "Thank you," she whispered.

Suddenly, Lennon let out a loud, joyful squeal, reaching out toward the gentle current. Taylor grinned as Sam held her steady. "She's getting the hang of it," she said with a chuckle. "Look at her! She's loving the water."

The sound of Lennon's laughter broke through the tension, and Janelle's face lit up as she gazed at her grand-niece. "She's beautiful," she said, her voice softer now. "So full of life. It's hard to remember what that feels like sometimes. You two are so lucky to have her."

Taylor's heart swelled as she looked at Lennon's excited little face. She thought, if she hadn't left her job at the sheriff's department, she would have missed all these moments with her daughter. If she hadn't made that decision, she would have been too caught up in work and cases, too distant to experience the joy of raising a child.

She felt peace wash over her as the four of them floated together. The case was still the priority for them being there, but this moment, right here with family, was enough. For now.

"Family," Janelle whispered again, this time with a smile. "It really is everything."

Taylor nodded, her fingers lightly tracing the edge of the tube. "It sure is."

She caught Sam's look. His gloating smile that he tried to hide. He'd told her for a few years that her job was sucking the life out of her, and he'd been right.

She'd never say it aloud though.

As they continued to float down the river, an unexpected voice broke the peaceful atmosphere. A woman, standing near the water's edge with her children, eyed Janelle with a mix of recognition and distaste. Her gaze lingered for a moment too long.

"Hey," She called out. "I know you."

Janelle smiled at her.

"You're the wife of Clem Tiffin, aren't you?" she said, her voice turning nasty, carrying over the water. "Who let's a man like that into her life? Then stands by him after he kills her own mother. You're a sicko, lady."

Janelle stiffened, her face flushing with a mixture of shame and anger. She immediately looked away, her hands gripping the edge of her tube.

Sam's expression hardened, his protective instincts flaring. But before he could say anything, Taylor gently placed a hand on his arm, her voice low but firm. "Ignore her, Janelle," Taylor said, looking at the woman and then turning her attention back to her aunt. "People like that don't matter."

The woman snorted and turned away, muttering something under her breath.

Taylor and Sam both gave Janelle a reassuring smile, but the moment had passed. Janelle, her face slightly pale, looked up at them. "I don't know if I'll ever get away from that. The judgment. The whispers behind my back."

Taylor squeezed Janelle's hand, her voice unwavering. "It's their problem, not yours. You're doing your best. That's all anyone can do."

For a long moment, Janelle said nothing, but Taylor could see the tension slowly leaving her shoulders. The water around them seemed to carry away some of the heaviness in the air.

As the four of them drifted along, the worries of the world momentarily faded, replaced by the quiet solace of family.

Chapter Six

Taylor's thoughts were still swirling from the previous day. It had been nice to spend a few hours with Janelle—seeing her begin to relax a little, to show that small glimmer of hope she'd long since buried under the grief cloud that always settled around her. But now, as she and Sam pulled into the parking lot of the state penitentiary, that fleeting sense of peace felt miles away.

"Do you think Lennon is okay?" She asked quietly as Sam maneuvered the car toward the designated visitor parking.

It's not that she didn't trust the world—it was that she knew too much of it to just walk away from her child without worrying.

"Yeah," Sam replied, his voice steady but tired. He glanced over at her. "Please don't look like I forced you to leave her, Taylor. We agreed, remember? And Janelle needs this. She needs to focus on something else for a while and know that we trust her. Besides, Lennon obviously loves her. I think they'll be just fine."

Taylor gave a small nod, glancing at the rearview mirror

where the baby car seat was empty. After dinner the night before, Janelle had offered to watch Lennon for them while they went to interview Clem today.

It wasn't easy, but Taylor knew this was a necessary step. For their investigation, and for Janelle's own healing. It didn't help her from obsessing over her daughter—and missing her—but she'd have to get through it.

"Okay," Sam murmured as they reached the entrance to the prison parking lot, "Let's get this over with."

After finding a space way too far away, they both stepped out of the car, and, as Taylor looked up at the towering gray building in front of them, she couldn't help but feel a wave of unease wash over her. It was as stark and imposing as expected. To think that a possibly innocent man had spent a decade behind these walls gave her a feeling of pity that washed over her.

If he was indeed innocent, it was going to be quite the travesty.

Taylor thought of her mother, and all the time she'd spent in jail, falsely convicted. Now it felt like a surreal story, something that had happened to a stranger. It was hard to imagine a time when Cate wasn't a part of their family.

As they walked toward the front gates, they were greeted by the usual hum of a busy correctional facility—the sound of clanging metal, the low murmur of voices, and the occasional shout or whistle echoing from behind the thick walls. The scent of institutional bleach and the faint metallic tang of the air clung to the atmosphere.

The officer behind the glass window barely glanced up at them as they arrived.

"Name?" he asked, his voice muffled through the thick security glass.

"Taylor Gray and Sam Stone," Taylor answered, feeling a

little out of place. The officer flicked through a stack of papers and nodded, then gestured for them to wait as he buzzed them in.

They passed through the metal detectors with only a cursory glance from another officer and then were directed to a small room for someone to go through their belongings. Taylor set her purse on the table, and Sam did the same with his wallet, his eyes scanning the sterile room. It wasn't much more than a holding area—a small, cold room with fluorescent lighting and a few uncomfortable chairs.

After that came the thorough body searches. After her own dignity-grabbing once over, she was taken to a place outside the room. Once Sam was cleared, they were led down a series of long hallways, the air growing colder with each step. Taylor could hear the muffled voices of inmates calling out from their cells as they walked past, but no one dared to speak as they passed with the guard.

The expressions the men wore hit Taylor hard. It was as if time stood still in this place.

They soon arrived at the interview room, a small space with one table and two chairs on either side. It was more comfortable than some of the rooms she'd been in through her law enforcement career, but it was far from welcoming.

The officer who escorted them to the door stepped out, leaving them alone.

Minutes passed, though it felt like hours. Finally, the door opened, and Clem was led inside, his hands cuffed to a chain that was fastened around his waist. He shuffled in, dressed in the standard prison jumpsuit—a faded orange that seemed to swallow him whole.

"Who are you?" he said quickly, his voice guarded.

They'd agreed not to forewarn him they'd become involved. Sam wanted his first reactions without having time to plan his words. Still yet, his breath caught in his throat. Despite everything, despite the ten years behind bars, Clem hadn't changed as much as he'd expected. He'd held onto his looks better than he thought he would—though there were deep lines around his eyes. But it was the look in his eyes that struck him the most. There was something lost there, buried beneath layers of weariness and regret.

He glanced at Sam, then at Taylor, his expression unreadable.

"You must be Clem," Sam said, his voice even, his posture relaxed. "I'm Sam Stone. Your nephew. My father is Samuel."

Clem's eyes flickered with recognition, but it was brief. He looked at Sam for a moment, a vague expression on his face. "Yeah, I think I remember you. You were just a kid when I went away." His voice was low, rough from years of disuse.

Sam nodded. "I know it's been a long time. I'm sure a lot's changed. This is my wife, Taylor—she's here to help us look at your case again. Janelle reached out to us."

Clem's eyes narrowed slightly, and he shook his head. "There's no point. This case is done. It's over. The courts have decided. There's nothing more to talk about, and I've told Janelle to let it go and move on with her life."

"Just talk us through it," Taylor said, her voice calm and soothing. She opened her notebook and began taking notes, though she didn't expect much from this meeting.

Still, they needed to hear it from Clem—his side, his story.

"We need the truth," Sam added.

Clem sighed, leaning back in his chair slightly. His chains rattled as he adjusted himself, and he winced at the noise of metal hitting his chair. "I've been telling the truth all along. I didn't do it. I don't know what else I can say. They had their minds made up before I even had a chance to speak."

Sam leaned forward, a slight frown creasing his brow. "You

were convicted based on Amy's statement—that she said the man who attacked her looked like you. Is that right?"

Clem nodded, a bitter chuckle escaping him. "Yeah, that's what they based it on. Her word. No physical evidence, no real investigation. Just her saying I looked like the guy. I've been sitting here for ten years because of that."

Janelle had asked them not to tell Clem about Ed Mannopi yet.

Taylor wrote down the details. "But Amy did recant, didn't she? She admitted she said that because you were the only man she could think of who fit the description."

Clem's face hardened slightly. "She was a kid. Traumatized. They didn't care about the rest of the details. They just latched onto that one thing. Amy's statement was enough to convict me in their eyes. No one cares that she recanted."

Sam's voice was blunt as he asked the question they both had on their minds. "So why do you think you're sitting in here, Clem, rotting away while the real killer walks around a free man?"

Clem's eyes darkened as he shrugged, his voice thick with frustration. "Because they were too focused on me. Amy's statement was enough to convict me in their eyes. They didn't look at other suspects. Not really. They didn't look at the details, the timeline, or even the possibility that someone else could have done this. In their minds the only plausible scenario is that I did this."

Taylor could see Sam trying to read him, trying to decipher the man in front of him—his uncle, a convicted murderer. "Who else could have done it?" Sam asked, his voice low.

Clem's shoulders slumped slightly, a look of hopelessness crossing his face. "I have no idea. But they never asked. They never bothered."

"Tell us about your relationship with Janelle's mom," Taylor said.

He shook his head. "I'm not going to sit here and say that we were one big, happy family. We weren't. Just like anyone, the family had drama. Alma didn't always like me and sometimes she downright hated me. For my part, I got tired of her poking her nose into my marriage. Does that make me a murderer? Hell, I know a dozen fellow inmates who hate their mother-in-law, but they didn't kill them because of it."

"You hated her?" Sam asked.

Clem ran his hand through his hair, his handcuffs jangling loudly. "No. I didn't hate her. As far as in-laws go, she was okay. She was a decent woman. Damn sure didn't deserve what happened to her."

Sam was quiet for a moment before asking another question, his tone sharp, yet not unkind. "So, if they got it wrong ... what's your life like now? What have you been doing all these years?"

Clem's face darkened even further. "It's prison. What do you think? Fighting for food, dodging enemies, surviving. I spend a lot of time in the library, reading law books. I help the guys write their lawyers, and sometimes even their family. We have a lot of illiterates here."

"Sounds like you keep busy," Sam said.

"Not busy enough. It's lonely. Most every day is the same. Dangerous, too. Despite my low profile I try to keep, I've made enemies. Had a few fights. But I keep to myself, mostly. I don't know what I'm supposed to do anymore. I don't understand how I got here. What did I ever do wrong enough to be punished for something I didn't do. It's a thought that haunts me every minute I'm awake, and most when I'm not."

The bleakness in his voice made Taylor easily see the toll it had taken—physically, emotionally. He was a man who had spent ten years fighting an uphill battle against a system that had already made up its mind about him.

"Sounds like an ugly existence," she said quietly.

Clem nodded. "That's putting it mildly. But what else am I supposed to do? Keep going. That's all I can do. One foot in front of the other until they're both in the grave."

Taylor sat back in her chair, processing everything Clem had said. There were still too many questions to answer, too many details left to uncover. But one thing was clear: the investigation had been rushed, and Clem had been left to rot in prison for a crime that hadn't been proven beyond a reasonable doubt. The justice system had failed him.

"What do you think, Clem? Would you like to give it one more try? Let us investigate?" Taylor asked. "Because if you don't, we don't want to waste our time. Nor do we want to get Janelle's hopes up. But I can tell you this. That woman believes in you. She will sing your praises and claim your innocence until the day she dies. Now, granted, I've only known her a day or so but I'm finding it hard to doubt her. That's how tenacious she is about the fact that you did not kill her mother."

His head lowered and he used his handcuffed fist to wipe a tear away. He didn't look up.

"I'm going to take that as a yes," Sam said. "We'll see what we can do, but, if you want us to help, you've got to help us, too. We need details. Everything. Even the things you think are insignificant. By tomorrow, we expect a complete list of where you were and who you were with, every minute the night Alma was murdered. Names, businesses, phone numbers. Everything you can think of because, you'd better believe, we'll be doing our own investigation, and if there's any lying about what you tell us, we'll find it."

Taylor cringed inwardly. Sam didn't need to be so harsh.

Clem looked at them both, a glimmer of something—maybe

hope—flashing in his eyes before they went back to a dark, dead color. "Sure, I'll tell you everything. But I don't know if it'll help."

Taylor stood, her chair scraping the floor. "I guess we'll see."

As the guards came to escort Clem back to his cell, Taylor and Sam exchanged a quiet, loaded look. The investigation was far from over, but at least now they had a start.

Chapter Seven

The ER had been rocking since noon. Anna pressed her palm flat against a seizing patient's chest. As her team rushed to stabilize him, the man's panicked wife sobbed in the corner. Orders out of the doctor's mouth flew back and forth like tennis balls, and Anna caught each one, delivering with crisp precision—oxygen, IV line, Ativan. Her scrubs were damp with adrenaline by the time the patient finally settled, breaths evening out as his body went slack.

"Nice save," a tech said, wide-eyed.

Anna gave a quick nod and exhaled only after she made it to the hallway. It wasn't her save. But she'd helped. And that made her feel like she was making a difference.

Then she remembered she hadn't yet checked back in on Kelsey Marshall since the beginning of her shift. She'd been subconsciously avoiding it.

Kelsey's diagnosis was an upper respiratory infection—one serious enough to warrant a few days of hospital rest and IV antibiotics. It didn't hurt that she had a great insurance provider. One that paid promptly without a lot of questions. Of course, she would get to stay, and the hospital would milk it for every cent they could, while pushing out a noninsured patient too soon, still sick and unable to get everything they needed to get well.

That part of her job wasn't fun. If she had her way, every person in the country would get free health care.

Anna had kept her distance from Kelsey's room since earlier that day, focusing on more urgent cases. But now, things had quieted.

She walked toward the room, brushing a stray curl from her face. Entering quietly, she had to admit Kelsey was beautiful—no denying it. Anna immediately noticed the fresh manicure, perfectly shaped brows, and expensive bedclothes she wore.

How had she managed to do it all from her hospital bed?

Well, she was a realtor, so that made sense. Always well put together. Maybe even had a glam squad to swoop in and fix it.

Kelsey's youth and success probably helped Pete feel like he still had it, even though his law career had crumbled to dust and he was now working mall security at probably minimum wage.

He'd had it all at one time. A doting wife, two kids and a McMansion in the most elite neighborhood of Hart's Ridge. But as the story goes, he lost everything because he just couldn't keep it in his pants. Now he had to find women, who seemed to go through his life like a revolving door, to support his vices of fancy cigars and top shelf liquor. Probably to pay his bills, too. God knows he was so far behind on child support that the kids would be adults before he ever got close to catching up.

But it was almost worth it to her to carry the financial burden alone to know that he was struggling. Not quite. But almost.

She could barely suppress a bitter smirk at the image of Pete busting teenagers for vaping near a food court. God help those kids. He'd always expected perfection—especially from Teague. Bronwyn had a softer ride by virtue of being "Daddy's little girl," but Teague? Her son had started pretending to be sick on his dad's weekends just to avoid going. She'd started bribing him. And still, Pete refused to consider that he might be part of the problem.

When they were married, he hadn't even allowed her to work. Made her stop nursing school, more than halfway through. Said her place was at home, managing the house, the kids, *the image*. Dinner hot and on time. Floors gleaming.

Anna had been more ornament than woman, painted and dressed and presented like a showpiece.

She hadn't told Kelsey who she was. There was no point. Their's would stay a professional patient-nurse relationship. Nothing personal. She entered the room quietly. "Hey, Kelsey. Just need to swap out your IV bag and check your levels."

"Sure," Kelsey replied, voice softer now. Despite the fresh makeup, if you looked close enough, she was tired. Even weary, though she was striking. She reminded Anna of Scarlet O'Hara, dark hair and piercing eyes.

Anna moved efficiently, adjusting the line. She focused on the routine—clean, click, check—keeping her thoughts contained.

She'd learned to see her own beauty differently since leaving Pete. The kind that didn't come from blowouts or makeovers. It had taken years to unlearn the reflex of staring into the mirror and cataloging her flaws. These days, she tried to see past them—to find the strength in her eyes, the patience in her smile, the softness in the corners of her face earned from motherhood, from grief, from growing.

She wasn't the woman she used to be—and thank God for that. She'd learned to stop trying to match society's rules of beauty and had finally begun to appreciate the kind that bloomed from the inside out—when no one was looking, when no one was grading.

The kind that didn't fade. The kind that didn't need a man's approval.

The door swung open behind her.

"Oh, wow," a voice said, thick with mockery. "Who would've thought. Anna Chambers doing something for someone else instead of pampering herself with two-hundred-dollar blowouts and weekly pedi manicures. And can I just say, this Anna 2.0 isn't looking too good."

Her blood iced, but she didn't turn around. She adjusted the IV drip, calm and deliberate.

"It's Anna Gray now," she said coolly. "You know I went back to my own name."

She finally turned, meeting Pete's smug grin. He looked thinner. Grayer. Still cocky. But there was something desperate beneath the surface now—something brittle.

Kelsey blinked, confused. "Wait ... Anna, as in your ex-wife, Anna?" She looked between them, a dawning horror crossing her face.

Anna gave her a neutral smile, but pity lingered behind her eyes. Poor girl. The cracks were starting to show.

Her phone buzzed in her pocket. She checked the screen—Bronwyn. FaceTime. Her stomach clenched.

"Sorry," she said, stepping back and turning toward the small bathroom, a few feet away. "I need to take this—it's my daughter."

"*Our* daughter," Pete spit back. "You don't own her."

She kept her back turned and answered in a whisper. "Hey, Bron. Everything okay?"

"I need a baby cow." Bronwyn was laid back against a mountain of purple pillows, her eyes bright and eager.

Anna sighed. "What are you talking about?"

"A calf, Mom. Like, an actual baby cow. You know Allie at school? She adopted one through a program. She named it

Milkshake. I want one. Mine will be George. Even if it's a girl."

Anna rubbed her temple. "Sweetheart, I'm at work."

Bronwyn looked sad. "But it's kind of an emergency."

"Unless the cow is inside the house, it's not an emergency," Anna whispered. "We'll talk later, okay? I love you."

"George loves you, too."

Anna smiled in spite of herself. "Bye, baby."

She hung up and slipped her phone away, catching Kelsey's wide eyes and Pete's sneer as she turned around.

Anna excused herself and left the room, pulse fluttering beneath her skin. She went straight to the nurses' desk and found her supervisor.

"There may be a conflict of interest with one of my patients," she said, voice steady. "Personal history."

The supervisor frowned. "Anna, we're short-staffed enough. Don't become another problem I have to deal with, please. Unless there's a legal issue, she remains yours."

Anna nodded tightly, feeling her face burn with embarrassment. "Understood."

She went back to work. Other patients needed her. A little boy with a split chin from the playground. A confused elderly woman who'd wandered into the waiting room alone. A newly diagnosed diabetic asking the same questions over and over again. These people grounded her.

Later, when she returned to Kelsey's room, Pete was gone.

Kelsey, however, had a new look in her eye—something sharp. Jealousy?

That would be insane. She was everything that Anna wasn't. No need for envy.

"I didn't know you were Pete's ex," she said, voice syrupy. "He mentioned you used to be quite the socialite. Guess things change."

Anna smiled politely. "They do."

"You were smart to go back to work," Kelsey added, her tone suddenly sarcastic. "I'm sure it's good for someone like you to stay busy."

Anna didn't know what she meant by that, but it couldn't be good. She finished checking her chart without reacting. She knew the game. Pete's words were leaking through Kelsey's voice, twisting around the edges of every sentence.

She would not let him get to her. Even through her patient.

A patient buzzed, asking for help to the restroom, and Anna headed that way. There was plenty more work to be done. No time for drama.

At the end of her shift, as she began logging her notes, she was called to the supervisor's office.

Security was there. A semi-retired man named Joe who was usually super friendly to her. Now he stood with his arms crossed over his chest, a mask of disapproval on his face.

"Anna, we need to speak with you," her supervisor said. "There's been a report. A patient claims a piece of jewelry is missing from her bag in her bathroom—a diamond bracelet."

Anna blinked, stunned. "What?"

"She said you were the only one in the room."

Her heart dropped. "I didn't take anything from any room. Who is saying that?"

"Room 284."

Anna ran her patient room numbers through her head, matching them with faces.

No.

She felt her stomach fall.

It was Kelsey's room.

"I'm sure you understand," the supervisor added. "But you're suspended until we complete the investigation. We need you to empty your pockets, and we'll be going through your locker and your purse before you leave."

Anna stood there, too stunned to speak. Too upset to argue. To explain about the toxicity of her ex-husband and how he'd do anything to make her look bad.

No, she needed to remove herself. Get to her car and lock the doors.

And cry.

But first she emptied her pockets onto her supervisor's desk. From one pocket she made a pile with her phone, lip balm, and a pen light. There were also a few small alcohol swab packets, and a pair of scissors.

"I bought those myself," Anna said, pointing to the scissors. She hoped they didn't think she was trying to take hospital supplies home with her.

The other pockets were packed full of pens, a few highlighters, and a notepad. Last to emerge was a pack of gum and a roll of antacid tablets.

But no diamond bracelet.

It was so humiliating to then walk with them to her locker and stand there while they went through every corner of it, as well as emptied her purse onto a table.

Joe was starting to look humbled, his gaze anywhere but at her.

Good. Let him squirm.

"We still have to investigate, Anna. We'll call you when you can come back. No more than a day or two, I'm sure," the supervisor said.

"I understand," Anna said, though she didn't. How could she be suspended without a shred of evidence? Just a complaint and accusation?

It wasn't fair.

As she walked out—badge turned in, eyes burning—some of

her coworkers looked away. Others watched her with quiet sympathy. A few exchanged uncertain glances.

No, she wouldn't cry, Anna decided. That would mean Pete won.

She kept her chin high.

She knew who she was.

Anna Gray, of the warrior Gray sisters.

And she wasn't going to let anyone—*especially Pete*—take that from her again.

Chapter Eight

By the time the school bus wheezed to a stop in front of the farm's gate, Anna had already changed into a soft T-shirt and yoga pants, her scrubs folded neatly on the washer. She stood on the porch with a mug of tea, the warmth a poor substitute for the heat still rising in her chest after the shift she hadn't finished.

Suspended.

The word had clung to her all afternoon, prickly and foreign. As if she were back in high school, getting sent home for talking back to a teacher. Only this time, her job, her reputation —her entire second chance—was on the line. Would it be recorded on her personnel file?

She assumed it would.

It felt like she was carrying a boulder on her chest.

The bus doors swung open with a hiss, and the Gray family spill-out commenced.

Alice was first, her long legs taking the steps two at a time. Fifteen going on twenty-two, blonde hair in a messy bun, earbuds still hanging around her neck. Then came Levi, all swagger and spurs, his Wranglers dusty from some kind of adventure he'd probably cooked up at recess. Puberty was hitting him like a truck, and Anna smiled at the small line of fuzz over his lip—his starter-stache.

Bronwyn emerged next, backpack half-zipped, her French braids having completely surrendered to the wind. And. finally, Teague—fourteen and broody, khakis and a button-down tucked in too neatly for anyone who didn't want to be labeled "class president."

"Mom!" Bronwyn called, her voice full of that untarnished joy that still caught Anna off guard. "You're home early!"

Teague looked surprised. "You okay?"

Anna pasted on a smile, hating herself for the oncoming lie. "I had a short shift. Caught up on some paperwork and came home."

She wasn't ready to tell them. She couldn't. Not when the dust hadn't settled, and there was still a part of her that clung to hope this was all a big mistake someone would soon apologize for.

"Mom," Bronwyn started again, tugging on her hand, "can we pleeeease talk about George?"

"George?" Anna blinked.

"The calf! I told you at lunch—well, kind of. It was a quick call. But I need him. Allie named hers Milkshake, and now I want one too. George. Isn't that the cutest name for a baby cow? And we can do it for free!"

Teague rolled his eyes. "You don't even get up before 7:30."

"Cows are early risers," Levi chimed in, kicking at a stone with his boot. "George'll have breakfast before you even open your eyes."

Anna laughed despite herself and hooked Bronwyn's backpack strap. "Let's go talk to Cecil about it."

The four of them trooped toward the barn, the kids chatting over each other, voices weaving through bits of the day: who got in trouble for swearing, what teacher was out sick, and how Levi had found what he swore was a fossil behind the soccer goal.

The barn doors creaked as they pushed them open, the scent of hay and earth washing over them in a way that felt like home. Inside, Cecil sat on an overturned feed bucket, mending a length of worn rope with patient fingers. His overalls were stained with evidence of work, and his ball cap sat low over his forehead.

"Well now," he said with a grin as they approached. "Look what the wind blew in."

Each kid made a beeline to him, hands already outstretched.

Cecil chuckled and reached into his overalls pocket. "One at a time, now. I know y'all ain't forget your manners."

He handed out butterscotch candies like gold coins. Alice tucked hers into her jeans and leaned against a post, arms crossed. Levi unwrapped his immediately, shoving it into his mouth with a grin. Teague nodded a quiet thank you. Bronwyn, of course, was already trying to butter him up.

"Cecil," she said sweetly, "do you think there's room in the barn for one little baby cow named George?"

"A calf, huh?" he drawled, scratching his beard. "And who's gonna take care of him? You?"

Bronwyn nodded eagerly.

"Then let's see what that means." He stood slowly, stretching his back. "First, you're up at 5:30. Every morning. Rain or shine. That calf's gonna want a bottle, right when he opens his big wet eyes—and not later. Then you're gonna be shovelin' out his pen. And I mean all of it. Fresh hay. Fresh water. Twice a day. You're gonna have to check his eyes, his ears, his stools—y'know what that is, don'tcha?"

Bronwyn's enthusiasm was starting to waver. "Like ... poop?"

"Exactly right," Cecil said with a wink. "You're gonna have

to track how much he eats. Keep a log. Might even have to give him medicine if he gets scours."

Bronwyn's nose wrinkled. "That sounds ... messy."

"Messy's just another word for life, child," Cecil added.

The others had started wandering off to see Apollo, the farm favorite and oldest animal resident. More than twenty years old, the horse had been through a lot but was living a dream retirement, spoiled and loved by many.

On his way out, Teague tossed his candy wrapper at Levi, who ducked and ran. Alice pulled out her phone and muttered something about a test tomorrow.

Bronwyn lingered, looking thoughtful.

"You don't have to decide now," Anna said, touching her shoulder. "Think about it."

When the kids disappeared into the back pasture, chasing each other between the oak trees, Anna stayed behind. Cecil's presence was calming, and she needed more of it.

He watched her for a beat. "You got a sadness on you."

She looked up sharply. "That obvious?"

He stood beside her, hands deep in his pockets. "Been around a long time. I can tell when a woman's carryin' something heavy."

Anna exhaled, long and quiet. Then, the words came.

"I got suspended today at work."

Cecil turned, his brows lifting.

"A patient accused me of stealing a bracelet," she said. "A diamond one. Said I was the only one in the room."

"You?"

She nodded.

"Well, I can tell you now, that wasn't true." He scowled.

"Of course not." Her voice cracked. "It was Pete's girlfriend. The newest one. She didn't even know who I was until he came in and opened his mouth. Next thing I know, I'm being pulled into the office and asked to turn in my badge."

Cecil let out a slow breath, then sat back down on the bucket.

"That man's been poison in your life for too long."

Anna sat next to him, staring down at her hands. "I thought I was past all this. I thought I'd done the work, made it out. I went back to school, I got my license, I built something again. And all it takes is one lie to put a crack in it."

Cecil nodded slowly. "The thing about liars is, they good at what they do. Real good. And you? You got somethin' he ain't got. Peace. Pride. A life you made your own. That kind of light makes a man like him real uncomfortable."

She looked over at him, tears threatening.

"I'm scared," she whispered. "That they'll believe him. That I'll lose everything. Again."

He gave her shoulder a gentle squeeze. "Even if you lost that job, you still got everything that matters. Your kids. This place. Your name, Anna Gray. You built all that from nothing. You will not let that tear it down, you hear me?"

She wiped her cheek and gave him a tired smile. "Thank you, Cecil."

He tipped his hat, then opened his arms wide. Anna practically fell into them.

"Anytime, baby girl."

The wind carried the sound of laughter from the pasture, and, for a moment, Anna let herself breathe again. Maybe everything was about to fall apart.

But maybe ... maybe it wasn't.

Chapter Nine

Some people woke with songs in their head, or the remnants of a dream, but Taylor always woke with a checklist. Today the morning air was crisper than usual. A few joggers passed by as Taylor and Sam pulled into the quiet park in Kokomo. Today, they were meeting with Detective Harrison again, and she hoped for some clarity—maybe even a breakthrough. Something the others had missed?

Would that be asking too much?

As she stepped out of the car, she adjusted the baby sling wrapped around her chest and Sam came around with Lennon, slipping her into it. Still a little sleepy, Lennon rested her head against Taylor, her tiny hands curled into the soft fabric of her shirt.

The rush of love that went through Taylor could move a mountain. She smiled down, taking comfort in the weight of her daughter, but the calmness was fleeting. There was too much uncertainty ahead. Too much to unravel.

"Let's hope we get something solid today," Taylor murmured to Sam as she swung Lennon gently, walking toward the picnic table where they were supposed to meet Harrison.

"I'm not expecting anything groundbreaking," Sam said, his voice low. The frustration in his eyes was clear. "But I hope I'm wrong."

They arrived at the picnic table, where Harrison was already waiting. He was seated, a large manila folder in front of him, his face grim. He looked up as they approached, offering a small nod. The lines on his face were deeper than they had been a few days ago. Taylor wondered if this case had been eating at him, too.

"Morning," Harrison greeted, shifting the folder to one side. He glanced at Lennon. "I see you brought a little one along. I hope she doesn't hear any of the gory details."

Taylor smiled tightly, adjusting the sling as she sat down next to Sam. "She's too young to understand."

Harrison pulled out a few pictures from the folder. "Let's get to it, then. I've got some notes, photos from the crime scene, and a few things they didn't follow up on when the case was first filed."

He slid the photos across the table to them, and, as Taylor glanced down, she felt a sickening lurch in her stomach and instinctively turned Lennon even more to the side, her view on the trees in case she opened her eyes again.

The pictures were gruesome. Alma, Clem's mother-in-law, had been assaulted and beaten so savagely that it would've been hard to recognize the woman.

"Are you okay, Sam?" she asked, putting her hand on his arm. It was his grandmother, after all. "Maybe you shouldn't look."

He nodded solemnly. "I'm okay, but it's horrific what a human will do to another. Especially to a defenseless woman. Or any woman, for that matter," he mumbled.

In the photo, Taylor could see the blood had soaked through the rug beneath Alma, her features distorted from the violence.

There was a particularly brutal shot of her face, and Taylor quickly averted her eyes. But then, her gaze fell on the next set of photos—the ones of Amy, Clem's niece.

The little girl's face was swollen beyond recognition. Part of her ear had been torn off during the attack, the lobe hanging awkwardly as if it had been ripped away. Amy's eyes, wide open, stared back in shock, terror freezing her expression. Taylor's heart twisted in her chest, and she felt a sting in the back of her throat as she blinked away the rising tears.

She set the photo down slowly, not wanting to linger over the horror. "God ... poor kid," she whispered.

"I know," Harrison said, his voice grim. "It's hard to look at, but it's part of the case. The biological evidence from both Alma and Amy was collected, but the samples weren't tested for DNA at the time. The police did their searches—Alma's house, Clem's house, even his car. There was nothing, not a single thing that linked Clem to the crimes. But then ... six days later, he was indicted on charges of aggravated murder, attempted aggravated murder, rape, and felonious assault."

Sam raised an eyebrow, clearly frustrated. "So, they had no physical evidence, but they went forward with an indictment?"

"Circumstantial evidence," Harrison confirmed, his face hardening. "The prosecution's case relied entirely on Amy's statement. She said the man who attacked her looked like Clem. But, at trial, the state admitted that no physical evidence linked Clem to the scene. It was all based on that one statement. That's it."

Taylor sat back in her chair, her mind racing. It was like the case was built on quicksand—one piece of testimony that was shaky at best. "And now? What are we working with?"

Harrison sighed, rubbing the back of his neck. "My superior won't let me dedicate more time to this case. He doesn't think there's anything there. But I'll help you as much as I can. I'm pulling up old interviews and evidence for you, though, I'll tell you now, there's not much more I can give you. This case is as cold as it gets."

"Thanks for what you can do, Harrison," Sam said, a note of genuine appreciation in his voice. He glanced at Taylor, then back at the detective. "We'll take your list of people interviewed. We'll start by going back to them. Maybe we'll get something new."

Harrison nodded, then handed over a file with the interviews and photos inside. "Be careful. Some of these people might not appreciate you reopening the case. Some of them are still around, and they don't like questions being asked about it."

Taylor looked at the pile of documents, her eyes narrowing. She was determined to get to the truth. But the longer they dug, the more she felt like they were chasing shadows. "We met with Clem yesterday," Taylor said, her voice quieter now. "I think he's telling the truth."

Sam's eyes flickered toward her, then away, as if unsure whether to comment. "I'm not convinced yet," he said bluntly. "It's hard to trust anyone in this situation, especially after all this time. The evidence—what little there is—doesn't exactly scream innocence. I mean—at six years old, Amy would know what her uncle looks like."

Taylor tilted her head slightly, her lips pressing together in thought. "I get that. But ... something in his eyes, Sam. There's a kind of desperation there. He hasn't given up on proving his innocence. And Janelle ... she believes in him. I just ... I feel it. Something's amiss in this case."

Sam shook his head slightly, a sigh escaping him. "I don't have your gut instinct on this. I need more. There has to be something concrete we can work with before I can believe him."

"Playing devil's advocate here, Sam, but it was dark when Amy saw the assailant."

Taylor reached into the sling to adjust Lennon, who had started to squirm in her arms.

"Let's see what we can uncover," she said firmly, looking at Sam and then Harrison. "We'll keep at it. But we're not walking away from this, not yet."

Harrison looked at them both, his expression weary but resolute. "Okay. Give me a few hours and I'll send you what I can. Just keep me posted on what you're up to."

As they stood to leave, Taylor adjusted Lennon again and turned toward the exit. They had a long road ahead of them. But, for the first time, she could feel a spark of hope. They weren't giving up on Clem, and they weren't going to let Janelle down either.

Chapter Ten

The high school library was quiet and chilly, its air thick with the smell of old books and polished wood. Being there brought back Taylor's high school days, with reminders that, back in her high school library in Hart's Ridge, tucked between dog-eared pages and overdue slips, was a version of herself who had believed that with enough ambition and hard work, anything was possible. She'd grabbed hold of a dream and made it possible, when everyone around her had thought she'd turn out to be nothing.

She and Sam sat at a corner table, the late morning sunlight streaming through the tall windows onto Lennon. She was sitting on a quilt between them, happily banging two plastic toys together. Every few moments, a librarian would glance over, but, when she saw the baby playing quietly, she gave a small nod of approval.

"I wasn't expecting Julie to be so ... defensive," Sam said, his voice low, breaking the silence. He folded his arms across the table and leaned back in his chair. "She's still angry at what Amy went through. It's like it's all still fresh for her."

Taylor nodded, her eyes focused on Lennon for a moment as

the baby made another round of clattering noise with the toys. She reached out to shush her gently, and the librarian, noticing, smiled in acknowledgment. "It's fine," she said warmly, turning back to her work.

"Julie's hurt," Taylor said softly, her mind still processing the conversation with Amy's mother. "Her mother was killed, and her daughter was traumatized, and it broke Julie's heart to see her little girl carry that burden, to this day. You heard what she said—Amy's been haunted by it ever since."

Sam said. "But at least she gave us permission to talk to Amy. It's all caused such a rift in the family. Janelle said she and Julie haven't spoken in at least five years. That's sad for sisters."

Taylor sighed, shifting in her seat. "I agree with Julie when she said she did what a mother would do—she believed her daughter."

Sam nodded slowly, glancing down at the pile of notes they had from their interview with Julie. "She's carrying a lot of guilt. The way she spoke about that voicemail Amy left with the neighbor after she woke from the beating ... 'I need somebody to get my mom for me. I'm all alone. Somebody killed my grandma.' Julie's probably never been able to move past it. It doesn't help that her mom told her once that she and Clem had an argument about how he treated Janelle, and she threatened to call the police on him when it got heated."

Lennon, who had been occupied with her toys, suddenly let out a small squeal of joy as she banged them together louder than before. Taylor couldn't help but smile. "She's full of energy today."

Sam chuckled. "She always is."

Just then, the door to the library opened, and in walked Amy. She was holding a cup of coffee in one hand and a book bag slung over her shoulder. Taylor instantly noticed how much older she looked—how normal she looked. Amy appeared to be like any other student, vibrant and carefree, as though she had left her troubled past behind her. It was hard to believe that this was the same girl who had been at the center of the case that had torn her family apart.

Amy's gaze flickered around the room, and, when she saw Sam, there was no immediate recognition. She stopped in her tracks for a moment, then smiled politely as she approached them.

"Hi," she said, setting down her coffee on the table before sitting down opposite Sam and Taylor. "You must be Sam and Taylor. My mom said you'd be here." Her voice was warm, though there was a hesitation to it, like she was bracing herself for what was about to come. "I only have fifteen minutes before my biology class."

Sam gave her a small, sympathetic smile. "We appreciate you agreeing to speak with us, Amy. I know it's not easy."

Taylor could see that Amy's left earlobe was scarred, and didn't quite match her right.

"I'm just hoping it helps," Amy said softly, her eyes flicking between them. She glanced down at the table for a moment before looking back at Sam. "I wasn't really sure what to expect."

Taylor's fingers rested lightly on the edge of the table as she set aside her pen and opened her notebook. "We'd like to hear your version of what happened that night, if you're comfortable. Anything that comes to mind."

Amy took a deep breath, her fingers tracing the rim of her coffee cup before she took a small sip. "That night ..." She paused, her brow furrowing as she tried to piece together the memory. "I don't remember all the details. It's still hard to think about. But I remember seeing the man standing over my grandmother—he was yelling at her, really loud. As I ran by her couch, I saw him standing there ... and I thought it was

Uncle Clem. They were fighting, and I thought it was over money."

Taylor jotted down notes quickly as Amy spoke, her mind racing to connect the dots.

"Was it definitely Clem?" Sam asked gently, though the doubt in his voice was clear. "I mean, was it really him, or was it just someone who looked like him?"

Amy looked down at her hands, her fingers fiddling with the edges of her coffee cup. "I was just a kid," she said, her voice quieter now. "I didn't say it was my uncle—I said it looked like my uncle. I wasn't around a lot of grown men, and he was the only one I could think of. He was the only reference I had. I was just trying to be helpful."

She paused again, lowering her voice as another student walked by, waving at her. Amy waved back with a forced smile before continuing in a whisper. "Or, at least, that's what I think I was thinking. It's all very hazy now."

Sam nodded, clearly not convinced. "And you recanted a few years after Clem was sent to prison?"

Amy's lips pressed into a thin line, and she nodded. "Yes, I did. But they wouldn't listen. They refused to give him another trial." Her voice trembled, and her eyes welled up with unshed tears. "I was just a kid ... how could I have known? But I don't think I'll ever forgive myself for what I said. I put a man in prison for something he didn't do."

Taylor's heart broke at the words, but she quickly shook off her own emotions, trying to focus on the task at hand. Lennon fussed and Sam handed her his phone to keep her occupied for the moment.

"I understand that you have that guilt, Amy," Taylor said softly, her voice filled with compassion. "But this isn't about blaming you. You were a child, and you were trying to make sense of something so terrible that had happened to you. It's important to acknowledge that, and you've already done a lot of healing."

Amy wiped a tear away with the back of her hand. "It doesn't feel like healing. It feels like I ruined everything." She looked up at them both, her voice cracking. "It's my fault he's in there. A man is spending the rest of his life behind bars for my mistake. And a murderer is running free."

Sam leaned forward slightly, his voice firm but gentle. "We don't know that for sure. And that's why we're here. We aren't here to clear Clem's name. We're just trying to get to the truth, to bring peace to Janelle. She's been fighting this for ten years, and she needs some closure, just like you."

At the mention of Janelle, Amy's tears spilled over. She bit her lip to keep from crying, her voice shaking. "I'm so sorry," she whispered.

Taylor reached across the table, placing a hand gently on Amy's. "You're not the one who should be apologizing. You were a child. You've already carried so much."

Amy looked down, her chest heaving with sobs. "I don't know if I can keep talking about it."

"Of course," Taylor said quickly, standing and pulling Lennon from the floor, then dropping her into the sling at her chest. "Take a moment. You don't have to do this."

Amy nodded, wiping her eyes as she stood abruptly, excusing herself from the table. "I just ... I can't right now." With that, she hurried out of the library, leaving Taylor and Sam to sit in stunned silence.

They exchanged a glance, the sudden exit settling heavily between them. Sam let out a slow breath, his eyes following Amy as she disappeared into the hallway.

"She's carrying all that guilt," Taylor said quietly, her eyes still on the door. "She doesn't deserve that. None of them do."

Sam didn't answer right away, his mind clearly processing

everything. Finally, he looked at Taylor and said, "I don't know. I need something more concrete. But you're right. She's a kid. She shouldn't have to bear this burden."

They sat for a few moments longer, both lost in thought. There was more to uncover, more questions to ask, before they could form solid opinions.

But for now, they had no answers. Only pieces of a puzzle that still didn't quite fit together.

The sun had barely risen on the day that Taylor and Sam were determined to get through at least four people on their list. The drive had been quiet, but, as they dropped Lennon off for her nap at Janelle's house, Taylor worried that they were missing something important.

"Let's see if we can get some answers today," Sam said, his voice focused as he adjusted the rearview mirror before pulling out of the driveway.

Taylor nodded, gripping her notebook in her lap as she prepared herself for what was ahead.

Their first stop was a local bar, where they hoped to talk to one of the guys who Clem had been with the night of the attack.

The bell above the bar's door jingled as they entered, the scent of stale beer and fried food clinging to the air. The place was nearly empty, with just a few regulars nursing drinks in the corner. The bartender, a middle-aged man with graying hair and a weary look about him, wiped down the counter with a cloth, his eyes flicking up when Taylor and Sam approached.

"Can I help you?" he asked, his voice gravelly but not unfriendly.

"Are you Tony?"

He nodded. "Sure am, last I checked."

Sam didn't smile. "We're looking for some information about a guy who was here the night of June 7th, ten years ago." Sam said, keeping the tone casual. "Clem Tiffin. He was here with some friends."

"Who wants to know?" the bartender asked.

"We do. Just taking another look at the case," Taylor said, introducing herself and Sam as private investigators.

The bartender squinted at them, surprise flickering briefly before he nodded slowly. "Yeah, ol' Clem was here that night, right up until closing time. He left with a couple guys—yeah, I remember now, he was with Brad and Randy. They were always a trio, but they didn't get into any trouble."

Taylor jotted down the names. "Do you remember what time they left?"

Tony rubbed his chin thoughtfully. "I've already testified to this a long time ago. I said it was about 1:30, I think. We were closing, and they were heading out. They said they were going to another bar that stayed open until later. I think it was something like ... The Iron Gate, maybe? I don't know. Been a while."

Sam made a note in his phone. "The Iron Gate? And while they were here, what was Clem's mood like?"

"Same as usual," Tony said. "Friendly. Glad to be out."

"Did Clem mention anything about his wife or mother-in-law?" Taylor asked.

He shook his head. "Not really. From what I remember, it was just the usual night out, you know? They were talking about old times, joking around. Clem's a stand-up guy, as far as I know. Never heard him say a bad word about his wife or her mom. They had a lot of issues, sure, but he always seemed respectful."

"Do you know where we can find Randy and Brad?" Sam asked.

Tony looked sorrowful for a second. "You can find Randy at

his junkyard, but you'll need a shovel to interview Brad. He died a few years back. Prostate cancer. The man refused to go to a doctor until it was too late."

Taylor glanced over at Sam. His expression was unreadable, but she could tell he was still processing everything. "One more thing," she said. "Have you ever heard of Ed Mannopi?"

He squinted upward, then shook his head. "Don't believe I have."

"Thanks for your time," she said, giving the man a polite nod. "We'll be in touch."

"Sure thing," Tony replied, already turning away to greet another customer coming in.

The heat of the day had started to settle in as they drove out of the bar's parking lot, the wheels of their car spinning over the cracked asphalt. Sam didn't say much as they headed toward the junkyard where they were supposed to find Randy.

The junkyard was just outside of town, the landscape dotted with rusted vehicles piled high like twisted metal sculptures. The air smelled of oil and gasoline, and the ground was dusty, with bits of broken glass and debris scattered around. A beat-up office trailer sat at the entrance, its faded sign reading "Reed's Salvage Yard."

"Nice place," Sam muttered under his breath as they parked.

"Let's see what Reed has to say," Taylor replied, her voice determined as she stepped out of the car.

They entered the office, where a man in his forties sat behind a cluttered desk. His shirt was dirty, and his hands were covered in grease, but his sharp eyes took in Sam and Taylor immediately. He stood up and wiped his hands on a rag before extending a hand.

"Randy Reed," he introduced himself. "Tony called and said you were on your way over. What can I do for you folks?"

"We're looking into the night of June 7th, about ten years ago," Sam said, after introducing the two of them. He began, his voice calm and steady. "Clem Tiffin was out that night, and we're gathering information about his alibi. We heard he was with you for part of the evening."

Reed scratched his beard, nodding slowly. "Yeah, damn shame what happened to Clem. We used to hang out. I was with him that night, along with Brad Cooper. We all left Tony's place at closing time and headed to the Iron Gate. Had a few beers there, too, then we went our separate ways."

"What time was that?" Taylor asked.

"Hmm ... just after one in the morning, when they closed. Hey—can't you read all this in the court papers? I thought they have it all written down, word for word?"

"They do, but we're doing our own interviews," Sam said. "We appreciate your help. Clem said you'd be easy to talk to," he added. "Did Clem talk about his wife? Anything strange about that night?"

Reed shook his head, a small chuckle escaping him. "Not really. His wife and him didn't always see eye to eye, sure, but he never talked bad about her. Never about Alma, either. He just seemed like a guy who was stuck in a bad situation. You could tell he was frustrated, but that's all. He was a stand-up guy who got a bad rap, in my opinion."

Taylor wanted to believe Randy, but every buddy called his friends stand up guys. Bro code. Allegiance. Or whatever you wanted to call it.

Randy ran his hand through his hair, looking off into the sky before answering. "Clem left before we did. Went to go help someone with a flat tire."

Taylor raised an eyebrow. "Yes, we read about that."

"Yeah. Adam Chandler had a flat on the side of the road and

called Clem," Randy explained. "Clem is that kind of guy you call when you're in a tight spot. Always been that way."

"What time did he leave?" Sam asked.

"I already said—somewhere around one a.m."

"And he was okay to drive after drinking all night?" Taylor asked.

Randy laughed harshly. "Yeah, he was okay. The man is built like a bear, and it don't matter how much he drinks, you can't even tell he's drunk."

"Does Adam still live on Oconee Drive?" Taylor asked, checking her notes.

"As far as I know," Randy said, shrugging his shoulders. "You'd better wait until early tomorrow to talk to him, though. No one is ever home at this time of day. They both work afternoons."

"Thank you for your time," Sam said.

When they got into the car and Taylor turned to look back, Randy was still standing on his porch, watching them drive away.

Chapter Eleven

The longer Taylor was gone from Georgia, the more she realized how much home was part of who she was. The drive to the Chandler residence was quieter than she'd expected. The morning sun was high, and the heat of the day was starting to seep into the car. Sam drove with a focused expression, eyes straight ahead, while Taylor stared out the window, her thoughts racing. She missed being home. The farm. Her family. Especially Alice. And Diesel.

She needed to focus.

Stop thinking about home.

She was tired. The day before had been exhausting—meeting with Tony. Then Randy. Hearing their versions of events, and trying to piece together Clem's alibi. But there were still so many holes. Taylor couldn't help but feel uneasy as they headed to the Chandler's house.

They had two more leads to chase before the day was done, but something else gnawed at the back of her mind.

"You think Randy was being honest?" she asked, her voice breaking the silence as they approached the suburban neighborhood where Adam Chandler lived.

"I think he believes what he's saying," Sam replied, his voice low. "But it's hard to trust anyone completely when they're that loyal to their friend. We still need Adam's version."

They pulled into the driveway of a modest, two-story house. The yard was well-kept, with a few kids' bikes scattered on the front lawn.

A woman in her early forties opened the door, wiping her hands on a dish towel. She had a tired but friendly expression, and her eyes flickered between Taylor and Sam as they introduced themselves. "I'm Mary Chandler," she said, her voice polite but wary.

"Hi," Taylor said. "I'm Taylor Gray and this is my husband, Sam. We're private investigators hired by Janelle Tiffin. We'd like to talk to your husband about Clem, if that's okay."

She looked uncertain. "Adam's not here—he's in Nebraska on a long-term welding job. He left about a month ago. Why is this being brought back again?"

Taylor explained. "We understand Adam had a flat tire and called Clem for help that night. We just need to go over the events that happened after."

Mary blinked, processing the question. She stepped aside, allowing them to enter. "Come in," she said softly. "I don't know how much help I can be, but I'll tell you what I know."

The house smelled of fresh-cut flowers and freshly baked cookies, though Taylor knew that this wasn't the time to get distracted by the homely comforts. They sat down at the kitchen table while Mary took a seat across from them, visibly nervous but trying to remain composed.

"We were at my sister's house that night. Cookout. Adam had a few beers, and things got a little heated between us. I thought he was rude to my sister, and we started arguing on the way home," she began, her voice distant as she recounted the events. "We were driving, and he let the wheel go off the road for a second—just swerved, but not too badly. But the tire popped. I was so angry, and Adam was frustrated, and he pulled over and called Clem because we didn't have a spare."

Taylor wrote down the details, her mind processing every word. "So, Clem came out to help him?"

Mary nodded. "Yeah. I told him we should just Uber home and deal with it in the morning, but Adam didn't want to leave the car on the side of the road. Clem brought a spare and followed us back home. We got to the house, and I went straight to bed. Adam and Clem sat out in the barn. Adam has somewhat of a man cave there. As far as I know, they were drinking and talking. I don't know exactly what time Clem left, but Adam told me it was around 2 or 2:30 a.m."

Taylor's stomach tightened. A half hour difference could make all the difference in this case. She leaned forward slightly. "Are you sure about the time? Is there any chance Adam could've been wrong?"

Mary's face grew tense, her eyes flicking downward. "I'm not sure. Adam said it was around 2:30, but honestly ... he was tired. And a little drunk. He probably wasn't looking at the clock. But that's what he said. He had no reason to lie about it."

"Okay," Taylor said, writing down the information. She could hear Sam's quiet exhale beside her, his own thoughts heavy. "Thank you, Mary. This helps."

Mary gave a small nod but didn't speak. Taylor stood, and Sam followed her as they made their way back to the car, the information swirling in their minds.

As they drove away from the Chandler residence, Sam turned to her. "It's all lining up, but I still don't feel like we're getting the full picture."

"I know," Taylor replied. "We're missing something. I can feel it."

Their next stop was Alma's best friend's house. The woman,

Marlene, was sitting on her front porch sipping lemonade when they arrived, a cat on her lap.

"I don't know what you expect me to say about Clem," Marlene said after they explained who they were. The cat took off as Marlene set her drink down. She looked between Sam and Taylor at the porch floor. "I'm not a fan and, to be honest, Alma hated him. And she wasn't shy about it. She didn't think he was good enough for her daughter, and she made sure Clem knew it."

Taylor studied the older woman carefully, her heart heavy. This wasn't going to be easy. "Did she ever say anything that might indicate Clem was dangerous?"

Marlene shrugged. "Not really. She'd call him all kinds of names when she was mad at him. And she'd tell me he wasn't worth a damn. She said he was lazy, always drinking. But she never said she feared him. Not really."

Sam leaned in, sensing an opening. "Did Clem hate Alma back?"

Marlene hesitated, looking away before answering. "I don't know. Probably. He'd complain about her getting involved in his marriage. Told her a few times to keep her nose out of his business."

Taylor felt the tension in the air, the lack of real information hanging between them. "Was there any indication that Clem and Alma had an especially big blow-up before? Any reason he might have snapped?"

Marlene shook her head. "They'd been at odds for years, but nothing like that. There wasn't anything unusual before the night she died. At least not that she told me. And that's really all I know."

"One last thing, Marlene," Taylor said. "Do you think that Clem is guilty?"

She nodded slowly. "I do. And Alma would roll over in her

grave if she thought he had a chance to be freed, so I hope you button up this latest inquiry and let her rest."

They left Marlene's house, the conversation still echoing in their minds. As Sam drove toward their next destination, Taylor could feel the day beginning to drag on them. Every person they'd interviewed had a different story, but no one could say for sure what had really happened that night.

Sam's brow furrowed with frustration as he drove. "I don't understand. Where's the smoking gun in all this?"

"There isn't one," Taylor replied, her voice flat. "Just a bunch of conflicting stories, timelines, and half-truths."

Sam's frustration was palpable as he ran a hand through his hair. "This whole thing is just ... off. Too many what-ifs. Not enough evidence for either way. We never should've agreed to come here. Now Janelle is going to be even more devastated when we can't help."

Taylor shook her head, her gaze focused on the road ahead. "Don't think about that yet. We're getting closer to figuring something out, Sam. We have to be."

But the closer they got, the more questions seemed to emerge. The investigation was far from over, but they were inching toward the truth—one uncomfortable conversation at a time.

Chapter Twelve

Three days had passed, and still—nothing. No call. No email. Not a single word from her supervisor. Anna glanced at the screen of her phone again, though she knew there was no point. The silence from the hospital had begun to feel personal. Like she'd slipped through the cracks, or worse—been quietly erased.

She straightened the clipboard in her hand and pasted on a smile for the woman in front of her. The latest customer at the Gray family boarding facility—a woman who introduced herself as Kelli with an i—was in the middle of a full-blown separation-anxiety crisis.

Not her own—but her dogs'.

"These two are not kennel dogs," Kelli said, one perfectly manicured hand resting protectively on her enormous handbag. The two purse-sized Yorkies inside it blinked up at Anna, bejeweled collars sparkling beneath their matching floral bandanas. "I mean that sincerely. They sleep with me. They eat with me. I have their meals labeled by day and time. Don't even think about microwaving their chicken—only stove top. No onions. Not even onion fumes."

Anna nodded patiently, biting back a smile. "Got it. No microwave. No onions. Chicken—pan-seared."

Kelli exhaled, looking ready to burst into tears. "I don't know if I can do this. You must wash their bedding every other day. Oh God—what if they think I've abandoned them?"

"You'll be cruising around the world," Anna said gently. "I promise they'll be just fine. We have a big private suite reserved just for them, and they'll get more snuggles than they'll know what to do with."

"I left a playlist," Kelli said. "They like classical during nap time. Nothing with violins—they find it shrill."

Anna stifled a laugh. "Of course."

Kelli gave the dogs a dramatic farewell—complete with kisses and whispered promises to FaceTime from Rome—before finally stepping out the door and heading toward her vehicle.

Anna gratefully watched her car drive off and then leaned against the counter with a sigh.

She loved the family business—caring for animals, helping out with rescue cases. It was meaningful, in its own way. But it didn't set her soul on fire the way nursing did. It didn't carry that sense of purpose. And it certainly didn't pay for two growing kids and one who was suddenly into the most expensive name-brand sneakers.

The door opened again, and her sister, Jo, stepped in, brushing windblown hair from her face and shrugging off a hoodie streaked with dog hair.

"Guess who we're picking up later," she said, reaching into the front desk basket for a peppermint. "It's a case that might interest you."

"Let me guess," Anna said. "A chihuahua who hates men and only responds to Taylor Swift songs."

Jo smirked. "Close. A three-legged lab mix. They found him limping near the edge of the park—looks like he was hit a while back and had a mean infection going. The bad leg had to be amputated."

Anna winced. "That poor thing."

"We already might have a home for him," Jo added. "Corbin's interested. Says Hank needs someone to tumble around with."

A warmth spread through Anna's chest. "Really? Hank's been a solo act for a while."

"Yeah, well, Corbin says he's starting to act bored on the road. Thinks a dog buddy might help."

"That reminds me. Are Corbin and Sutton still a thing?" Anna asked, leaning against the counter again. "I haven't seen them around here lately."

Jo nodded. "Yeah, they're still going strong. No ring on her finger, though, that I know of."

They both fell into that comfortable rhythm that came so naturally—sisters musing, half gossiping, half soul-searching. Giving a little but holding some back, too.

There would always be secrets.

"I wonder why he hasn't asked," Anna said. "He seems so into her."

"He is," Jo replied. "But you know Corbin. Took him two years to say yes to singing at county fairs again. He's not rushing anything."

Anna smiled. "Hank and Sutton helped him so much through all that. I remember when he couldn't even play in front of twenty people without shaking."

"Now he's out there every weekend. Playing the little honkytonks, roadside bars, anywhere that lets him feel grounded. He found his comfort zone."

"Back to the small stages," Anna said, almost wistfully. "Kind of like the rest of us."

Jo gave her a look, one brow raised. "Hey—about that. How

do you have so much free time to hang out here lately? Not that I'm complaining, but you're usually juggling three things at once."

Anna hesitated, heart stuttering. She wanted to tell her. Wanted to get the words out and let someone else carry the stress for just a minute.

But shame crept in like a slow fog. She couldn't bear to say it aloud. That she was under investigation. That someone thought she was a thief. That it might cost her everything she'd worked for.

That her accuser was Pete's girlfriend.

It was just too much.

"I just needed a few lighter days," she said instead, brushing imaginary lint from the counter. "Figured the dogs wouldn't mind having me around more. Mom sure was happy. She's already had me reorganizing the supply closet and putting together a budget for a second well to be dug. She's afraid the one we have will go dry and leave us in a bind. Wants to have a backup, even though I told her it's going to be expensive."

Anna was jabbering.

Jo didn't push, but her eyes lingered longer than usual.

Anna turned the conversation. "Speaking of Corbin and Sutton, what about you? Any sparks lately?"

Jo rolled her eyes. "You know me."

Anna did. Jo was quiet. Protective. Always carrying more than she let on. Since Eldon—since that whole nightmare—she'd thrown herself into the rescue. Into Levi. Into survival.

Anything to keep her from confronting the guilt she carried.

"You're allowed to be happy, Jo," Anna said gently. "It wasn't your fault."

"I know that," Jo said, her voice short. Then she sighed. "I just ... I don't know if I want to go down that road again."

Anna didn't press. Jo wasn't wired like that. She didn't talk it out—she carried it, stuffed it in her back pocket, and worked around it.

Jo looked toward the barn. "Anyway, I'm too busy trying to put food on the table. Levi's eating me out of house and home."

Anna chuckled. "That sounds about right."

"And when he's not eating, he's asleep or glued to that phone. I miss him. I miss our movie nights and talking about weird animal facts. Now it's all grunts and memes."

"He's a teenager," Anna said. "It's a phase."

"I know," Jo said, but her voice was thin. "Still. What if it's not just that? What if something's really wrong, and I'm just chalking it up to hormones?"

Anna paused. "Maybe he needs to see us handling our stuff out loud. Teague, too. If we show them how to open up ... maybe they'll try, too."

Jo didn't answer, but the thought settled between them like dust motes in sunlight.

Before either of them could say more, the door chimed.

A tall man in a baseball cap stepped in, smiling broadly. "Hey! I'm here to pick up Diabo—black lab, white chest, answers to 'treat' more than his own name."

Anna reached for the check-out sheet. His exuberance had thrown her off. And maybe his brown eyes with delicious eyelashes, too. "Of course. She's been waiting for you."

Jo caught her eye, raised her eyebrows. Anna blushed.

Diablo's dad leaned over the counter, propped on his elbows.

"So tell me everything. Was she a good girl? My name is Jack, by the way."

As Jo disappeared to fetch the cat, Anna kept her smile up, her pulse racing for the handsome man giving her the eye, and her heart thudded heavily under everything left unsaid to Jo.

Maybe tomorrow she'd hear from the hospital.

Maybe tomorrow she'd find the strength to tell her family the truth.

But today, she had critters to care for.

And sometimes, that was enough.

Chapter Thirteen

Taylor walked into Janelle's kitchen, inhaling the delicious scent of home-cooked food. The smell of garlic and onions filled the air, mixing with the rich, savory aroma of something slow cooking on the stove. Cate had once mentioned to her that a kitchen alive with activity was the soul of a home, where every meal should be a gesture of love. She'd talked of how, when Taylor and her sisters were young, they'd spent so much time around the table, not only eating but playing games or drawing, just lots of family time before the fire ruined it.

The memory was a gift from her mother, remnants buried by ashes but pulled from the wreckage, cleaned up and handed over to her daughters for them to cherish. It always made Taylor's heart smile to take it out and enjoy it again. Janelle stood at the counter, chopping vegetables, her movements steady and practiced. The soft clink of her knife against the cutting board was the only sound besides the occasional giggle from Lennon, who was sitting on Sam's lap at the kitchen table.

Sam bounced Lennon gently on his knee, making exaggerated "ouch" sounds as the baby tugged at his hair, her face lit up with delight. "Oww, you're hurting Daddy!" he said, wincing dramatically. Lennon cackled in response, delighted by her father's antics.

Taylor couldn't help but smile at the scene. Sam was so natural with their daughter, and it was moments like this that made the investigation feel like a distant thought. Sam had enjoyed a day of working on odd jobs around the house, fixing things up for Janelle. The porch had been renailed and repainted, and the garage door was finally working again. He'd also patched a few holes in the drywall of a back bedroom, evidence left behind of brothers fueled by testosterone and horseplay, marks of a childhood from long ago.

The normalcy the tasks brought to them was a welcome change to the tense interviews of their investigation the day before. Now the comforting smells of home-cooked food filled the kitchen as Janelle worked steadily at the stove, dropping in the cut vegetables, the stirring of sauces creating an almost soothing ambiance.

Taylor stood by, watching her, grateful for the change in Janelle's mood.

Janelle glanced up from her cooking and sighed contentedly, her hands moving with confidence. "You know, it's been years since I've cooked like this," she murmured, her tone soft with nostalgia. "I didn't even realize how much I missed it. This house hasn't felt like a home in so long."

Taylor nodded, her heart tightening for Janelle. She could see the small, quiet victory in her face. Cooking was something Janelle had loved once, something that had been buried under years of hardship. And now, there it was again—something that could be a small piece of her, something she could reclaim.

"Glad to see you back in your element," Taylor said, stepping closer and offering a small smile. "And we get to reap the benefits. I can't wait to test that spaghetti sauce."

Taylor lingered over the kitchen counter, sipping on iced tea, and asked Janelle about her two grown sons. It was a soft question, meant to guide her into a safe conversation. But the mood in the room shifted immediately.

"I rarely see them anymore," Janelle said, her voice tinged with sadness. "They're both grown, and they have their own lives now. They've gone through so much trauma. It's hard for them to even step foot in this house."

Taylor waited, giving Janelle space to continue.

"My oldest son, Derek, he keeps telling me to walk away from Clem. Start a new life. He wants me to just let go. But Aaron ... he can't even talk about his father without breaking down. He shuts down every time I bring him up. He's never really gotten over it."

Sam's expression softened as he listened. It was clear how deeply the family had been torn apart. Taylor's gaze shifted to Lennon, still giggling on Sam's lap, her innocence a stark contrast to the pain Janelle was carrying.

"It's hard to see them like that," Janelle continued, stirring a pot on the stove absentmindedly. "But it's harder knowing I can't fix it for them. I've been so focused on Clem all this time, I didn't realize until they were gone how much of their childhood I missed out on. I've hurt them and didn't even mean to. I guess when they have children of their own, I won't get to be involved. Clem and I always joked about when we'd become grandparents, and how much revenge we'd get on the boys for giving us a hard time. We promised we'd spoil our grands so much that it would make up for all the sweat and tears the boys put us through. But honestly, considering everything, they were good sons. *Are* good sons."

Taylor exchanged a glance with Sam, both understanding the complexity of Janelle's struggles. She wasn't just fighting for

Clem's innocence—she was battling to repair the shattered bonds within the entire family.

"Well, we were able to interview several on the list," Sam said, breaking the silence. "But it's hard to know if we're getting closer."

Janelle glanced up from her cooking, raising an eyebrow. "Closer to what? Finding something to prove Clem's innocence?"

"Closer to the truth," Taylor said gently. "We're getting pieces, but no one seems to be able to tell us much more than what's already in the reports. We need to talk to everyone we can—get as many angles as we can. Are you sure your mother didn't have any enemies?"

"None that I know of," Janelle said.

They fell into a silence for a moment, but Janelle eventually spoke again, her voice growing cold. "And Marlene?" she asked, the name dripping with disdain. "That woman's a bitter old gossip. Always trying to stir things up. Did she tell you about the time she tried to get Julie in trouble?"

Both Sam and Taylor were startled by her words. "What do you mean?" Taylor asked, leaning forward slightly.

Janelle's lips curled into a thin smile. "She called child services and tried to get them to open a case when Julie agreed to let Amy be hypnotized. Marlene said it was abuse. Claimed it was dangerous for a child to go through that kind of thing."

Taylor's eyes widened as she glanced at Sam. "Amy was hypnotized?"

Janelle nodded, the frustration clear on her face. "Marlene was against it from the start. She's always had a chip on her shoulder about Clem. Julie was just trying to help Amy remember things more clearly, but Marlene couldn't stand it."

"Why wasn't that in the detective's notes?" Sam asked, his brow furrowing.

Janelle's shoulders sagged as she sighed. "I don't know. I can show you the transcript from the session, though. Hold on."

Sam leaned back in his chair, glancing down at Lennon, who had settled into a content giggle, still trying to tug at her father's hair. Sam smiled softly and shook his head, the brief moment of levity helping to clear some of the tension hanging in the room.

Taylor took over stirring the pot as Janelle quickly left the kitchen, returning shortly with a large notebook. She opened it, flipping through the pages before pulling out a thick stack of papers. "Here," she said, handing it to them. "This is the transcript."

Taylor and Sam sat down at the kitchen table, flipping through the papers carefully. As they read, Taylor felt an electric tingling start at her shoulders and streak down to her fingertips.

It was clear that the session was an attempt to help Amy recall more details of that night—details she had trouble remembering. But what stood out in the transcript was the confusion that seemed to pervade her recollection. The hypnosis had been an attempt to sharpen the blurry edges of her memory, but, instead, it seemed to have complicated things further.

"I think I was just a kid, and I didn't say it was my uncle, I said it looked like my uncle," Amy had said under hypnosis, as the therapist guided her through the events that had happened.

Taylor read aloud, her voice quiet as she passed the paper to Sam. "'I wasn't around a lot of grown men, and he was my only source of reference. I was trying to be helpful.'"

Sam's expression darkened as he read, then looked up at Janelle. "But why wasn't this used in court? Why wasn't it considered?"

Janelle's eyes filled with frustration. "Because it didn't fit the narrative. The prosecution had already convicted Clem. They didn't want anything to mess with that. They dismissed it, and Amy recanted years later, but it didn't matter. The system had made up its mind."

Taylor set the transcript down and rubbed her eyes, feeling the tension settle back in her bones. "It wasn't enough to stop the train. And yet, we're left with so many unanswered questions." As they read more of the transcript, Taylor began to recognize the inconsistencies in the case that were becoming clearer with each passing day.

In the transcript, Amy, under hypnosis, walked through what was happening to her the night her grandmother died. She recalled first coming out of the bedroom and seeing a man standing over her grandmother's body. Her recollections were fuzzy, but she spoke clearly about the man's features—brown eyes, a rough voice. But the most shocking part was her description of the attack. She had originally believed the man to be her Uncle Clem, but, under hypnosis, she recanted, saying that she wasn't sure anymore. It seemed that the hypnosis had helped her recall more details, but the truth seemed even harder to pin down.

As the session went on, Amy's words describing how she'd been beaten until she'd blacked out, then woken to find herself alone with her grandmother's body the next morning. She'd tried to waken Alma, then realized she was dead, and used Alma's phone to call and leave a message with a neighbor. When no one came, she decided to walk over to the closest house and knocked on the door.

She recalled the neighbor opening the door, being shocked at all the blood on Amy, and telling her to wait right there while she got her shoes on, so she could drive Amy home. She chronicled sitting down on the porch steps, and watching a line of tiny black ants marching across her path while she waited. She even recalled that one was carrying what appeared to be a piece of white rice, carrying it high like a trophy while the others followed. She described a mail truck going by, down to the hat and shirt the man wore as he stopped at the neighbor's mailbox, not noticing a blood-covered child on the porch.

Taylor had always found the subject of hypnotism to be interesting, and she was enthralled at the tiniest of details that Amy was led to remember.

The transcript mentioned that after the session Amy had expressed doubts about her initial identification of Clem, and that she was no longer sure who had attacked her and her grandmother.

"This is a game-changer," Sam murmured, pointing at the notes. "But what could it mean for Clem's case?"

Taylor nodded, her thoughts churning. "It means we need to dig deeper into those memories. And we need to get to the bottom of why Amy ever believed it was him in the first place."

Janelle sat back down, folding her arms, her eyes dark and deep-rooted conviction in her tone. "All I know is that my husband didn't do it. And I'll do whatever it takes to prove it."

Chapter Fourteen

The drive to Shelly Sexton's place was longer than Taylor had expected. The woman no longer lived across from Alma's old place, and it had taken a call to Detective Harrison to get her last known address. Her new neighborhood felt desolate. The houses along the street had seen better days, their paint chipped and peeling, the lawns overgrown and wild. Shelly's home was at the end of the block, tucked between two run-down houses that seemed like they were barely holding together.

The house was a tattered old thing, sagging in places, with broken window shutters and a sagging porch that looked like it hadn't been touched in years. The paint was faded, chipped to the point that it hardly resembled the color it had once been. There were piles of junk in the yard—old tires, rotting furniture, and a broken-down car up on cinder blocks. The place reeked of neglect.

Taylor's heart tightened as she stared at the house for a moment. Sam didn't say much either, his face dark with something unreadable, but Taylor could feel it.

Anyone living in a situation like this was in a bad place in life.

As they got out and approached the door, Taylor could hear faint music coming from inside—something heavy and slow, the kind of sound that didn't fit the atmosphere of the house at all. She knocked twice, and, after a moment, the door creaked open.

Shelly stood there, looking like she hadn't slept in days and at least a decade older than her forty years. Her face was gaunt, her eyes hollow, with deep bags under them. Her hair hung in oily, unkempt strands around her face. She was wearing an old, faded robe that barely hung from her shoulders, and Taylor could smell the faint scent of stale cigarettes and something more pungent.

She blinked at them for a moment before recognition passed through her foggy expression. "What do you want?" Her voice was hoarse, and she rubbed her eyes as though trying to wake up from a bad dream.

Taylor introduced herself. "Do you have a moment to talk?"

"About what?"

"The death of Alma Jennings."

She looked confused for a second, then scowled even more. "Why?"

"We're just looking at the case again, trying to see if anything was missed. We'd appreciate your help."

Shelly stepped back, her movements slow and sluggish, then waved them in. "I already said everything I know but, sure, come on in. I've got nothing else to do today." She closed the door behind them, then immediately slumped onto a chair near the window, looking out at the street.

Taylor couldn't help but feel a pang of pity for the woman. According to Janelle, back then, Shelly was a busy mother of three. Always on the go. But now, she seemed like a shadow of herself, trapped in some kind of emptiness. The house was bare, except for a few old mismatched pieces of furniture, and the air felt stale, as though it hadn't been aired out in a long time. There were empty bottles of pills scattered on the coffee table.

"So, Shelly," Sam began, his voice calm but direct, "we need to talk about the morning Amy showed up on your doorstep."

Shelly leaned back, rubbing her temple with her fingers. Her gaze flickered between them as she thought for a moment, but Taylor could tell she was struggling to pull together a coherent thought. It was as though she were operating in slow motion.

"Yeah ... that. I remember ... it was scary opening my door and seeing her standing there," Shelly said slowly, her voice barely above a whisper. "She was covered in blood. In the oversized nightgown she wore, she looked so ... small, so scared. And so very serious. No hysteria. Or crying ..." Her voice trailed off, as if she were lost in the memory, her eyes unfocused.

Taylor could see Shelly's fingers twitch, as though she were trying to hold onto a memory that kept slipping away. Taylor didn't want to push her too hard, but they needed the details.

"Do you remember what she said?" Taylor asked gently. "Did she say who did this to her?"

Shelly seemed to shrink back into her chair, sighing loudly. "It was such a long time ago. From what I remember, she just kept asking for her mom. She wanted me to take her home."

Shelly paused, and there was a deep, heavy silence in the room. Taylor waited, watching her, feeling a deep sadness for the woman in front of her. Shelly had once been a witness to something so tragic, and, now, it was like she was lost in her own life, haunted by the past.

"We read the interview notes," Sam pressed, trying to get more from her. "You'd mentioned something about her uncle Clem."

Shelly shifted uncomfortably in her seat, her hands gripping the edges of her robe as she stared down at the floor. "She said she thought it was her uncle Clem."

"Or did she say *he looked like* her uncle Clem?" Taylor asked.

"Could you possibly have had it confused?" Sam added.

Shelly's brow furrowed. "I don't know. Like I said, my memory is fuzzy from so long ago. I know she wasn't making a lot of sense. I'm sure she was in shock." She wiped her forehead with the back of her hand.

"Did you ever talk to Amy about it after that day?" Taylor asked, her voice soft, like a balm to Shelly's frayed nerves.

Shelly looked up, meeting their eyes before staring at the floor. "No. They sold Alma's house to a little family from out of town. I never saw Amy again. Well, except on the news. I wish I had more to tell you, but I just don't."

Taylor's stomach tightened. It was clear that Shelly was trying to reconcile her own role in the confusion and guilt that Amy carried. Maybe she thought she should've done more.

Shelly looked down at her hands, shaking her head. "I'm sorry you wasted your time coming here. I don't know how to help anyone anymore."

"Are you married, Shelly?" Taylor asked.

"No. Never was. I've had men in my life but, for the most part, I raised my kids on my own. A lot of good that got me. Never hear from any of them anymore. They couldn't care less that I'm here in this hovel while they're in the well-manicured cookie cutter neighborhoods. I'm an embarrassment to them."

Taylor could see it—the unraveling of a life, the exhaustion of a woman who hadn't had an easy life.

"Did your children talk to Amy that day she came to your door?" Sam asked.

She shook her head. "They didn't even see her. I made sure of that."

Now and Then

"Thank you for your time, Shelly," Sam said, his voice steady. "We appreciate your honesty."

As they left the house, Taylor couldn't shake the feeling of pity she had for Shelly. Once a woman with a family, now a shell of her former self, struggling to hold onto fragments of a life that had slipped through her fingers. It wasn't a particularly productive interview, but she knew one thing for sure—every piece of the puzzle mattered.

Chapter Fifteen

Anna sat in the small conference room just off the administrative wing of Hart's Ridge Community Hospital, her hands folded neatly in her lap. The scent of disinfectant clung to the air, mixing with the metallic click of a wall clock that seemed louder than usual. She'd come dressed in her scrubs, hopeful they'd be put to use.

Across from her sat three people: her immediate supervisor, the head of nursing, and a representative from human resources. Their expressions were unreadable, but the folder on the table and the way no one had offered her coffee told her everything she needed to know—this wasn't a warm welcome back.

"We've completed the preliminary review," her supervisor began, clearing her throat. "And while there's no evidence linking you to the missing bracelet, we wanted to meet in person before reinstating you."

Anna nodded, her face calm even as her pulse drummed beneath her skin.

"Kelsey Marshall is still admitted," added the head of nursing. "She's continuing treatment for the respiratory infection, but she's been advised you're no longer assigned to her care. We'll have someone else managing her case."

"I understand," Anna said evenly.

"We're allowing you to return to work," the HR rep cut in, her tone clipped. "But we want to be transparent. You're not off the hook—not entirely. This incident isn't closed. Should any new information surface—"

"There is no new information," Anna interrupted before she could stop herself. Then, softer: "Because I didn't do anything wrong."

There was a brief silence. Her supervisor offered a tight nod.

"Still," the HR rep continued, "you need to be aware that Thatcher Chambers—the soon-to-be father-in-law of Kelsey Marshall—has made several calls. He's a donor to the west wing, as you probably know."

Anna froze. Her breath caught.

Thatcher. Her ex-father-in-law was an indulgent and crooked man who she'd never trusted. His interaction with his grandchildren all but stopped once they were out of the cute toddler stage.

Of course he'd want to throw his money around to her detriment.

"He believes you took the bracelet out of malice toward his son. Claims you've been out to destroy his life for years. That this—robbery—is only the latest example."

Anna felt heat rise in her face, a flush that had nothing to do with shame. She clenched her hands beneath the table.

"With all due respect," she said quietly, "His son, Pete, was the cause of our family's collapse due to his lying and cheating. Now he has ambushed me in a patient room, insulted me in front of my patient, and, since then, I've been accused of theft. I've cooperated fully. I have nothing to hide and I will continue to say, I've stolen nothing. I love my job. Why would I jeopardize it for something I don't even want? Believe me, Pete's jewelry always comes with a hidden price tag. I never want anything he's touched again."

"We appreciate that you love your job," her supervisor said, her voice more sympathetic now. "Truly. But when someone like the senior Mr. Chambers makes waves, it puts us in a difficult position."

Anna nodded again, even though she wanted to scream.

They didn't see it—how far the roots of Pete's manipulation stretched. How it always looked like he was the one being wronged. And how he had powerful people like his father willing to clean up every mess he made. And his mother powdering his butt in consolation.

"We're hoping this entire incident ends here," the head of nursing said. "And we'd like you to return this afternoon. Get back into your rhythm."

"Thank you," Anna said softly, rising to her feet. "I had hoped"—she paused—"I appreciate the opportunity."

She left the room with her shoulders squared and her jaw locked. They sure didn't give her a vote of confidence ... that they had her back.

At the nurses' station, her badge was waiting for her in a plain envelope. No welcome back card. No fanfare. Just a thin piece of plastic, the metal clip cold against her skin as she attached it to her scrub top.

"Hey," whispered Liza, one of the few who'd looked her in the eye during her suspension. "Good to see you back."

Anna managed a small smile. "Thanks."

She forced herself into motion. Down the hall. Into the rooms. Check-ins. Vitals. Soft words. Gentle hands. Her body knew the rhythm even if her mind was still tangled in the meeting from earlier.

She walked into a room where an elderly man with a breathing tube was dozing, his granddaughter sitting nearby with a tattered paperback. Anna smiled, checked the monitor, adjusted the flow. Then into the next room—an anxious teenager being prepped for an appendectomy. She called and checked on transport.

They'd be there shortly.

And the next room—a new mother with her baby who had colic. She needed the support and encouragement only another woman could give. Anna took the baby, and told the mother to go downstairs and get a cup of coffee, or outside for some fresh air.

The mom hesitated but, when she saw how expertly Anna handled her daughter, she nodded and promised to be back in ten minutes.

Anna moved in a gentle figure-eight motion, and the baby calmed. It was a relief, especially if she could get the baby to go to sleep before the mom returned. She breathed deep, then tried to exhale all the negative energy she was carrying. The child didn't need to be next to that, not if there was any hope of her sleeping. So, Anna envisioned an azure ocean, and soft waves crashing on the beach. A book in her hand and the wind lifting her hair.

But beneath it all, her thoughts kept drifting back to Thatcher Chambers. His voice echoed in her head even though she hadn't heard it in years.

She wants to destroy my son's life.

As if Pete's unraveling hadn't caused his own downfall. As if Anna hadn't spent years covering for him, smoothing over his lies, apologizing for bruises she hadn't caused and accusations she hadn't made.

She'd thought she'd escaped it all when she left him.

Thought she'd carved a new life out of the rubble. But there it was again—the same storm, just in a new form.

The scary part wasn't that Pete was still trying to destroy her.

It was that she wasn't sure she could withstand it this time.

The kids needed her. This job was her lifeline. And her nerves—strung tight from the moment she was called into that room—were starting to fray.

The baby was asleep when the mom returned, her eyes wide and mouth hanging open.

"But how—" she started.

Anna put her finger to her lips, then lay the baby down on the bed and lifted the safety bar slowly and quietly.

"I'll work on finding a crib," she said, then excused herself. She paused outside the next door and rested her forehead against the cool wall.

You're okay, she told herself.

You didn't do anything wrong.

You are not the woman they think you are.

You're the woman who came back. Who started over. Who got up, even after it all.

Pull up your big girl panties and keep on trucking.

She straightened and walked into the next room, a smile on her face for a patient who had apparently just soaked her sheets.

Chapter Sixteen

The small, cluttered office felt like a relic from another era. Taylor was in the rear and stood in the doorway for a moment, taking in the dimly lit space before stepping inside. The walls were lined with bookshelves that had once held rows of legal texts but now seemed to hold more memories than case law. There were dusty old tomes, half-closed file folders stacked on the corner of a desk, and framed photos of what looked like a much younger man in judicial robes, his face beaming with pride.

The office was semi-retired, much like the man who ran it. A long, wooden desk sat in the center of the room, cluttered with papers, a half-finished cup of coffee, and a framed certificate for some legal accomplishment long past. The leather chair behind the desk looked worn but comfortable, and the light from a small desk lamp illuminated the few clean spaces. Taylor couldn't help but notice how everything had a faded, nostalgic air to it—like a place that had seen its glory days and now settled into a quieter, more reflective existence.

Michael Guptill, the attorney who had defended Clem Tiffin ten years ago, sat across from them in the worn leather chair, leaning back with an almost reluctant air. His attire, though expensive-looking, was a little too relaxed—he was clearly not interested in a life of stress anymore. His salt-and-pepper hair was neatly combed, and his face bore the tired yet experienced expression of someone who had seen more than his fair share of courtroom drama over the years.

"Well, would you look at that pretty girl," he cooed at Lennon. "I've got a granddaughter just about your age, I think."

Lennon smiled back at him. She was being so good. Clearly captivated by the new setting, all the books, and stacks of stuff. She was probably thinking how much damage she could do if her dad would only let her on the floor.

This time Janelle was with them, as only her call and special request had opened the door for a conference with the man who rarely took meetings now. They were directed to sit in the three chairs on the other side of the expansive desk.

"Hi, Janelle. So nice to see you again," he said, looking over the desk with a warm smile. "I remember you well—your loyalty and persistence. I don't know many spouses who would fight as hard as you have."

Janelle's eyes softened, a small smile breaking through her solemn face. "Well, I've learned a lot over the years, Michael," she said, her voice steady. "More than I ever thought I would."

Guptill chuckled, leaning forward slightly in his chair. "I imagine you have. You should be a professional detective by now." He paused, glancing over at Sam and Taylor. "Her husband had the best advocate, no doubt about it. It's rare to see someone so committed to finding the truth."

Janelle nodded, her fingers gently clasped together in her lap. "Thank you. Who knew that all my true crime shows would come in so handy. Especially *Forensic Files*. It taught me a lot in trying to see every angle."

Taylor listened with a sense of admiration, knowing how much Janelle had put into this over the years.

Janelle introduced them and then shifted in her seat, coming back to the task at hand. "We wanted to talk to you about Amy," she began. "About the hypnosis session she underwent years after Clem's conviction. We were hoping to get your take on it."

The attorney raised an eyebrow, clearly intrigued. "The hypnosis, you say? Yeah, that was a defeat for sure. Ultimately, the judge declared that Amy had been exposed to too many people who held a biased interest in the outcome, and he refused to give Clem another trial."

"I don't understand how they can just throw out evidence like that," Taylor said.

Guptill shrugged. "Well, dear, there's been a lot of controversy around the practice of hypnosis, especially in the courtroom." He leaned back in his chair again, folding his hands over his stomach. "In fact, hypnosis-based testimony hasn't been accepted in most courts for a long time. I'll admit, I myself have seen it fail too many times. I'm not surprised it was thrown out."

Janelle's brow furrowed slightly. "But Amy was so certain ... why aren't her memories valued?"

Guptill gave a small, understanding sigh. "It's not that the memories don't hold any value. But there's something about hypnosis that makes it unreliable in legal settings. You see, courts have ruled for years that hypnosis can't always be trusted as a tool for recalling accurate memories. Take the 1968 case of *Harding v. State*, for example. The court allowed testimony that had been enhanced by hypnosis, but jurors were explicitly told to question its credibility."

Taylor wasn't fully understanding the complexities. "But Amy's original testimony about Clem—it's not the same now. She recanted."

"She even admitted under hypnosis that she was just trying to help by identifying him," Sam added, glancing at Janelle before focusing back on the attorney.

Guptill nodded, as though he had anticipated that response. "Yes, and that's the problem. In cases like these, hypnosis often creates what's called memory hardening—false memories that are so vivid the subject starts believing them completely. The lines between what actually happened and what's been suggested can blur." He paused, letting the words sink in before continuing. "The issue is that hypnosis often fills in the blanks. That's what we call hypermnesia—when the subject's mind creates false memories, sometimes based on personal beliefs or suggestions they've been exposed to. It can lead to confabulation, where the subject, under the influence of hypnosis, fills in the gaps with things they believe to be true but are actually false."

Janelle seemed to absorb this, her expression a mixture of confusion and concern. "But Amy's a good girl. She would never lie about something like that," she said, her voice softening.

"I'm sure she believes what she said," the attorney replied, "and of course I'd hoped we could use it, but the issue is, once you've had something implanted in your mind under hypnosis, it's hard to separate what's true from what's been suggested. And that's why it's not admissible in most courts."

Taylor's mind raced as she processed his words. "So, there's a very real possibility that Amy's memory of the attacker was skewed to what she wanted to believe happened?"

"That's exactly it," Guptill said, leaning forward. "And it's not just about what she said. It's the entire process of hypnosis that makes it unreliable. Amy wanted to be wrong about her uncle, so some could say that, under hypnosis, her brain painted a new memory to make that happen."

Janelle exhaled slowly, her face a mixture of disappointment and frustration. "So all these years, I've been fighting for a false memory?"

His eyes softened. "Not false—misguided, maybe. But I'm afraid it's the reality we're dealing with. It's not that anyone's intention was bad. Amy was trying to be helpful. But hypnosis is a flawed tool in this situation. We just don't know how reliable her memory is under hypnosis."

Sam's eyes narrowed slightly. "So, what do we do now? What's our next step?"

He gave them a thoughtful look. "You need to focus on the facts. Look at everything with fresh eyes. Go through every witness's statement, check the timelines again, and make sure the alibis are airtight. You really need to get them to test the pubic hairs and skin cells recovered from Alma's body. If it doesn't match Clem's DNA, that's your key. There's a lot to untangle, and the truth is often buried in the details. I still regret that I couldn't get that ordered. Focus on that and, in the meantime, meet with everyone who was ever connected to this case."

"They have been interviewing people from the case," Janelle said. "And they've read all the trial transcripts now."

He sighed, rubbing his chin. "So, it sounds like you've already got a decent start. But the truth won't be found in a courtroom. It'll be discovered in the little details. So go back to the beginning. Get back to the scene. Talk to more people who were around back then. Maybe you'll uncover something you missed the first time."

Janelle nodded slowly. "We'll do whatever it takes," she said, her voice steady but still tinged with the exhaustion of years of waiting.

"I'd also suggest that, if you really want to open this case up again, you hire a new defense attorney. I'm sorry, but I'm just not the one who can get this going. But I have someone in mind who just might be exactly who you need. He's the son of an old colleague."

"I can't afford a new attorney," Janelle said, her voice so low it was almost inaudible.

Taylor glanced over at Sam, who was silently taking it all in. There were no guarantees. But with every step, they were digging deeper into the truth. And as much as the journey had drained them, it was the only path worth walking.

"Then talk to the prosecutor again. See if she's softened at all," he said.

"Well," Taylor said, standing up and gathering her things, "thanks for your time. We'll take your advice to heart, and we'll talk about your referral. Hopefully, this helps us get closer to the truth."

The attorney smiled faintly. "Good luck, and don't let this drag you down too far, Janelle. You've already given more of yourself than any other spouse I've ever known in this kind of situation."

Janelle thanked him and he embraced her at the door.

As they left the office, Taylor felt a sense of quiet determination settle over her. So, the hypnosis wouldn't be any help. But they weren't finished yet—not by a long shot.

Chapter Seventeen

Janelle, Sam, and Taylor sat around a polished wooden table in the conference room of Thompson and Thompson law firm. What was coming could be a pivotal moment. A moment that, for the first time in ten years, might actually have a chance to change Clem's fate.

Janelle sat at the edge of her seat, her fingers nervously folding and unfolding a tissue in her lap. Sam had his arms crossed, his face a mask of focus, while Taylor's thoughts ran deep, everything they'd learned so far pulling her in all directions.

The door clicked open, and in stepped John Thompson, proudly carrying his reputation for getting things done when it came to flawed cases. He exuded confidence, wearing a sharp suit that contrasted against the casualness of the room. His eyes flickered over to Janelle, and there was a glimmer of something like respect there—perhaps admiration for her persistence.

Taylor took that as a good sign.

Sam sat beside her, his usual easygoing demeanor replaced with a quiet, focused energy that matched her own. They'd done everything they could on their end. Now it was time to get a real shot at justice for Clem.

Janelle glanced around the office. This was probably really her last viable hope. Taylor could see the desperation in her eyes, the toll taken by years of fighting for a man she believed in, even when no one else did.

The meeting room wasn't the usual pristine space of a high-powered corporate attorney, but Taylor liked it. It was a place that spoke of experience, of battles fought, and perhaps battles still to come.

John Thompson was well into his late forties, with salt-and-pepper hair and a strong jawline. His eyes were sharp, but not unkind. He had an edge that came across making Taylor confident he was the right man for this case. She felt a glimmer of hope when she saw him. He had already reviewed the case, they'd had one phone consult, and today they'd find out if he was willing to fight.

"Taylor, Sam, Mrs. Tiffin," he greeted, extending a hand toward each of them. "I'm glad you're here. Let's get to it." He sat down, pulling a folder from his briefcase and pushing it to the center of the table.

"As you know, I've had a chance to look through the case in detail," John started, glancing at the papers in front of him before holding their gaze. "It's my belief that Clem is innocent."

Janelle let out a breath she was holding.

He continued. "But more importantly, there's no evidence—no concrete evidence—to say otherwise." He locked eyes with Janelle. "I'm totally surprised that they were able to convict Mr. Tiffin. I must say, Mrs. Tiffin, looking through everything we've got here, what you've done so far is remarkable. You've fought for your husband tirelessly. And your persistence has made this possible. I'm here because you deserve another shot at justice for your husband."

Janelle's lips trembled, but she nodded and whispered "Thank you."

"Don't thank me yet. It's going to take a miracle, and I'm in the business of finding evidence to refute a conviction. Right now, we just don't have it. Not only do we not have it, but the prosecutor in this case is a bulldog when it comes to crimes like this, and I don't know if she'll play ball. It's evident that she hasn't budged in previous attempts."

"She's terrible," Janelle said softly, then lowered her eyes and blushed.

Thompson shook his head. "No, she's good at her job is what she is. She has a passion about it that some never find, and, between us, it's because long before she went to law school, she was abducted at knifepoint. She got away but not before her assailant put a fear in her that would never quite go away. A fear that makes her a formidable opponent in the courtroom. You have to understand that most women do try to protect their men, by lying or even taking responsibility for their crimes. Prisons are full of women doing time for what their partners did."

"That's true," Taylor said. "But considering that it was her mother who was brutally murdered, she should've gotten a bit more benefit of the doubt. That maybe she—nodding to Janelle—was telling the truth, that Clem couldn't have done it because he was with her."

Before anyone could respond, the door opened again, and in walked Prosecutor Rosana Calloway, the woman who had convicted Clem ten years ago. Taylor felt a quick tension snap into place as soon as she saw her—the prosecutor's eyes scanning the room, taking stock of everyone present as she shut the door behind her with a soft click.

The night before, Taylor had read a lot about her. Calloway had been the rising star of the prosecutor's office, and her hard-line stance on convictions had earned her both admiration and animosity.

"Good to see you again, John," Rosana greeted, her voice as tight as her posture. She didn't offer a handshake, just a slight nod. Her gaze slid over to Janelle before resting back on Thompson. There was a flicker of something—maybe regret or pity?—but it quickly disappeared. She was back to all business.

"Ms. Calloway," Taylor greeted, her tone polite but firm. "Thank you for agreeing to meet. I think we're all aware of what we're here to discuss."

"I'm here simply because John and I go way back, and he pulled in a favor for this meeting," Rosana said flatly. "What I'm not here to do is revisit a case that's already been decided. Mr. Tiffin's guilt has been settled in court. And the appeals have been declined."

Janelle shifted uncomfortably beside Taylor, and Taylor placed a reassuring hand on her arm. "I understand that, Ms. Calloway," Taylor began, her voice calm but steady. "But I think you'll agree there are some issues that have never been fully addressed. Especially when it comes to the evidence—or lack of it—that was used to convict Mr. Tiffin."

The prosecutor's eyes narrowed, and Taylor could feel the walls going up around her. "I'm very aware of every detail of the case," Rosana replied evenly. "A jury of twelve peers found enough evidence to convict him. The system works, and it worked then."

"But did it, though?" John interjected, his voice cutting through the prosecutor's firm stance. "You see, what I've learned is that there was no direct physical evidence linking Mr. Tiffin to the scene. And the child witness, soon after, expressed doubt over her identification. You can't ignore that, Rosana."

"Only after there had been time for people to coach her,"

Rosana said. "To appeal to a young girl's conscience about her uncle spending the rest of his life behind bars."

"Or conscience that she'd misconstrued what she saw?" Sam said.

Taylor quickly added, "In addition, pubic hairs recovered from Alma's body, skin cells beneath her fingernails, and cells from her genital area were tested, but the results were inconclusive. No follow-up testing was done when requested later."

Calloway's jaw tightened, but she remained stoic. "When that request came through, Mr. Tiffin was already convicted. The evidence spoke for itself."

"Not really," John replied with a slight shake of his head. "The problem is the police had tunnel vision from the start. They built a case around Mr. Tiffin, and you know very well that they didn't look into other possible suspects. This is what happens when law enforcement gets fixated on one person without doing the proper legwork."

Calloway's eyes flicked to John, her voice deadpan. "Mr. Tiffin had the means and opportunity. He was seen at the scene by his niece, and that's all we need."

"What about motive?" John asked. "Isn't that usually a vital part of an investigation."

She nodded confidently. "Witnesses said the relationship between the victim and Mr. Tiffin was tenuous at best."

John leaned forward. "Hearsay. And they also didn't have a lineup that was properly conducted. Amy identified her uncle because she was a child—and he was the only man she knew. That's not a fair process. They didn't match the description first—they matched the lineup to the person they already thought was guilty."

Calloway's face remained stoic. "We did what the law allows. This is a matter of public record."

"Let's go back over a few things. I mean, while we are

already here," John said, smiling slightly at Calloway, nearly flirting. "Tiffin lived about an hour away from Alma's place. He came home that night around 2:40 a.m. and we know this because Janelle was awake with one of their children—Aaron. He was sick with strep throat, right?"

"Yes, he was," Janelle confirmed softly.

John nodded. "So, let's say he comes home when he says he did. The estimated time of Alma's death was between 2:30 and 5:30 a.m. There's no way he could have left, driven an hour to Alma's house, attacked her and Amy, and returned without anyone noticing whether he was home. And that's why I'm asking you, Rosana, to give us another chance. The DNA tests that were done ten years ago were inconclusive, but testing methods have improved. We could test the evidence again. We could eliminate Clem if he's guilty—or prove he's innocent."

The prosecutor crossed her arms, staring at John with cold resolve. "It's been ten years, John. Don't you have better and more productive cases to work on? This case is locked up tight."

"Not if we can do something about it," John pressed. "You have to admit, the county's DNA testing methods have become more refined in the last decade. It might still be inconclusive, but we can at least try again, can't we?"

"And whose budget do you think that's going to come from? Even if I wanted to say yes, it would be downvoted so fast your head would spin."

"I'll find a way to pay for it," Janelle said.

"Yes, we'll come up with the money," Taylor said. Sam nodded beside her. How they would do it, she had no idea. Janelle was already tapped out, and she and Sam didn't have that kind of disposable funds to work with. Testing again could cost anywhere from hundreds of dollars to tens of thousands. They just didn't know.

"Mrs. Tiffin, how are you going to feel if the DNA comes

back positive to your husband this time? Will you then let it go? I'm tired of seeing chatter about this case with my name attached to it," Calloway said.

"That's not going to happen," Janelle replied, not blinking an eye.

"Yes," Taylor elaborated, "If the DNA belongs to Clem Tiffin, then we'll all agree to let it lie. Janelle will stop fighting."

"Won't you, Janelle?" Sam said softly, urging her to agree.

She faltered. It was obviously hard for her to do, but she finally nodded her head in agreement.

Calloway still wasn't budging.

"Think of it like this, Rosana," Thompson said. "If you are as confident about this case as you come across here, then you have no reason to fear running the DNA again. Right?"

Good play, John.

Taylor was impressed at his cat and mouse game. With a colleague, no less.

Her resolve not wavering, Calloway's expression softened slightly. "Fine," she said reluctantly. "It's your dime. But I'm secure in my decision. Tiffin is where he belongs."

"I'll have the paperwork drawn up," John said, standing up and offering a handshake. "We'll take it from here."

Calloway stood, her gaze lingering on the group for a moment before she turned and walked out of the office without another word. The door clicked shut behind her, and the room was still.

Taylor looked at Janelle, her heart heavy for her. This was it. They had a chance. Maybe. But it would take everything they had to see it through.

Chapter Eighteen

The break room smelled like burnt coffee and the unmistakable tang of disinfectant wipes. Anna leaned her elbow on the chipped laminate table, stirring the creamer into her mug with mechanical focus while her coworker, Melinda, sat across from her, venting into her yogurt cup.

"I swear, I've got a patient who is milking her stay," Melinda said, stabbing her spoon into the fruit on the bottom. "I mean, respiratory infection, yeah, but her oxygen's been stable for days. Her appetite's back. Vitals are perfect. She's just lounging now."

Anna sipped slowly. "Then why hasn't she been discharged?"

Melinda leaned in slightly, voice lowered even though they were alone. "Because Dr. Fletch says she still needs monitoring. And you know no one questions Fletch. You breathe too loud and he'll write you up for insubordination."

Anna raised a brow. So Melinda was lucky enough get Kelsey. First, she hadn't thought it was Kelsey, but Dr. Fletch was her doctor. And the respiratory infection—had to be her.

Melinda was right, too. Fletch had a reputation. Old-school, arrogant, and never wrong—even when he was.

She continued, "And the patient's boyfriend? God, Anna. He's the real problem. Has DoorDash showing up twice a day with steak, sushi, once even Thai food. She doesn't eat it. He does. And, I swear, he thinks we're his personal waitstaff."

"Let me guess," Anna said. "He asks for extra pillows, fresh ice, Diet Coke, and someone to plug in his charger?"

Melinda nodded emphatically. "Exactly! Yesterday he asked if we had sugar packets for his coffee like we're a hotel. Poor Avery—she's a CNA, barely twenty. He scared her into bringing him snacks from the staff fridge. She's practically hiding from him now."

Anna's stomach sank.

Pete would never change. Once an asshole, always an asshole.

Melinda sighed. "I want to report him, but something about him gives me the creeps. Like he'd make life hell for anyone who stands up to him. You ever get that feeling about someone?"

Anna stirred her coffee again and nodded, choosing her words carefully. Melinda didn't know how close her instincts were. "I'd let it go if I were you. For now. Better to have a story about an annoying visitor than become part of a bigger one."

Melinda looked surprised. "You think it could go that far?"

Anna shrugged. "Some people collect grudges like trophies."

Melinda rolled her eyes. "God. Why are the worst ones always the ones who think they're above the rules?"

Anna didn't answer. She didn't have to.

On her way back from break, Anna moved through the main corridor toward the nurses' station, trying to organize her thoughts. The patient load had been somewhat manageable today, and she wanted to keep it that way. One room at a time.

Stay present.

Stay grounded.

But just as she rounded the corner near the elevators, she spotted them.

Thatcher Chambers and his wife, Elizabeth.

Walking side by side, dressed like they were headed to the most exclusive country club in Georgia. He wore a white sweater draped over his shoulders, sleeves knotted at his chest, and tennis whites that probably hadn't seen a real court in a decade. Elizabeth wore her signature oversized sunglasses indoors and carried a purse that likely cost more than Anna's car.

They saw her. She knew they did. She caught Thatcher's sideways glance, the quick nudge he gave his wife. They both paused just slightly, long enough to make the next part feel deliberate.

As they passed, Elizabeth hissed it under her breath but loud enough that it hit Anna like a slap.

"Town trash."

Anna froze for a split second but didn't turn.

Didn't flinch.

Didn't give them the reaction they wanted.

Instead, she crossed her arms and turned slowly, watching them walk away.

Let them see her. Let them feel her eyes on their backs.

She wore a smug smile—not because she didn't feel the sting, but because she refused to let them think they'd landed a blow.

They thought they were so high and mighty, but, truth be told, they hadn't earned one dime of what they had. Their wealth had been inherited from Elizabeth's family, a dynasty of landowners and banking elites that made them feel entitled to look down on people like Anna. People who worked. People who struggled. People who crawled out of where they began, only to become something no one would expect.

They'd hated her from the moment she entered their world. Expected Pete to marry someone like them—well-bred, soft-spoken, with generational wealth and an unblemished name. Not the daughter of a woman who once served time. Not a Gray.

But Anna would put the Grays up against the Chambers any day. Her family might not have tons of money, but they had respect. They had grit. And most of all, they had each other.

Taylor had protected half the people in this town before she ever hung her badge on the wall. Jo ran the rescue with the kind of quiet tenacity that made people trust her with their hearts. And even their mother—Cate—had become someone others looked to for advice, for support, for truth. A convicted felon turned respected elder. That didn't happen by accident.

It happened because they earned it.

And that was something the Chambers would never understand.

Still, Anna's chest tightened as she turned back down the hall.

They could sneer and snub all they wanted, but, beyond that, Thatcher had more. Connections. Influence. And she knew the storm wasn't over yet.

She checked on her next patient—a diabetic woman recovering from a foot ulcer. Changed the dressing, made sure the pain meds were working, and took a minute to review the chart. But she couldn't focus. Not fully.

Not with Pete three doors down. Not with his parents hovering like vultures. Not with her job still hanging in the balance, no matter how quietly they'd reinstated her.

She could feel the eyes. Even if no one was watching, she felt them.

And for the first time in weeks, she wondered if coming back had been a mistake. Not because she didn't want to nurse. But because she didn't know if she could keep doing it under this shadow.

She checked her watch. Another four hours.

She could get through four hours.

Then she could go where no one whispered behind her back, where the dogs barked too loud and her kids left all their school stuff in the hallway. She'd listen to requests and then complaints about dinner, and she'd smile through it and give thanks for the nowhere-near-perfect new life she'd made for the two most important people in her life.

Teague would be playing a video game.

Bronwyn would probably be drawing plans for a calf palace she couldn't possibly build.

Yes, her heart was hurrying her along so she could go home.

Where she was safe.

Where she was Anna Gray.

And not someone Pete Chambers was trying to ruin—again.

By the time Anna's shift ended, she felt wrung out—body, mind, and soul. Her feet didn't even feel like feet any longer. They were heavy, solid blocks of pain. She was going to have to invest in a better pair of shoes. Ones that lasted more than half her shift.

It was times like these she wished she had a partner at home, waiting to give her a foot rub. Or at least have dinner waiting.

Either of the two would be heaven.

The last few hours had been the usual ER chaos: a child

Now and Then

with a gaping dog bite and panicked parents who couldn't stop crying, a college kid brought in after fainting at track practice, dangerously dehydrated and still arguing about finishing his next race. An older man with chest pains who'd insisted on driving himself in, and now had three nurses working to stabilize him while his blood pressure swung like a pendulum. She'd even had to calm down a woman convinced she was having a stroke, only to find out she'd taken five caffeine pills and half a diet shake without eating.

Anna had been too busy to breathe, and, for that, she was grateful.

It meant less time to dwell on the sick twist in her stomach every time she passed Room 284.

Or to replay the hissed words of Elizabeth Chambers: *town trash*.

It was nearly dark when she finally slipped away to the locker room. Her feet ached, and her shoulders were stiff from leaning over patient beds all day. All she wanted was to grab her keys, maybe cry in her car for five minutes, and drive home to the predictable chaos of kids and dogs and dinner.

But as she turned the corner, she saw them.

Her supervisor, Monica, stood with arms crossed, face unreadable. Next to her was Patricia from HR, holding a clipboard and wearing the same stiff expression she'd worn during the disciplinary meeting a few days ago.

Anna's stomach dropped like a stone.

"Can we speak with you a moment, Anna?" Patricia asked.

"Of course," she said carefully. "What is this about?"

Monica exchanged a glance with Patricia, then turned back to Anna. "Thatcher and Elizabeth Chambers have contacted us again. Their insurance company is refusing to pay out on the bracelet."

"They're claiming it was stolen under negligent circumstances," Patricia added. "As such, the Chambers have requested we search your locker one more time."

Anna felt like the breath had been knocked out of her.

"I already told you—I didn't steal anything," she said, her voice tight.

"I understand," Patricia said. "But we need to proceed."

A nurse Anna barely knew walked past just then, eyeing the three of them with open curiosity.

"Can we speak somewhere private?" Anna asked quietly, fighting the rising heat in her face. "This doesn't need to be done in front of everyone."

"We'll keep it discreet," Monica said. "We just need to follow protocol."

Anna swallowed hard and turned to her locker. She unlocked it with trembling fingers, pulling the door open.

Inside was everything she always kept there.

Her fleece zip-up jacket. A spare pair of tennis shoes. Her half-used packet of gum.

A travel deodorant.

Her water flask with a worn "Nurses Heal" sticker.

A granola bar she'd been meaning to throw out for days.

And her canvas tote with her planner, wallet, and a couple pens.

Monica reached in and began removing the contents one by one, laying them neatly on the floor. She turned the pockets of the jacket inside out. Opened the tote bag, sifting through receipts and lip balm.

Anna stood still, every muscle in her body vibrating with embarrassment. A different nurse walked by this time, slower, her eyes flicking between the women and the contents on the floor.

"Let me just ..." Monica unscrewed the top of the flask.

Anna started to speak. "There's just water in that—"

Monica tilted it toward the light, peering inside, then upended it over the floor.

A soft splash of water hit the tile, and with it came a glittering object—small, silver, and unmistakably expensive.

The bracelet hit the ground with a sharp clink, skidding just slightly before it came to rest near Anna's shoe.

No one spoke for a moment.

Patricia's eyes went wide. Monica froze, her fingers still gripping the bottle.

Anna stared at it, numb. Her vision blurred at the edges, her ears ringing.

"What ..." she whispered. "What is that? That wasn't—That wasn't in there. I didn't—"

Monica slowly stood. "Anna ..."

"I didn't put that in there!" she said, louder this time. Panic flared through her chest like a sudden fire. "It wasn't in there. Someone—someone put it there."

She looked between them, heart pounding, throat dry.

"Please. I've never seen that bracelet in my life. Why would I hide it in my own water bottle? That doesn't make any sense!"

Monica looked shaken, but Patricia had already begun writing something on her clipboard.

"We'll need to document this," she said. "And discuss next steps."

"Wait—wait," Anna said, voice cracking. "You don't understand. Pete—he's been trying to ruin me. His parents—they've never liked me. I left him because of what he did to me, and now they're still coming after me."

Monica exchanged another glance with Patricia.

"Can we please talk in private?" Anna begged. "Please. Let me tell you what's really going on."

Patricia hesitated, then nodded. "Let's move this to the conference room."

But Anna couldn't move yet. She stared at the bracelet still lying on the floor—glistening, accusing—and felt the ground tilt beneath her feet.

She had survived a lot.

But right now, for the first time in a long time, she didn't know if she could survive this.

Chapter Nineteen

The tension in Janelle Tiffin's living room was thick, an almost tangible dread hanging over the gathered family members. The sun was high in the sky outside, but the room felt as dark as the topic they had to address. Everyone stood, reluctantly, in their positions. Some with arms crossed, others fidgeting, unsure of where to look or how to behave. The only sounds were the shuffling of feet and the occasional sigh as family members exchanged glances, unsure how to begin.

It felt like a funeral.

Janelle stood at the front, her hands nervously clasped in front of her. Sam and Taylor stood to the side, the presence of two outsiders creating an almost unnatural distance. Sam was a stranger to many of them, and, while Taylor had met some of them briefly, they hadn't yet made their impact as part of the family dynamic.

One of the teenage cousins was playing with Lennon on the back porch.

Janelle cleared her throat, stepping forward.

"Thank you all for coming," she began, her voice shaky but firm. "This has been a long ordeal. I know that everyone has their own thoughts, and it's not easy to talk about what happened. But we're here because we still want answers. For Clem. For Amy. For all of us." She glanced at Sam and Taylor. "This is Sam. My nephew. And his wife, Taylor. They're private detectives, and they've come to help."

The room shifted slightly, as if the introduction of outsiders made everything feel more real. Derek, Janelle's oldest son, shifted uncomfortably. His face was hard with skepticism, arms crossed tightly. His wife stood next to him, a hand resting on his shoulder, her face sympathetic but uncertain.

"Why are we bringing this back up again?" Derek asked, his voice tight with frustration. He looked to his wife for comfort before looking back at Janelle. "Let it rest, Mom. Let Clem rest. Let Grandma rest. This ... this isn't doing anyone any good. It's been ten years."

His wife, standing beside him, reached up to rub his back, comforting him with the touch.

Janelle's face softened with emotion, but she didn't back down. "Derek, I can't let it rest. Not after everything. You don't understand, and I don't expect you to. But I can't just let him stay there when I know, in my heart, that he didn't do it."

Aaron, Janelle's younger son, who had been leaning against the wall with his arms crossed, stood up straighter and faced Derek. His expression was more aggressive, a fire burning in his eyes. "Let Mom talk, Derek. She's been fighting this alone for too long. She deserves to be heard."

The air seemed to crackle with tension as Derek shot a glare at Aaron. Taylor worried that a physical feud was brewing. Before anything more could be said, Clem's brother, George, cleared his throat and spoke up.

"This has been a miscarriage of justice for my brother and

for Alma," George said, his voice gravelly but passionate. "No one deserves to have this kind of thing happen to them. Not Clem, not Alma. One day in prison for an innocent man is too long. Ten years? That's way too long."

There was a silence that followed, as George's words settled in the room. It was a blunt truth, and everyone in the room knew it. Even Derek seemed to wrestle with the reality of the situation, his face showing the conflict within.

Clem's elderly mother, who had been sitting quietly at the far end of the room, suddenly started to sob, her body shaking with the force of her grief. She covered her face with her hands, unable to hide the pain that had consumed her for years.

Janelle turned away, her eyes filled with tears, and she began trembling. She turned to Taylor, her voice breaking. "I can't do this anymore. I can't be the one to hold all of this together. Please, Taylor, take over."

Taylor nodded, stepping forward. Her heart ached for Clem's mother. And especially for Janelle, who had fought so long and so hard for a man who was lost in the system. A decade lost and she still couldn't let go.

She placed a hand on Janelle's shoulder and gently guided her to sit down before turning to the others.

"Listen, everyone," Taylor said, addressing the room. "You're here today because we had an appointment with a new attorney yesterday. A fresh pair of eyes. We really believe Clem deserves one last chance at justice. The prosecutor has agreed to let us have the DNA found on Alma tested again. But to get it done, Janelle needs money. For the attorney, and for the testing. She needs our help."

As soon as the words left her mouth, the room erupted into noise. Derek shook his head. "Money? You're asking for money?" His voice was rising, frustration clear in his tone.

"Mom's been through hell. Why drag us all back into this mess? Just to throw more money at it? It's been a decade!"

"It could clear Dad, Derek!" Aaron yelled.

Julie, Amy's mother, who had been sitting quietly in the corner, stood up and walked over to Derek. "Stop it, Derek," she said, her voice firm but comforting. She placed a hand on her arm, then turned toward Janelle, her eyes soft. "I know how much you've sacrificed, Janelle. I also know that we've sacrificed our relationship because of this horrific situation. Some of that is my fault. But if you really believe in Clem's innocence, then I'll help."

Derek's eyes widened with surprise, but, before he could protest, Amy—who had been silently standing in the back, watching the argument unfold—whistled loudly to get everyone's attention.

Everyone turned to her, her face pale, eyes wide with emotion.

"Amy?" Janelle's voice cracked as she looked at her niece, surprised to hear her speak up.

Amy's lip quivered, but she pressed on. "I ... I can't live with this anymore," she said, her voice choked with tears. "If there's even one tiny sliver of a chance that Uncle Clem is innocent, and my testimony put him there ... I can't live with myself." She wiped at her eyes, clearly struggling to keep it together. "I just want the truth to come out. Let them hypnotize me again. Maybe I'll remember something else. I'll give you all my college money. And I'll get a loan. Don't care what it costs, I want to make things right so I can move on with my life!"

She was sobbing as she finished.

The room went silent, her words hanging in the air. Every set of eyes was on Amy now, and the affection they all shared for her was evident in the stillness that followed.

Sam took a deep breath and stepped forward, his hand

resting on Amy's shoulder. "We need to at least get together the retainer for the attorney. Janelle has given everything she has, but, if we're going to go down this road, we need something to show we're serious. That's where you all come in. As family. To help with this last push."

Janelle's voice was barely above a whisper. "I'll sell this house," she said, her voice shaking. "I'll do whatever it takes. This house ... I've clung to it because it was supposed to be here for Clem when he got out. But if it means getting him the chance he deserves, I'll let it go. We could live in a box, for all I care."

Derek's face turned nearly purple with anger, and he stomped out the front door, letting it slam behind him.

The tears came quickly for Janelle as she broke down, the trauma of her sacrifice too much to bear. Julie walked over and enveloped her in a warm embrace.

"You're not selling the house. Not yet. We're doing this together, Janelle," Julie said softly, rubbing her back. "One last try to circle the wagon and make sure Clem gets a fair shot. We can do this. All of us."

Aaron, who had been mostly silent up until now, wiped his eyes and turned to the others. "I'll set up a Facebook page. We can ask for leads. And donations. I have five grand I can put in once I sell my truck," he said. His voice was steady now, though his emotions were clearly raw.

Julie's husband, who had been quiet until now, stood up. "We can put in ten," he said, his tone matter-of-fact. "Let's finish this so this family can start to heal."

Julie looked at everyone, then turned to Janelle. "But this time, if we get shot down, we stay down. Janelle, you have to agree to that. This isn't healthy for you."

Janelle nodded, her voice hoarse. "I agree. I'm not healthy.

This is killing me, but we have to try. We owe it to Clem. If the DNA comes back to him, I'll stop. I promise."

Aaron came to his mom and put his arm around her.

A few of Clem's brothers stood up, offering what they could toward the retainer, and moral support, of course. The room was still, the sense of unity finally settling in. They were ready, for better or worse, to give this one last shot.

Chapter Twenty

Anna looked around the farm from her perch on the porch steps of Taylor's house, and she wondered how an adult could love a place so much that they'd hated as a child. Obviously, the human psyche was complicated. Once, the land beneath her had felt heavy with silence and sorrow—echoes of slammed doors, whispered arguments, and things no one dared talk about. Back then, she'd dreamed of running far, far away. Becoming someone totally different and leaving behind her difficult childhood. But now, the same porch frequently creaked beneath them with laughter. The barn was filled with rescued animals instead of tension. Her own children ran barefoot across the same wooden dock she'd once cried on, and the house they gathered in—patched and worn—held warmth instead of secrets. Somehow, thanks to Taylor never letting go of the property and allowing all of them to embrace it and turn it into something wonderful, they'd rewritten what this place once meant.

The land itself hadn't changed.

But they had. And maybe that was the most powerful kind of healing.

Down by the lake, laughter drifted up faintly through the trees, the voices of Cate, Ellis, Jo, and the kids as they fished, everyone competing for the first catch of the weekend.

Anna wrapped her arms loosely around her knees as she listened to the crickets tuning up in the dusk. Taylor sat just behind her on the swing, one leg tucked beneath her, Lennon asleep in her crib inside the house. Sam leaned against the porch railing, nursing a bottle of beer, eyes flicking toward Taylor every so often with that quiet concern he never voiced until necessary.

Dinner had been good—Jo's garden squash, breaded and pan-fried, with grilled chicken and wild rice. Comfort food. No one had noticed Anna pushing the same piece of squash around her plate all night. She hadn't said much, but she could feel Taylor watching her.

"So when do you go back to Indiana?" Anna asked. She knew they had a case of possible false arrest and conviction that they were working on, but so far both Sam and Taylor were mum about the details.

"Soon. We're waiting on news about DNA, and a witness is going to be hypnotized for the second time, to take her back to the incident. We're also following up on calls and leads from here, but, when the forensics is back, we'll go."

Sam nodded. "It's complicated. But it could be the DNA results or even the hypnosis session will confirm what the jury believed, and we won't go back at all."

They fell into stillness again.

Taylor finally broke the silence. "Okay. Out with it."

Anna blinked. "Out with what?"

"You've got that look," Taylor said, tone dry. The voice she used when she was mothering them. "The one where you're holding something in so hard I can practically hear the pressure building. So just ... spill it."

Anna let out a slow breath. "Something has happened at work."

Taylor straightened. Sam turned his full attention to her.

Once she got going, Anna couldn't stop, and, by the time she got to the first locker search and getting suspended, she was in tears.

"But they didn't find it, right?" Sam asked.

"Not that time," Anna replied. "I went back to work a few days after the first meeting. Everything was fine. Awkward, but fine. They told me I wasn't assigned to Kelsey's care anymore, and I kept my head down. Did my job."

"And?" Taylor asked.

Anna swallowed. "At the end of my shift, Monica—my supervisor—and HR were waiting for me in the locker room. Said Thatcher Chambers had called again. That their insurance company wasn't going to pay out on the bracelet unless they could prove it had been stolen."

Taylor sat up straighter. "You're kidding me."

"They asked to search my locker again."

"Again?" Sam said. "Didn't they already do that and find nothing?"

"Yeah." Anna stared out at the lake. "But this time ... they found it."

"What?" Taylor's voice was sharp.

"In my water flask," Anna said. "Monica unscrewed the lid and when she turned it over—along with the water—the bracelet fell out."

Taylor was silent for a full beat. "No. No way. There's no way you—"

"I didn't do it, Tay."

"Of course you didn't," Taylor snapped. "Jesus, Anna, they know you didn't do it. Or they should. Did you tell them?"

"I told them I've never seen the bracelet before. That someone had to have planted it."

"Let me guess," Sam said quietly. "They suspended you again."

Anna nodded. "While the board reviews the incident. I mean, what if they try to arrest me? Could I go to jail? Oh my God, what if I lose my nursing license?"

Terror struck a chord through her.

Taylor stood, arms crossed, pacing the porch. "This is insane. It's Pete. He's behind it. Has to be."

"I think so too," Anna whispered. "But how do I prove that?"

Sam rubbed his jaw. "You said the flask had water in it?"

Anna nodded. "I drink from it constantly. If the bracelet had been in there all day, I would've noticed."

"Exactly. So someone must've slipped it in while you were with patients," Sam said.

Taylor stopped pacing. "Are there cameras?"

Anna blinked. "What?"

"Cameras," Taylor repeated. "In the hallway. In the staff lounge. Outside the locker rooms. Ask if they've reviewed the footage. Ask who else has keys to your locker."

"I didn't even think—"

"You shouldn't have to," Taylor said, her voice rising. "Because this is ridiculous. Pete is doing this on purpose. And his father's just fueling the fire. Trying to make you look like the problem."

Anna's throat tightened. "I thought about calling Pete. Just to ask him to stop. Maybe offer something—waive the back child support he owes, just ... anything to make a deal."

"No," Sam said immediately.

"Absolutely not," Taylor echoed. "You don't negotiate with

someone like Pete. He'll twist it and say you're harassing him. He'd love that to go down on your record, too."

Anna let her head fall into her hands. "I just want this to be over. I'm so tired."

Taylor sat beside her, wrapping an arm around her shoulders. "Listen, you've come too far to let him drag you down again. You didn't steal anything. We're going to find a way to prove that."

"Start by demanding to know if there's security footage," Sam added. "And who had access to that locker room during your shift."

Anna nodded slowly, the beginnings of something unfamiliar stirring in her chest—maybe not hope, but something close. A flicker of strength. Of fight.

She just hoped it was enough.

Later, Anna stood in her hallway with folded laundry cradled against her hip. The house was dim and quiet, the dishwasher humming in the background She pushed open Bronwyn's bedroom door and found her sprawled on the bed in mismatched pajamas, hair a wild mess of waves from a long day.

"Teeth brushed?" Anna asked.

"Sort of."

Anna raised a brow. "Try again."

Bronwyn sighed dramatically but slid off the bed. As she passed her mother in the hallway, she paused.

"Mom?"

"Hmm?"

"Are you okay? You've had that weird 'don't worry, everything's fine' face on since dinner."

Anna paused. How was everyone so good at reading her emotions? "I'm just tired."

Bronwyn didn't look convinced. "Is it about the bracelet thing?"

Anna blinked. "What?"

Bronwyn said, turning back toward her, "Someone at school said you stole a diamond bracelet from a patient and that it was worth a million dollars."

Anna froze. "That is absolutely not true. Who told you that?"

"My friend Susie said her mom works in the cafeteria at the hospital, and she told her. That's a rumor, right?"

"First, of course I didn't steal anything. I'm also sure it's not a million-dollar piece of jewelry that is up for grabs, but let's go sit down on your bed and talk."

Once they sat, Anna put her arm around Bronwyn and released a long, pent-up sigh. She had no intention of bringing her daughter into another battle between her parents, so she'd have to tread carefully.

"Part of that story is true, Bronwyn. A patient of mine did say that her bracelet was missing. But you know I don't take things that don't belong to me."

"I know! That's what I told Susie!"

Anna smiled slightly before the frown took over. "Thanks, but the patient did accuse me of it and stirred up a lot of trouble."

"Just tell them you didn't do it," Bronwyn said, looking shocked.

"I did tell them that. But, somehow, the missing bracelet ended up in my locker. I didn't put it there, but someone did." Anna felt sick at her stomach, worried that her daughter would lose faith in her at this point and wonder if maybe she was a thief after all.

Bronwyn tilted her head. "In second grade, someone put a note in Jack Pesch's backpack that said I love you, with a bunch of stupid hearts. Everyone said I did it. I didn't, but they all teased me anyway. Since then, he thinks I like him, and I don't. He's a nerd."

Anna nodded. "So you understand how that can happen. But now they must investigate and decide if they think I'm guilty."

"That's so not fair, Mama. I'm sorry."

She sounded so sad that Anna squeezed her close, kissing the top of her head. "I'll get it figured out. Don't worry. You concentrate on school stuff."

"And George?" she looked hopeful.

Anna laughed. "I didn't say that."

The tense moment was broken, and Bronwyn pulled a notebook from her nightstand, turning the cover toward Anna.

"See, I think this is what he'd look like," she said, grinning.

A brown and white cow was clumsily drawn, along with a collar and nametag. George the Calf had cow print boots on, which also made Anna smile, knowing that her daughter didn't see the irony.

"Alright, go brush those teeth, young lady. Stop cow-dreaming," Anna said, playfully tugging at a strand of Bronwyn's hair. "And you tell those kids at school that, here in America, we are innocent until proven guilty, and to stick their opinions up their nose."

"I will," Bronwyn said, then turned serious. "But I just thought of something. Remember our video call that day we first talked about George? You were at work, and I saw someone behind you. A man. He was going through a purse. Was that the room the bracelet was from?"

Anna's heart began to pound. "What purse?"

"It was on a table, in the hospital room behind you. I didn't think much of it at the time. But now ..." Bronwyn looked up at her.

Anna's breath caught.

"You're sure you saw that? What did the man look like?"

What if it was another patient? Or someone from the cleaning staff?

Bronwyn grimaced. "I couldn't see him good but, from what I did see, he looked kind of like Dad. He also wore a dumb black watch like Dad always wears. I remember because it glinted when he reached into the bag."

Anna sat slowly on the edge of Bronwyn's bed. Her hands were shaking. This changed everything. At least now she knew for sure that Pete did it, but would anyone believe her if she said her daughter might've been a witness?

Pete would claim she coerced Bronwyn into it.

"Okay, Mom. Really, I think it was Dad. You didn't mention him being there, so I didn't either. I also didn't want to say anything bad about him," Bronwyn added, quieter now. "I know you don't like it when we do that. But Susie, she got me thinking about it. Are you mad?"

Anna's throat tightened. For years, she'd worked so hard to protect her kids from Pete's damage. She hadn't told them the ugly truth. Hadn't laid it all bare. Any negative feelings they had toward their father was because of what they'd experienced themselves.

But maybe ... maybe her protecting him had given him the cover he needed to keep hurting people.

To keep hurting her.

She reached for Bronwyn's hand and held it tight. "You did the right thing, sweetheart," she whispered. "You always tell me the truth, okay?"

Bronwyn nodded.

"You aren't going to jail, are you, Mom?" she asked next, her eyes round as saucers.

"No, I'm not going to jail." Anna felt the need to reassure Bronwyn, but the truth was she didn't know what would come next.

But she had something she hadn't had before.

Proof.

And maybe that was finally enough to start turning the tide.

Chapter Twenty-One

Amy sat in the soft, cushioned chair, her legs crossed, and her hands neatly folded in her lap. The room was calming, with soft lighting and pastel-colored walls. A faint aroma of lavender hung in the air, a comforting and gentle presence meant to ease the nerves of anyone who entered. She looked at the therapist, a kind-looking woman with short, curly hair and glasses that perched on the tip of her nose.

This was an entirely different experience than when she'd been hypnotized so long ago. Then she was a frightened little girl, who had no idea what was about to happen. She'd believed the scary man was going to find her, and do to her what he'd done to her grandmother.

Now she was ready to really allow herself to go deep.

There was no longer a huge scary shadow lurking in her imagination. For the last few years it had taken the form of a question mark.

Her mom sat waiting outside the office, nervously fidgeting with the sleeve of her sweater, not happy to be there. but Amy insisted on doing this. She had to know the truth—everything was already tangled in her mind, and she felt like she'd never truly be free of it until she could understand what happened that night and free her uncle.

"Okay, Amy," the therapist spoke in a soothing voice. "I'm going to start by asking you a few easy questions. I want you to feel completely comfortable. You're in control, and you can stop at any time. This is just a way to help you relax and open up, to help you recall memories in a safe and gentle way. Are you ready?"

Amy nodded, her hands twitching with anxiety, but she was determined. "Yes, I'm ready."

The therapist smiled kindly, her hands resting gently on her lap. "Alright, Amy. Just take a deep breath for me. In through your nose, and out through your mouth. Slowly ... and again ... in ... and out ... Good. Now, with each breath, let yourself relax more and more."

Amy followed the therapist's words, the rhythm of her breathing slowing as she let herself sink deeper into the chair. She could feel her muscles unwinding, her mind slowly quieting. Her thoughts drifted as she answered simple things, like her name and where she was born, though they kept returning to the same old memories—the same night.

"Now, Amy," the therapist's voice was soft, "I want you to think back. I want you to remember the first thing that comes to your mind. Take yourself back to that night. When you were with your grandmother. Just let the memories come, however they do. Can you do that?"

Amy swallowed, her throat dry. She could already feel it— the pull of the memory, the familiar ache in her chest. She closed her eyes and let the memory flood in, as though a door had been opened, and the past rushed in.

Amy could remember the excitement of the afternoon so clearly. It was a special time. It was just her and Mawmaw. She was six years old. She could hear the soft hum of the car as they drove, her grandmother's voice humming along with a song on the radio. Mawmaw was laughing, telling her that they were going to get pizza. Just the two of them.

They'd gone to their favorite little shop, a hole-in-the-wall place that made the best pepperoni pizza. The memories of the warm, cheesy pizza brought a small smile to her face. Then they went to the store for ice cream, a little treat to end the day. Mawmaw had said, "It's a special night, honey. Just you and me."

"She drew me a bath, and put bubbles in it," Amy said, her voice slow and quiet. *"My hair was in a fancy turban-thing. When I got out, Mawmaw let me wear her long, pink nightgown and she painted my toenails red. I felt like a real lady."*

She loved her grandmother so much.

"Okay, so you were getting all pampered up," the therapist said softly. "Then what happened?"

Amy remembered crawling into Mawmaw's big, cozy bed, settling under the covers with the soft glow of the TV playing in the background. Mawmaw had brought her a bowl of ice cream and told her to enjoy the movie. "I'll be in the living room later," Mawmaw had said, her voice kind and calm.

"I love you, Mawmaw," she said, feeling so special.

"I love you too, sweet girl."

She'd eaten the ice cream slowly, savoring every bite, set the bowl on the nightstand, then drifted off to sleep. The plot of the movie broke into her dreams, sending her on the same adventure as the character in the Disney cartoon. She was flying. On a magic carpet. Or was it a unicorn?

The therapist's voice broke the trance, bringing Amy back, but the memory stayed vivid, like a painting in her mind. "Now, Amy," she continued gently, "I want you to keep going. What happened next?"

Amy stirred in her grandmother's bed. The movie had been

playing, but now the screen was black. She felt a strange tension in the air, like something was wrong. She heard voices. Angry voices.

She climbed out of bed, still wearing the oversized nightgown. Her bare feet padded softly on the floor as she walked quietly into the living room. It was there, in the dim light, she saw him.

A man had his back to her while he stood over Mawmaw. She could hear him yelling, though his words were too muffled to understand. Amy felt the fear rise in her chest, her heart pounding in her little body.

Were they fighting about money? Her grandmother never had much of that.

Amy remembered the seven dollars in her backpack. She'd earned it by helping her dad rake leaves. She could offer it to the man!

Before she could act on her idea, he hit Mawmaw across the face! Hard with his fist, like a boy should never hit a girl! Amy trembled as the man turned to face her. He was so tall. Big shoulders and a face scrunched and red with anger. He had brown hair, a scruffy look, and his eyes were a dark brown. His eyes locked with hers before he turned back to the couch.

Amy gasped, her breath caught in her throat, and the man punched Mawmaw again.

Mawmaw slumped against the couch, unconscious.

Before Amy could move, the man turned to her, his face twisted with fury. She tried to run, but he grabbed her. His hands were rough, and he was so strong. His grip was painful.

He yanked her toward him, and she could feel his breath against her face. But then everything went black.

Amy gasped aloud as the therapist spoke again, her voice soft and reassuring. "You are okay. I want you to keep breathing deeply, Amy. Take your time. Then let's talk about what happened next."

Amy's head throbbed and her body felt heavy. The soft carpet under her made her groan as she tried to sit up. She didn't know where she was, but she was no longer in Mawmaw's bed.

Looking around, she realized she was beside the bed. Stiffly, she crawled on her hands and knees into the living room. The room was still dim, the shadows stretched across the floor. Her heart skipped a beat when she saw Mawmaw.

She was lying motionless on the couch, blood around her.

Amy's eyes filled with tears as she approached, her little hands trembling as she touched Mawmaw's arm.

"Mawmaw?" she whispered, but there was no answer.

Mawmaw's face was purple and swollen. It didn't look like her.

In a daze, Amy pulled the blanket up over Mawmaw, as though trying to protect her. She reached into her grandmother's purse, her fingers fumbling with the phone. She dialed the number for the neighbor. The message she left still echoed in her mind: "I need somebody to get my mom for me. I'm all alone. Somebody killed my grandma."

"No one answered the phone," she said softly. *"I have to go find someone."*

"Okay. So you are leaving the house," the therapist said. "You're outside. Which way do you go?"

"I'm going across the street. Why is it so bright out here? Everything feels normal, but I know it's not. Not back there," she said, weakly waving a hand behind her head.

Amy crossed the street to Shelly's house, her legs shaky but determined. The neighbor opened the door.

"I need my mom," Amy said, her voice breaking. *"Can you take me home?"*

Shelly stared at her for a moment, taking in the sight of the bloody nightgown, before she nodded. "Just wait right there. I'll put my shoes on."

Amy sat on the wooden steps, watching ants. She couldn't go inside and look at her grandmother anymore. The thought of Mawmaw's lifeless body was too much. She also didn't want to think about the angry man.

She watched ants march by her bare feet.

So much blood.

No! She didn't want to think about what had happened. A mailman in a van went by. He didn't see her. She wanted her mom. She wanted everything to be normal again. A hawk over her head screeched, but Amy couldn't spot it in the sky.

Shelly returned, and Amy was taken to her car.

"Did you see who hurt you?" Shelly asked, her voice gentle.

Amy shook her head. "No."

Shelly pressed on, "Was it a big man, like your uncle Clem?"

Amy's eyes widened. *"Yes ... he was big,"* she whispered.

Shelly pressed, "Did he sound like him?"

Amy hesitated. *"He had a deep voice, like Uncle Clem,"* she murmured. *"Brown eyes and big, bushy eyebrows."*

"What was he wearing?"

Amy frowned, confused. *"A green shirt with some letters. There was an angry cat on it ... it looked like a football shirt."*

Shelly nodded, looking thoughtful. "Let's get you home, Amy."

The drive back felt slow, but, when they reached her house, Shelly helped her inside. Amy's dad was there and was shocked at the sight of the blood all over her.

"Oh my God, Amy! What happened? Where's Alma?" he asked.

Amy swayed a bit, nearly fell. All her energy was gone, and she felt sadder than she'd ever felt in her life. She wished she could've done something to save her grandmother. Her mom would be so mad.

"Daddy, Mawmaw is dead."

He was speechless, looking back and forth between her and the neighbor.

"She told me she thinks her uncle Clem did it," Shelly said. "You need to call the police."

On the therapist's couch, Amy became restless.

"You've done well. Now it's time to take you out of this, Amy. When I count to ten, you'll open your eyes and be back in the present time, in my office with me."

Chapter Twenty-Two

Hart's Ridge County Sheriff's Department had changed in the year since Taylor had left, but the familiar hum of the place still had its grip on her, pulling her in. The scent of coffee and paper hung in the air as she pushed open the door and stepped inside with Lennon in her arms. Her daughter's giggles filled the space, a welcome distraction from the wait for the DNA from Alma's crime scene to come back, an anticipation that had been gnawing at Taylor's thoughts.

After the family meeting that Janelle held, things began moving at a fast pace. Everyone put money into the pot and they had enough for the attorney retainer. Most shocking, Cate had reached out to someone at the Innocence Project, and they'd gifted a grant to pay for the testing.

As she walked through the lobby, Sheriff Dawkins was the first to spot her. His face broke into a grin at the sight of the little girl in her arms.

"Well, if it isn't Taylor Gray and her little bundle of joy!" he boomed, a wide grin spreading across his face. He straightened up from the desk where he had been speaking with one of the deputies. "Come on in. I've missed you!"

Lennon, who had been sucking on her pacifier and staring around, lit up at the sight of Dawkins. She stretched her tiny arms toward him, a big smile playing across her face. He immediately walked toward them, bending down to scoop her out of Taylor's arms.

"Well, look at you! You're getting so big!" Dawkins chuckled, holding Lennon close before looking up at Taylor. "We all miss you around here, girl. This place hasn't been the same without you. You ever think about coming back?"

Taylor laughed lightly, brushing it off as if it were the most casual thing in the world. But, internally, her heart recoiled. "Oh, Sheriff, I don't think so. I'm enjoying my new path in life just fine, trust me."

He raised an eyebrow, clearly not convinced. "You sure? We could use you back here, especially now that some of these new deputies are—well, let's just say they don't quite measure up."

Taylor shot him a teasing smile. "You miss me, huh?"

"More than you know," he said, his voice turning a little more serious. "But, hey, you do what you need to do. Just know that the door's always open for my favorite deputy of all time."

"Thanks, Sheriff," Taylor said, giving him a warm smile before taking Lennon and turning toward the bullpen area.

She walked toward where her old desk was. The once familiar place now felt almost foreign to her. As though she'd never spent most of her waking hours there. She really did miss the routine, the adrenaline of a good case, but she couldn't let herself fall back into that world. Not now. Not with Lennon in her life.

Her old cubicle was still there, tucked beside Deputy Penner's desk. Someone had been using it, and it felt strange to see items scattered around it that didn't belong to her.

Now and Then

But Penner was there, still at his same desk, looking like a comfortable sweater.

He looked up and a big grin spread across his face.

"Taylor! How've you been, partner?" he said, standing to greet her.

"Good to see you, Penner," Taylor said, walking over to him. She let Lennon squirm in her arms before lowering her down onto a blanket on the floor with some toys. The little girl immediately began pulling at the plastic rings, giggling as she banged them together.

"You've been keeping this place running while I've been gone?" Taylor asked, settling into her old chair beside Penner's desk.

"Hey, somebody's gotta do it," he said, his voice light, his eyes twinkling with amusement. He leaned back in his chair, holding up a thick folder. "You'd be amazed at some of the stuff that goes down in a small town like Hart's Ridge. Second thought, you wouldn't, but, hey, look at these recent blotters."

He handed her the folder, and Taylor thumbed through it, laughing at some of the incidents. Penner had always had a knack for adding a little humor to the mundane. There was one about a cow that got loose and rampaged down Main Street, scattering traffic and causing chaos. Another one was about a neighbor complaining that a dog had "tried to drown" his dog in a backyard kiddie pool.

"Good ol' Hart's Ridge," Taylor murmured, shaking her head, amused by the simplicity of it all.

Penner grinned and slid another paper toward her. "And get this one—there was a guy caught wearing nothing but a bathrobe and slippers, trying to steal a basket of laundry from the laundromat at three in the morning. The guy's excuse? He was 'looking for his lost socks.'"

She snorted. "I see some things haven't changed."

"Yeah, we definitely keep busy," Penner said with a wink, still chuckling. "But enough about that. What brings you back to this side of things? You looking to get back in the game?"

Taylor hesitated, then shook her head. "No, just checking in, really. I'm actually working a case right now. But it's not something I can talk about with anyone here." She shot him a sideways look.

Penner nodded in understanding. "I get it. Always got my ear if you need me, though."

Taylor smiled at him gratefully. "I know, Penner. You've always had my back."

Her smile faded slightly as she shifted the conversation. "Speaking of which, what's the latest gossip around here? Anything juicy?"

Penner leaned in, dropping his voice. "Well, if you really wanna know ... There's been a revolving door of deputies trying to replace you. We haven't had much luck. Some of them can't handle the pressure. The worst part? Weaver doesn't like working with any of them so now he's having to solve crime all on his own and he's all in his feelings about it. I think you spoiled him." He raised an eyebrow. "But, in other news ... Dottie's retiring soon and we have a new dispatch in training. Have you met her?"

Taylor nodded. "Yes, I met her. She seems nice, though I can't imagine this department running without Dottie."

Penner grinned. "Agree. We'll see if she really does retire this time. Anyway, Shane's been spending a lot of time up there, talking to the new girl. Might be flirting a little, if you ask me. He hasn't been the same since you left, but maybe now he's found someone to take the edge off."

Taylor felt a flutter in her chest at the mention of Shane's name. She knew she'd left without looking back, but the thought of him—always the distant, intense figure—still made her feel a little ... unsettled.

Just then, Shane himself appeared in the doorway, looking a little distracted. He glanced at Taylor, his face a little closed off, but, as soon as he saw Lennon on the floor, his expression softened. He crossed the room, kneeling down next to the blanket where Lennon was happily playing.

"Well, well, if it isn't Taylor's mini me," Shane said, his voice warmer than before. He smiled at her, and Lennon immediately reached out for him.

Shane laughed softly, lifting her into his arms. "You sure grew up fast, kiddo."

He'd only seen her once, and that was right after she was born, but he sure acted familiar.

Taylor felt her discomfort increase, but she kept it under control, shifting slightly in her seat. "She sure did. What are you up to these days?"

Shane stood up, bouncing Lennon lightly on his hip. "Same old, same old. Everything's great with the new deputies, things are going smoothly." His tone was clipped, and Taylor could sense that he was holding something back. "But I guess you didn't come here to talk about that. What're you working on with your new big time investigations business?"

Taylor hesitated at the slight sarcasm she picked up from his tone, glancing at Penner before speaking. "I'm not at liberty to discuss it, Shane. It's ... professional. But thanks for asking."

Shane looked at her for a long moment, his gaze lingering as if trying to read her. "You're really serious about this new life, huh?"

"Yeah, I am," she said, a little too quickly, and then quickly added, "It's just ... more flexible, you know? I have Lennon to think about now. And this is something Sam and I can do together. He's actually good at it."

Shane's eyes narrowed, then he caught himself, but he skirted around the subject of Sam. "I get it. I do." There was a long silence before he finally broke it. "Well, I have a call to take. But don't be a stranger, alright? It's good to see you."

Taylor nodded, though her discomfort was palpable. Shane excused himself, his usual guarded nature back in full force as he stepped out of the room.

After a few moments of awkward silence, Taylor turned to Penner. "I need a favor," she said, trying to keep her tone casual. "Can you do a deep dive into the national system? I need a list of sex offenders released around the Kokomo area on the night of the attack on Alma."

Penner's eyes widened slightly. "You've got it. I'll get it to you as soon as I can."

Taylor nodded. "Thanks, Penner."

As she and Lennon left the sheriff's department, the past and present collided, and she knew that, no matter how hard she tried to move on, the department was always going to try to pull her back in. Not just the people, but the place. The environment where she'd gone from being an awkward and uncertain girl, to a capable and confident woman.

In a sense, it was like leaving home. She'd loved her job for a long time, and had worked hard to get where she'd gotten. But it was no longer enough. To get credit for how good of a detective she really was, she wouldn't be able to find it under the helm of small-town politics, even if she did love the sheriff like a father. The fight to abolish gender discrimination in law enforcement had come a long way and was successful in many places around the nation, but it would take much longer to find its way to every small southern town that bubbled over with outdated attitudes and traditions.

She'd spent too many years proving herself, pushing through every obstacle, every doubt cast her way because of her gender. Her instincts were sharp, her record solid, but it was hard to gain the respect she deserved in a department where old biases lingered like ghosts. No matter how many cases she solved, how many lives she saved, it wasn't going to change the core of the Good Ol' Boy culture.

So, yes. She'd made the right choice—stepping away from it to build something where her worth wasn't measured by outdated standards, but by the results she could deliver on her own terms. As she maneuvered Lennon into her car seat and fastened her in securely, her phone beeped. She finished, shut the door, and pulled her phone from her pocket.

It was a text from Janelle.

> Call me. The DNA results are back.

Chapter Twenty-Three

The hospital looked different when you entered it with something to prove. Anna walked through the polished glass doors just after eight, her work badge still clipped to the inside of her bag. Her scrubs were clean and pressed, but she wasn't there to clock in.

Not yet.

Keeping her eyes to herself, she made her way past the main desk and into the quieter admin wing, where the walls were bare and the floors quieter, and the air always seemed a few degrees colder. A woman with a headset gave her a sympathetic nod from behind the reception desk, then buzzed her through to the back hallway.

Anna took a deep breath outside the small conference room, the same one they'd dragged her into after the bracelet turned up. Her hands were damp despite the cool air, and she clenched them together as if she could wring the anxiety out of her body.

She wasn't just fighting for her job anymore.

She was fighting for her name.

Monica—her supervisor—was already seated at the table, a thick binder open in front of her. Patricia from HR sat beside her with a tablet and clipboard, her expression unreadable as always. Neither woman offered her a smile.

"Anna," Monica said, her voice clipped. "Thanks for coming in."

Anna nodded. "Thanks for making time."

"Please," Patricia gestured to the chair across from them.

Anna sat, slowly and deliberately. This time she didn't fold in on herself. This time she didn't offer weak apologies or play defense. She kept her shoulders squared and her eyes level with theirs.

"Before you say anything," she began, "I have something new to report. And I need you to listen closely."

That caught their attention.

Patricia picked up her pen. Monica looked up from the binder.

"My daughter, Bronwyn," Anna said slowly, "remembered something from the day the bracelet went missing. It was during a FaceTime call with me, sometime that afternoon. I know I'm not supposed to take calls when I'm with a patient, but she so rarely tries to FaceTime me that I thought it might be an emergency. I turned away, toward the bathroom and took the call. Bronwyn said she saw someone in the background of the hospital room I was in. A man. He was going through a purse."

Patricia lifted her head, brows narrowing. "And she's just now saying something?"

"She's only just now heard what is going on. Seems the rumor mill got down to the cafeteria, then over to an employee's child who my daughter goes to school with. Once she heard about it, she thought what she'd seen on the call could be important." Anna took a breath, choosing her words carefully. "But what stood out to her—and to me—is that the man looked like Pete Chambers. Her father."

There was a pause.

"She could see his profile well. Also, she said he was wearing his signature watch—thick black band, glints in the light when he moves. She saw him reaching into the purse."

Monica leaned back in her chair slightly. "That's a serious allegation."

"I'm aware," Anna said tightly. "But if that purse in the video belonged to Kelsey Marshall, and you know it must have, then we have a situation that goes beyond a 'missing item.'"

Patricia adjusted her glasses and bit her lip. "This is not good."

Anna clenched her jaw. "Yes, I know that it's a difficult situation for you, considering that Pete had involved his influential parents. Believe me, I don't want to bring my daughter into this nightmare, either. But now kids are talking about it at school. She's being teased. And she came to me in tears, wondering if I was going to jail."

She let that sit. Watched as Monica's expression faltered—just slightly.

"Look, I've protected Pete for years," Anna continued. "Covered for him. Lied to keep the kids' illusions intact. He has tried at every turn to be vengeful toward me. And now he's trying to ruin my career, and it's bleeding into my daughter's life. I'm done staying silent."

Patricia cleared her throat. "Your daughter's testimony—"

"Mr. Chambers could've been only retrieving something from the purse that his wife asked him to get," Monica added.

"She's not his wife and my daughter is not giving a testimony," Anna said quickly. "Especially against her own father. She's a child. She told me what she saw, and that's it. I'm not asking you to drag her into this. I'm asking you to use your resources as a hospital to follow up."

"Such as?" Monica asked.

Anna sat up straighter. "Surveillance footage. The Face-

Now and Then

Time call happened around 2:20 that afternoon. I can give you the exact timestamp from my phone. Compare the visitor log and see if Pete was in the room at that time. Then you check hallway cameras. Nurses' station. See who entered or left Kelsey's room during that window."

Patricia scribbled something on her notepad.

"And not just that day," Anna added. "I want to know who else accessed the staff locker room the day the bracelet was found in my water flask. That item wasn't in there during my shift. I drink from that bottle constantly. Someone planted it— after I used it. I want to know who has access to staff lockers. Cleaning crews? Staffers? Anyone who could've slipped it in when I was with a patient."

Monica hesitated. "We hadn't reviewed hallway footage from that day yet."

Anna blinked. "Why not?"

"Until now, the investigation was limited to the locker search and your written statement."

"Which I gave," Anna said firmly. "And which you ignored in favor of the Chambers' accusations."

"We're following up on all angles," Patricia cut in.

"No, you're protecting a donor," Anna said, before she could stop herself. "Thatcher Chambers called and leaned on you. And instead of treating me like a valued employee, you treated me like a liability and a criminal."

There was a beat of silence in the room. Patricia's pen froze mid-scribble.

Monica exhaled. "Anna, I can't undo what's been done. But I hear you. I do. And if what your daughter saw is accurate, it does change things."

"She saw him," Anna said. "And if you follow the footage, I believe it'll show you more than you're expecting."

Patricia flipped a page in her folder. "We'll begin pulling

security logs and access records today. If your timeline holds, we should be able to match it."

Anna stood. "I hope you do. Because I'm not letting my daughter grow up thinking the system always sides with who has the most money."

Patricia nodded slowly. "We'll be in touch."

Anna turned and left without another word. This time, she didn't cry in the elevator.

This time, she wasn't leaving in shame.

She was leaving in motion.

And motion was how change always began.

Anna leaned against the fence, holding an apple out for Apollo. He took it and she climbed up and sat on the post, staring out over the late afternoon fields as he ate.

The horse always reminded her of tenacity, and how they all had it within them to get through the hardest of times, to find the reward on the other side. Apollo came to them from a bad situation. Neglected and abandoned, he didn't even seem to have the will to live.

It was touch and go, but they'd spoiled him. With comfort, the best food and care, and a lot of attention from everyone in the family. Especially the kids.

Levi and Apollo had bonded more than anyone. Every day, by three o'clock, the horse was waiting in the same corner of the field, up against the fence as close as he could get to the view of the driveway of the farm, eyes open wide until he sees the big yellow bus come chugging around the curve. Only when Levi stepped off and held a hand up to wave would Apollo swoosh his tail, then relax and go back to grazing.

It was special to see their commitment.

A boy and his horse.

Though the other kids also claimed Apollo, they all knew without saying that he preferred Levi over anyone.

Now the wind played in the trees, ruffling the tall grass and stirring the wind chimes into a gentle tinkle. It should have been peaceful—should have made her feel grounded. But today, it was nothing but background noise to the endless loop of questions and what-ifs running through her mind.

Her phone was on the railing beside her, face-up, silent.

No calls. No messages. No news.

She'd been told she'd hear something by the end of the week. It was now Friday afternoon. The silence was stretching like a rubber band ready to snap.

Every time her screen lit up with a notification, her stomach twisted. Every time it didn't, her nerves frayed even more.

Inside, Bronwyn and Teague were arguing over who got to pick the movie for pizza night. Their voices echoed off the walls, a reminder of how close to normal everything could still feel—how easy it was for a kid to bounce back from things that would wreck an adult.

The bracelet. The accusation. The fact that Bronwyn, her own daughter, had seen something on that FaceTime call—something no one else had.

Anna closed her eyes and took a deep breath. She had followed Taylor's advice. After her conversation with Bronwyn, she'd called Monica the next morning and requested another meeting. She calmly, but firmly, relayed what Bronwyn had seen: a man rifling through Kelsey's bag during a video call. Pete. Monica had seemed skeptical (HR even more so), saying it was no more than Pete just retrieving an item Kelsey had asked for.

"But why didn't you mention this before?" the HR rep asked, arms crossed in the conference room.

Anna had swallowed her frustration and calmly explained that her daughter had only remembered it after the rumors had reached the school. "It was a FaceTime call. A background detail she hadn't realized was important. But it could be the key to everything."

They'd agreed—grudgingly—to pull additional security footage and promised to reach out to IT. But Anna could feel the tension in the room. The subtext.

They still weren't sure she hadn't done it.

The sound of tires crunching on gravel drew her attention back to the present. A silver Subaru pulled up near the barn, and Anna sat straighter, uncertain.

When the driver stepped out, Anna's brow furrowed. It was Carina, the Maternity Care Manager from the hospital—someone Anna had spoken to only occasionally, mostly in passing, or during rushed reports between departments. Except for the recent conversation they'd had about neglectful parents.

Why was she here?

Anna rose and walked down the porch steps to meet her.

"Carina?" she asked, brushing her hands on her jeans.

"Hi," Carina said, offering a tight smile. "Sorry to drop in unannounced. I asked Monica for your address."

Anna blinked. "Is everything okay?"

Carina nodded. "Yes. I mean—no. I mean ..." She huffed and waved a hand. "Can we sit?"

They went back to the porch, Anna offering her a bottle of water from the cooler near the swing. Once seated, Carina finally met her eyes.

"I heard about what happened," she said. "The bracelet. The suspension."

Anna tensed. Was the entire hospital talking about it now? Would it soon be all over town?

"And I need you to know ... I believe you."

Anna blinked, stunned. "You do?"

Carina nodded slowly. "I worked with Pete when he first came in with Kelsey. I wasn't part of her care team, but I saw him in the nurses' lounge ... more than once. Acting like he owned the place. Asking for things. Getting snacks. Flirting. Making comments that made a few of them uncomfortable."

Anna shook her head, disgusted. It was all so—so Pete.

"I didn't come forward at first," Carina continued, "because, honestly, it didn't seem relevant. Just another arrogant man who thinks he's charming and the rules don't apply. But when I heard that the bracelet was found in your locker ... that they think you might have stolen it?"

Her voice tightened. "I remembered something else."

Anna leaned forward. "What?"

"I came back late from a meeting. Around 3:30. I went to the lounge to have ten minutes before my shift to put my feet up. Pete was there alone. I was irritated and wanted some privacy. I was going to tell him visitors weren't allowed in there, but then I saw him leaning over a chair. A water flask was sitting open on the table next to him."

Anna's breath caught.

"What color was the flask? Can you describe it?"

"It was green, with a pink flamingo sticker on it. Was it yours?"

"Yep, that sounds like mine." Anna felt rage course through her. Pete was a yellow-bellied coward snake. Always was, and always would be.

No respect for the mother of his children. Ironic since she was their only support and, if she lost her job, they'd have nothing. Once again, they'd have to depend on her family to step in and take up his slack.

Add shitty father to the list, too.

Carina continued. "And he was muttering something, like ...

'Let's see how the uppity bitch likes this.' At the time, I thought maybe he was talking to someone on the phone, or just venting to himself. But now …"

Anna could hardly speak. "Are you willing to tell Monica?"

Carina nodded. "I already did. I filed a formal statement this morning. And I told them I'd be happy to speak to anyone else if it comes to that."

Anna blinked rapidly, emotion rising like a tide.

"I don't even know what to say. You don't know what this means to me."

"I think I do," Carina said gently. "I know we haven't really spent a lot of time getting to know each other, but you are one of the most compassionate nurses I've seen come through that ER. We need people like you. Not people like him."

They sat in silence for a moment.

Finally, something was going Anna's way.

Chapter Twenty-Four

After leaving Lennon with Cate, and a message for Alice to go over there, too, after school, Taylor and Sam made record time driving back to Kokomo. Now John Thompson's conference room was quiet except for the soft hum of the fluorescent lights above them.

Taylor shifted in her seat, glancing at Sam and Janelle, whose hands were clenched tightly on the table. Her nerves were starting to spike as the results started to sink in. They had come so far, and now this—now they had the evidence, and, yet, it didn't feel like enough. Not enough to change the outcome, not enough to undo the damage done.

John Thompson, the attorney who had agreed to look at Clem's case, stood by the window, hands clasped behind his back as he gazed out at the bustling Kokomo street below. When he finally turned to face them, his expression was grave, his tone measured.

"We know now that the DNA found on Alma Jennings is not from Mr. Tiffin," John said, his voice low but steady. "This time, it wasn't inconclusive. The DNA gathered is definitely not his."

Janelle's eyes widened, a smile slowly spreading across her face. "I knew it! That's fantastic!" she asked, her voice rising with both disbelief and hope.

Taylor felt a rush of relief. Sam patted her leg under the table in a show of triumph.

"But that's not enough," he said.

"What do you mean it's not enough?" Janelle looked deflated.

John sighed, running a hand through his hair. "It means this is just the first step. They're not going to reopen this case on DNA alone, Janelle. They're going to want more. You've got to understand that."

Janelle slammed her fist down on the table, her face flushed with frustration. Sam immediately reached over to comfort her, placing a gentle hand on her shoulder. "I know, I know it's hard," he said softly. "But we're not done yet. We just need to figure out where to go from here."

Taylor watched the exchange, her thoughts racing. The idea of reversing a conviction was a monumental task, one she had seen only a handful of times in her career, and almost always with great difficulty. If anyone knew how hard it was, it was she after doing everything that she did to help with her own mother's case.

Even with the news that Clem's DNA didn't match the assailant's profile, it felt like a mountain they still had to climb.

"This doesn't just get overturned that easily," John continued, his voice harder now. "There's a long legal process for this. A trial would be required, and you can't just walk into court with that news as your only evidence. The prosecution will fight back. Hard. Remember, the prosecutor convicted Clem based on the compelling eyewitness testimony from Amy. That means that a court might rule that a jury would have reached the same conclusion even if it had known his DNA didn't match that found at the crime scene.

Taylor's stomach twisted. "So this won't get him another trial?" she asked, her voice tinged with the exhaustion she felt creeping in.

"It's a very slim possibility," John replied. "But first, we need to find the right evidence to prove Clem's innocence. We need more than the fact that the DNA found was not his. If we have a real chance at freeing him, we need to show, beyond a reasonable doubt, who actually committed the crime."

Janelle's brow furrowed, and she shook her head. "This is ridiculous. We know Clem didn't do it! The police had tunnel vision, only looking at him. There was no effort to investigate other possible suspects. So what do we even have to go on?"

"Exactly," John said, his gaze narrowing. "That's why we're going to dig deeper. We need to look at who else was around at that time. We need a new direction."

Sam spoke up, his voice quiet but firm. "A real bad man had to have done this. Someone like our suspect doesn't just do one crime and stop. They usually live a life of crime before they're caught."

"If Alma's assailant was convicted of anything in the last decade, his DNA would be in the system," John said, flipping through some papers on the desk. "But our sample didn't get even one hit."

"No, not necessarily true," Sam interjected, his voice a little more urgent. "I did some research last night. Indiana's laws mandate that DNA samples from felony arrests cannot be tested or placed into the statewide database until there's a finding of probable cause by a court."

John blinked, processing what Sam had said.

"Is that true?" Taylor asked, her mind racing.

"Technically, yes, Sam's right," John confirmed, running a

hand over his face. "The system is broken in that way. So, this doesn't mean the killer isn't already incarcerated or has a past arrest record. It just means his DNA hasn't been cross-referenced or archived in a bigger system."

Janelle's eyes widened. "So, do you mean the killer's DNA could be in an individual prison system, but it's not showing up in a state database?"

Taylor could see the hope creeping back into Janelle's expression.

"Exactly," John said. "That's why we need to keep pushing. But first, we need to start from scratch. Go back and interview people again. Maybe there's something we missed the first time."

"Didn't we already do that?" Janelle asked, crossing her arms over her chest. "I went through the list of sex offenders in Kokomo already. Ten years ago and several times since."

Taylor nodded, remembering Janelle's diligent research. "I know you did but we need to look at every angle again, even the ones that might seem like dead ends. We need fresh eyes on every piece of this."

John leaned back in his chair, letting out a long sigh. "We can keep trying, but we can't afford to waste time. And, frankly, we need money to keep this going."

Janelle's expression hardened. "How much do you need?"

Taylor watched as John's eyes flicked to Janelle's tear-streaked face. He knew she had nothing left to give.

John let out a breath and met their gazes. "I feel terrible talking about this part, but it's my job to tell you that it's going to be expensive. Legal fees, further testing, possibly another trial. It's going to cost more than you expect."

Janelle stood, pacing for a moment. "I've given everything to this case," she said, her voice thick with emotion. "I thought I was saving my husband, and all I've done is watch my family fall apart. But I can't just let this go, not when we're so close."

Sam stood and placed his hand on her shoulder. "We're not asking you to do this alone, Janelle. We're in this together and we'll figure it out again."

Janelle's eyes filled with tears, but her resolve remained strong. She turned to John. "Besides more money, what's next?"

John leaned forward. "We need to start from scratch. Go over everything. Interview more people, or interview the same ones again. There's a lot of work ahead of us."

Taylor nodded, knowing the road ahead was long.

Janelle exhaled, wiping her eyes. "I don't know how much more I can take."

"You've come this far," Sam said. "Keep doing what you have—believe and take one step at a time."

The determination in his voice was enough to ignite a spark of hope in Taylor, even if she didn't fully believe it herself yet. They had to push on. For justice. For Clem. For the family.

Finally, even Sam was invested and on their side. He was a believer now, and this wasn't just a case any longer. This was his family, and she knew her husband wanted to prove himself on this one. But as she glanced at Janelle, still standing there, lost in thought, she knew it was going to take more than hope and wants.

Chapter Twenty-Five

Anna stood outside the administrative wing of the hospital, her palms sweaty despite the chill of the morning. The air conditioning hummed like a warning, rattling inside the metal vents above her. She tightened her grip on the strap of her bag and took a steadying breath.

This time, she wasn't walking in with her tail tucked. She wasn't there to beg.

She was there to be heard.

Inside the conference room, Monica was seated with a cup of tea, her usual neat hair pulled back in a tighter bun than usual. Patricia from HR sat beside her, tapping notes into her tablet. Anna took the seat across from them, unclipping her badge from her shirt and placing it silently on the table between them.

"We've been reviewing the information you gave us," Monica started, skipping pleasantries. "The FaceTime call. The possibility that your daughter witnessed someone in Kelsey Marshall's room—potentially your ex-husband—going through a bag."

Patricia nodded. "We've pulled internal footage and checked timestamps around that call."

Anna leaned forward, heart pounding. "And?"

Monica's expression shifted slightly. "We can't verify the identity of the man from security footage in the hallway outside Kelsey's room—it's too grainy. But there is one fifteen-second clip where a man left the room shortly after your call started. Tall. Male. Black watch."

Anna's pulse kicked. "That's Pete. He always wears that watch."

"We don't know that it's him for sure," Andrea interjected, "but we do know that Pete Chambers didn't sign in as a visitor that day."

"I'm surprised that he ever signs in. He always thinks the rules don't apply to him," Anna said.

Monica sighed. "Right. But we can't confirm it was Pete coming from the room during the time right after your call ... but the lack of a visitor log entry is suspicious."

Anna's lips parted, but she paused. Measured. "What about the staff lounge?"

Patricia blinked. "What about it?"

"I was told a nurse—Carina Martinez—saw Pete in the staff lounge the same day the bracelet was found. Near my water flask."

Monica glanced at Patricia. "She did submit a brief statement, yes. It came through Friday night. Unfortunately, we don't have cameras in the staff lounge, so we can't see if anyone else accessed your locker."

"It was weird he was in there," Anna added.

Patricia looked back down at her tablet, scrolling. "She said she thought it was your water bottle, but she didn't exactly see anything happen. Just that he was there. Near the flask. And it was odd."

"That flask," Anna said, voice steadying, "is the one the bracelet was later found in."

There was a long pause.

Finally, Monica leaned back. "Yes, we know. While we're not ready to say everything's cleared up, I will say this—something isn't adding up. And the more that comes to light, the more I believe we owe you a real review. Not just a reaction."

Patricia's tone softened, but it still carried that HR polish. "We've notified the board that we're reopening the investigation with new evidence. While that process continues, we're lifting your suspension—but with adjusted duties. No direct patient care for now. We're assigning you to the intake and discharge team."

It wasn't ideal. But at least it wasn't a termination.

Pete would be livid. And, no doubt, Thatcher Chambers had more tricks up his sleeve.

Anna nodded slowly. "Okay."

Monica's eyes met hers. "We also want to acknowledge that we know you've been through a lot. And you probably feel like we didn't have your back."

"I did feel that," Anna admitted. "I still do. But I understand you have protocols. I just hope, now, you're also seeing a pattern."

Patricia looked mildly uncomfortable, which Anna took as a small win.

"We'll continue reviewing footage," Monica said. "And for what it's worth ... I'm glad you pushed for it."

Anna stood, her knees wobbly but her spine straight. "Thank you both."

As she left the conference room, she passed a fellow nurse, Liza, in the hallway.

"Hey," Liza said, eyebrows raised. "Well?"

"They're reinvestigating. I'm back ... kind of."

Liza grinned. "Good. Because this place sucks without you."

Anna gave her a tired smile and kept walking. The sterile hallways didn't feel quite so hostile this time. Still distant, still professional—but not aimed at her like the barrel of a gun.

At the exit, she paused to check her phone. No messages from Pete, which was both a relief and a worry. He'd gone silent before pulling stunts in the past. Silence was never peace—it was just the inhale before another strike.

She was unlocking her car when her phone buzzed. Unknown number.

Hesitant, she answered. "Hello?"

No one answered, but she could hear breathing on the other end.

She ended the call, hands trembling, and leaned her forehead against the steering wheel. She wouldn't let this deter her. What she had with Carina's statement was another crack in Pete's carefully polished lie.

And maybe—just maybe—a way to break the whole damn thing wide open.

Chapter Twenty-Six

The discharge desk wasn't where Anna expected to end up after all she'd been through. But here she was—clocked in, scrubs on, and pretending she didn't feel like she'd been demoted in her own life. Carina, thank goodness for her new friendship, had let her know that Kelsey Marshall had been admitted to a room on the third floor. Her infection had turned to viral pneumonia.

Anna didn't wish harm to anyone, and, as a matter of fact, felt sorry for Kelsey that she was so sick and the partner she had beside her was Pete Chambers, of the Selfish Clan. A toddler would do better to help care for her than he would.

That wasn't her business, though. Kelsey was a grown woman. Smart. Successful. Just the kind that Pete went after, and then tried to ruin.

Not her circus. Not her monkeys.

The waiting area buzzed softly with activity. Families sat in clusters of uncomfortable chairs, murmuring to one another, occasionally glancing toward the triage doors with hopeful eyes. A toddler wailed in the corner while his mother juggled a diaper bag and dug for a ragged insurance card. A teenage boy with a

Now and Then

sprained ankle from football tryouts hobbled past her desk, glaring at his crutches like they were the enemy.

Anna reviewed the next file in front of her. Mr. Colin Reese, sixty-seven, short of breath with a history of COPD. He'd been brought in by his daughter, was treated, and now resting in Room 3 while his oxygen levels were monitored. His daughter was losing patience for them to get the discharge finalized.

She scanned his chart. There was a medication discrepancy —an inhaler brand listed on the intake paperwork that wasn't in his hospital chart. Something about it nagged at her. If he was prescribed a newer med but was still using the older one, it might explain the recent flare-up. The note said to clarify with the attending before discharge.

She flipped through the orders and found the attending's name: Dr. Hartley.

Anna frowned slightly. That name sounded familiar.

She picked up the desk phone and punched in the four-digit extension listed.

"Dr. Hartley," came the voice on the other end—warm, steady, and low.

"Hi, this is Anna Gray, down at intake. I'm reviewing the discharge for Colin Reese, and there's a medication discrepancy I was hoping to clarify before I release him."

"I'll head down," he said. "Be there in a few."

Anna hung up and turned back to her screen, double-checking Reese's vitals, allergies, and home equipment. A few minutes later, she heard footsteps behind her. She turned—and froze.

There he was.

Jack.

She remembered him instantly.

Same broad build. Same rugged stubble and easy posture.

And those familiar warm brown eyes that sparked with recognition the second they met hers.

"Hey," he said, a crooked grin lifting one side of his mouth. "I know you."

Anna gave a sheepish half-smile. "You do."

"Gray Escape—the pet boarding place. You helped me when Diablo came home from his little doggy vacation."

"He was a good boy," Anna replied, straightening a stack of intake forms unnecessarily. "How's he doing?"

"Still thinks he owns my couch," Jack said with a laugh. "But he's good. And you—Anna, right? I didn't know you worked here."

"Yep. Well, not usually doing this job. I'm just off suspension. Now being punished with desk duty," she said lightly, then winced. "Temporarily, I mean."

She saw his gaze sweep over her left hand, specifically on one naked finger, then raised his brows but didn't press. "Well ... it's good to see you again. So what's going on with Mr. Reese?"

They slid back into professional mode and went over the chart together, leaning over the same tablet. Their shoulders brushed, just for a moment, and Anna felt a flicker of something she hadn't felt in a long time. Not the full-blown butterflies of a crush—like she'd felt with Hazard—but maybe the cautious flutter of curiosity.

A breath of interest.

Jack asked a few follow-up questions, nodded thoughtfully, and scribbled a correction on the med order. "Thanks for catching that."

"Just doing my job."

He smiled—genuine and easy. "Still. Not everyone would've noticed."

They stood there a beat too long, the silence stretching like thread between them. Jack shoved his hands into the pockets of his white coat. "You mentioned suspension. That sounds ... like a story."

Anna tilted her head. "You could say that."

"Well," he said, his voice low and a little softer now, "if you ever want to tell it—maybe over coffee sometime—I'd listen."

Anna blinked. That definitely hadn't been in her forecast for the day. She peeked at his left hand now, and saw no ring. Still, you never knew. She sure didn't want to get caught up in the same old cliché, a doctor-nurse flash affair that would most likely end badly.

"I don't know," she replied, offering a slow smile. "My life is sort of ... complicated right now." That was putting it mildly, but hopefully enough to scare him away.

But Jack's eyes only crinkled at the corners. "I'm a trauma doc. Complicated doesn't scare me."

She laughed despite herself. "That might be the most dangerously attractive thing someone's said to me in a while."

He chuckled, then glanced at his pager. "Gotta run. But I meant it. Take care of yourself, Anna."

And just like that, he started to step away.

But before he could round the corner, the doors to the ER burst open and two security guards rushed past them toward a commotion just outside the triage area.

Anna stood up as shouting erupted across the room. Two young men—blood on one's knuckles, the other with a broken nose and an attitude to match—had broken into a full-blown altercation in the waiting area. A nurse tried to intervene, but one of the men shoved past her, knocking a rolling IV stand to the ground with a crash.

"Hey!" Anna shouted. "Back up! Security's here!"

But just as she stepped forward, one of the men swung blindly in frustration—not at her, not even toward her—but his elbow caught her squarely in the cheek.

The room tipped for a second. The tablet she held clattered to the floor as the impact stunned her. She stumbled back into the wall behind the desk, stars dotting her vision.

Before she could recover, Jack was there.

He crossed the space in seconds, stepping between Anna and the flailing man with a fury that froze the entire room. One hand braced the young man's chest, the other motioned to security.

"Enough!" Jack's voice cut through the noise like a scalpel. "Sit. Down. Now."

The force in his tone made even the most belligerent of the men blink, then stagger to the nearest chair. The other followed, muttering curses under his breath as security closed in.

Jack turned, his face tight. "Anna. Are you—"

"I'm fine," she said, even though her cheek throbbed and she felt the flush of embarrassment more than pain.

"You're not fine. Let me see." He gently reached out, tilting her face toward the light. "You're going to have a bruise. That was a solid hit."

She waved a hand. "Just a bump. I've been through worse."

"I'm sure you have," Jack said, not moving away. "But that doesn't make this one hurt any less. Call your supervisor and tell them to get someone down here to take your place. You're going to need to fill out an incident form, then I'm ordering you to go home. You'll still be paid, of course."

Their eyes locked for a second too long. Anna's breath hitched—and this time, it wasn't because of the blow. Random kindness wasn't something she encountered much lately. But Jack was full of it.

He dropped his hand and stepped back, finally letting her have space. "Go ice that. And when you've recovered ... you should think about that coffee."

He gave her a half smile and walked away, this time for real.

Anna slowly bent to retrieve her clipboard, her fingers trembling. She looked up as the security guards escorted the roughhousers away, the waiting room already beginning to settle again.

And yet ... something had shifted. Not just in the atmosphere—but inside her.

She wasn't sure what Jack Hartley wanted with her, but she felt a need coming from him. Was he looking for a distraction? To be a protector?

Or something more?

All she knew was that, for the first time in a long while, she didn't feel entirely alone.

And that ... that was something.

Chapter Twenty-Seven

Anna adjusted her oversized sunglasses and tried not to wince as Teague stomped past the endcap of neon-green high tops. He was clutching a pair of pricey sneakers like they were golden tickets to manhood, his jaw tight and his eyes darting toward her every few seconds as if daring her to say no again. Once upon a time, she wouldn't have even looked at the price. In their old life, nothing was too much to keep her kids in the latest fads and name brands.

But that was then, and this was now. For all the money they'd spent on designer clothes and shoes, they'd still been miserable in that life.

Money wasn't everything.

Though a bit more of it would sure make her life easier.

"I told you," she said, her voice calm and measured. "Those shoes are over two hundred dollars, Teague. That's not even close to our budget."

"But everyone wears these now!" he insisted, holding them up. "These aren't just shoes. They're, like … social survival."

"Try 'luxury advertisement for Nike,'" Anna said, arching a brow. "Do they also come with a trust fund?"

Bronwyn giggled beside her, holding a sensible pair of shoes and eyeing her brother with quiet amusement.

Teague groaned and ran his hand through his hair. "I knew you wouldn't get it. You never listen to me."

"I do hear you and I do get it," Anna said patiently, pushing her sunglasses up the bridge of her nose. The bruise on her cheek throbbed with every movement, and, though it wasn't as swollen today, it was a mottled blend of purple and green. "But I'm your mother. My job isn't to fund your popularity. It's to keep your feet covered and your head on straight."

Teague rolled his eyes so hard they practically clicked. "Forget it. I don't need shoes."

Anna sighed. "You do. You've outgrown your current pair. But we're not spending well over the budget just because some famous basketball player endorsed these. A cheaper brand will fit your feet the same way, I promise."

He sighed heavily and rolled his eyes to the ceiling.

Bronwyn tugged her sleeve. "Mama, he can have my budget."

Anna blinked. "What?"

Bronwyn held up her already worn-down sneakers. "Mine still fit. And they don't hurt or anything. So if Teague really wants those, he can use my money. I don't need new ones."

It hit Anna right in the chest. Sweet, selfless, and just like her daughter. But also—this was how monsters got made. She gave Teague a sharp glance.

"Don't even think about it," she told him. "That's your little sister being kind. But I'm not raising a boy who takes advantage of that kind of heart."

"I wasn't going to!" Teague snapped, though his flushed cheeks betrayed him.

A voice chimed in beside them. "Yikes. Shoe negotiations. Brutal terrain."

Anna turned.

It was Jack Hartley.

He wore a faded T-shirt and joggers, a pair of worn Nikes slung over one shoulder, and he was grinning like the whole store wasn't about to explode into adolescent tantrums.

She blinked. "Jack?"

"Guilty. I swear, I'm not stalking you. I'm here under duress. Got roped into joining the new men's basketball team at the hospital. Supposed to improve 'team cohesion' or something," he said, miming air quotes. "Only realized this morning I haven't bought new sneakers since the Obama administration."

Anna laughed—really laughed—for the first time in days.

"This is Teague," she said, turning toward her son, who was eyeing Jack with suspicion, "and Bronwyn. Guys, Jack was the one who kept your mom from getting her face rearranged yesterday."

Teague's posture shifted slightly, his interest piqued. "You're a doctor?"

"Emergency medicine," Jack said, extending a hand. "You into basketball?"

Teague shrugged but didn't shake. "I guess."

"Oh, don't let him fool you," Anna said dryly. "He reads stats like bedtime stories, and thinks Steph Curry walks on water."

That broke the ice.

"Did you know Curry averaged 42.3% from the three-point line last season?" Jack asked.

Teague blinked. "That's not right."

"Sure, it is. But you'll tell me the real number, won't you?"

And just like that, the floodgates opened. Stats, player comparisons, the finer points of vertical leap and court strategy. Anna stood back and let her son glow in the attention. He was still too cool to show it, but she saw the slight lift of his shoulders, the rare smile tucked into the corner of his mouth.

Jack finally glanced down at the expensive sneakers in Teague's hands. "Those yours?"

Teague nodded. "I wish. But my mom won't buy them."

"They are kind of pricey, you have to admit," Jack said. "Tell you what. How about you earn half, and your mom matches it?"

Teague's expression soured. "I don't have a job."

Jack gave Anna a quick look, then back to Teague. "You do now. If you're up for it. I've got this project at my place—a boat that needs some patching, sanding, and painting. Not a lot of dirt, but definitely some sweat."

Teague hesitated.

Jack leaned in. "There might be power tools."

That sealed it.

"Okay," Teague said, trying not to sound too eager.

"Great. You can do just enough for your half of the shoes, and I'll handle the rest myself. I mean, if it's okay with your mom."

Anna folded her arms, watching her son nod seriously as if he'd just signed a labor contract. She smiled—because it was the first time she'd seen him look grounded in weeks.

"I guess that'll be okay," she said. "Bronwyn, we'll get yours today and we'll come back for Teague's later this week."

As they all made their way toward checkout, Jack glanced at her. "Ice cream next door?"

Bronwyn's eyes lit up. "Please, Mama?"

She didn't even hesitate. The kids were behaving amazingly while Jack was present. She could use a few more minutes of peace before they began arguing over the front seat. "Sure. I'll meet you over there after I pay for these."

They went through the line quickly, then went out and over to the Cookiebird Ice Cream Bar. The kids ordered first, and she debated but decided not to tempt the lactose gods, and chose a fruit smoothie instead.

They sat outside on a slatted bench beneath the striped awning, the kids' cones dripping under the late summer heat. Jack had opened every door, offered to pay, and somehow managed to charm both kids without even trying.

Teague talked more in ten minutes with Jack than he had all week at home. Bronwyn, in turn, had drawn Diablo the cat on a napkin and offered it to Jack as a gift.

Anna nursed her smoothie and tried not to get too comfortable. But her guard was slipping. Once the kids wandered a few steps down the sidewalk to peek at a window display, Jack turned his attention to her.

"You're good with them," he said. "Even when one of them's acting like an absolute punk."

Anna smiled. "You mean Teague?"

He laughed. "I wasn't going to name names."

"They're good kids," she said. "And they've had to deal with more than they should."

He nodded, then hesitated. "I hope it's not out of line to bring this up ... but the bracelet thing. I heard more about it today."

Anna tensed. "What did you hear?"

"Just hospital gossip. I know your ex has something to do with it. You don't have to say anything if you don't want to. I just didn't want to pretend like I didn't know."

She sighed, eyes on her cone. "My ex-husband, Pete ... he's angry I left him and he can no longer control me. Even though it's been a few years, he's still salty. But, lately, it's like he's found a new level of vindictive. I never thought he'd go this far, though. Come after my job? Plant evidence? I swear, he's trying to ruin me."

Jack was quiet for a moment. "I believe you."

Her eyes flicked to his. "That simple?"

He nodded. "I've seen enough manipulation to know it when I see it. My own father's a master of it. Old money. Political ambitions. I walked away from that world when I left law school."

"You were in law school?" she asked, surprised.

"Until my second year," he said. "Then I witnessed a car accident on my way home. Elderly couple. I got out to help, but ... I couldn't do anything. No one showed up for ten minutes. I felt useless."

"So you became a doctor."

"I wanted to be someone who could make a difference. Not just argue bills or rewrite contracts. My father hated the decision. Then he thought I should go into cosmetic surgery. Needless to say, we don't talk anymore."

Anna watched him for a moment, his words settling somewhere deep inside her. "It's hard to walk away from power. Even harder to live with the consequences."

Jack met her eyes. "Yeah. But sometimes walking away is what saves you."

He had a point there.

They sat in silence, the buzz of traffic and kids' laughter floating on the warm breeze.

Anna wasn't sure what this was between them. A spark? A coincidence? A kindness she wasn't used to?

All she knew was—it felt good to be seen. To be treated like someone worth defending.

Even if she wasn't ready for more, it was ... nice.

Jack stood and called to the kids. "Ready to roll?"

Teague grinned, cone gone. "Only if you promise to take me out on your boat when we have it ready."

Jack laughed. "Deal."

Anna followed them down the sidewalk, the ache in her cheek dulling beneath a warmth she hadn't felt for a long time.

Chapter Twenty-Eight

A week had passed since the DNA bombshell, and Taylor and Sam were still in Kokomo. They'd spent the better part of their time interviewing everyone they could think of—those involved in Clem's case and others who might have seen or heard something the first time around. Some faces were familiar, some new, but the pattern remained the same: frustration, dead ends, and a quiet sense of helplessness creeping in.

Now they sat across from Clem in the small, dimly lit interview room, watching as the man's face shifted between disbelief and hope when they told him the news.

"The DNA from Alma's body doesn't match yours," Taylor had said softly, watching as Clem's eyes widened with a glimmer of something unfamiliar—relief.

"I always knew it," Clem muttered under his breath, as if the words had been trapped inside him for a decade. "I knew I didn't do it, but hearing it ... hearing it finally, it's ... it's a weight off my chest."

Sam shifted in his seat, watching Clem carefully. "I know it's a relief, Clem. But this is still not going to be easy. The system isn't built to overturn convictions on just one piece of evidence."

Clem's shoulders slumped, but his gaze remained steady. "I didn't expect it to be easy. But after all this time ... part of me doesn't think anyone will ever believe me. No matter what the DNA test said. I just don't know if they'll help me."

Taylor leaned forward, her voice firm. "We're not giving up, Clem. We're doing everything we can to get the truth out there. But it's not going to be an overnight thing."

Clem nodded slowly. "I appreciate it. I just ... don't know how much longer I can hold on to hope."

They left him that day with a mix of triumph and sorrow—he'd finally heard what he'd been longing to hear, but the journey to freedom wasn't over.

The next morning, Taylor and Sam planned to interview Shelly again. Ask her to think hard, and maybe Amy had said something else that morning that could be helpful. Before they got to her side of town, they decided to do one last round of interviews with the neighbors who lived close to where Alma had been attacked.

They knocked on doors, but many weren't home, and the ones who were there seemed more interested in avoiding their questions than answering them. The day wore on, and their hope began to dim until, finally, they knocked on one last door.

It was a property at the end of the street Alma had lived on. There was a gate, and an old house set back at least an acre. They took a chance and climbed the gate, headed up the driveway and knocked on the door.

At first, there was no response. Taylor's eyes scanned the yard, hoping to catch a glimpse of anyone who might be inside. Suddenly, the sound of a dog growling reached their ears, followed by the furious rustling of fur as the animal charged toward them from the side yard.

Taylor instinctively took a step back, hands raised, but the dog's snarls grew louder. Sam got in place in front, ready to defend her. Before they could react further, an elderly man in worn overalls appeared from behind the house. His hands were covered in dirt, and his face was weathered with age and sun, but his eyes were sharp and knowing.

"Down, Atticus!" he called out, and, just like that, the dog stopped growling, sitting down obediently beside the man as if he were a king and the dog his loyal subject.

He waved them toward the door. "Come on in, folks. I'll get you a glass of iced tea. No need to stand out here in the heat."

Grateful for the unexpected reprieve, Sam and Taylor followed him inside, their eyes still adjusting to the dimness of the small, cluttered home. The man led them to the kitchen, a sturdy, rustic room with a few aging appliances and walls lined with pictures of family. The air smelled faintly of tomatoes and fresh herbs.

"I figure it must be damn important if you're willing to trespass to speak to me, so take a seat. I could use some company anyway." He gestured to the table, and headed into the kitchen. "I'm Leon. Make yourself comfortable."

"We're lucky we didn't get eaten by that dog, or even shot," Sam whispered behind her.

As they sat down, and he returned with three glasses of lemonade, not tea, Taylor couldn't help but notice the old man's demeanor, quiet yet sturdy, like someone who'd lived a long life with a lot of stories to tell.

"So, what brings you out here?" he asked, his voice rough despite his hospitality.

Taylor introduced herself and Sam. "We're investigating the death of Alma Jennings, and we're hoping you might remember something about that night," Sam said. His tone was polite but direct, and Taylor felt her shoulders tighten. They had to get something useful from this conversation, something that could give them a new lead.

Leon paused, his weathered face turning solemn. He placed his glass down, his eyes narrowing as he thought. "More than ten years ago, yet I remember it like it was yesterday. Damn shame, what happened to Alma. She was a good woman, always kind to me. Shared my garden bounty with her every summer."

Taylor nodded, urging him to continue.

There was a pause as the man's gaze turned distant, remembering. He shook his head slowly. "Not like these days. Back then, folks used to talk to their neighbors, help each other out. Now, people don't even wave. There's crime, distrust. Everything's gone to hell."

Sam leaned in slightly, trying to steer the conversation back to the matter at hand. "Do you remember Shelly, the woman who lived across the street from Alma? Amy went to her house the morning after the attack."

Leon nodded slowly, his eyes narrowing again. "Yeah, I remember her. Didn't know her too well, but saw her and her kids out in the yard from time to time. A different guy around nearly every week. To be honest, I always found it strange how when Alma's granddaughter knocked on that door, that Shelly left her standing on the front porch while she finished feeding her kids. What kind of woman does that? That child needed comfort, not to be left sitting on the porch all alone. What if the killer was still around? She was a sitting duck. Then again, I don't believe that Shelly's elevator goes all the way to the top. Or at least it didn't. She don't live around these parts now."

Taylor did recall that Shelly had said she had to go get her shoes on before she'd taken Amy back to her own house. But Leon was right, why hadn't she let Amy wait inside? Where she was safe and a little comforted?

Sam's brows furrowed. "Do you remember if Shelly had a man around the time of the attack? The night Alma was killed?"

The man chuckled dryly, "She always had a man. But, yeah, I remember that one in particular. He looked like a mean son-of-a-gun. Used to sit on her porch, smoking and doing nothing, when he should've been out working. Could've helped her with those kids. But, no, he was content just letting a woman take care of him. Back in my day, we'd have called him a drifter. He took off not long after Alma's death, but there was a quick replacement."

Taylor's curiosity piqued, but she kept her tone steady. "Do you remember his name?"

"The replacement?" Leon asked.

"No, the drifter."

Leon scratched his chin, thinking for a moment. "Yeah, it was Ed ... something or other. Saw him at the Tractor Supply and he introduced himself. Don't remember his last name exactly, but Ed something. That's all I know."

Taylor and Sam exchanged a glance, the pieces of the puzzle slowly clicking into place. Ed. That name was too familiar to ignore.

She pulled out her phone and searched for Ed Mannopi on the internet. A mugshot popped up immediately. She turned the phone around and showed Leon.

"Could this be him?"

Leon pulled his glasses up from the chain that hung around his neck and perched them on his nose, then squinted at the photo.

"It might be," he finally said. "I didn't see him up close much, just that one time when I was picking up some deer feed. But, yeah, maybe."

"Thanks for your time," Sam said as they stood, his voice calm but purposeful.

Before they left, the old man handed them a bag full of ripe tomatoes and cucumbers from his garden. "Take these," he said with a grin. "Better than store-bought. You're gonna need your strength."

They left the house with the vegetables in hand, a strange weight in their chests. They were closer, they knew that much. But, now, they had a name: Ed. What a coincidence that the man who had been around Shelly at the time of the attack had the same name as the man that Janelle suspected.

Probably nothing but another lead, another vague clue in the tangled mess that had been Alma's death.

As Taylor and Sam drove away, the suspense of it all hung thick in the air. They couldn't ignore what the old man had said. They had to find out more about this Ed.

But in the back of Taylor's mind, a nagging question kept spinning: Was Ed really the one they were looking for? Or was this just another dead end in a case full of them?

And if he was the one, could they prove it before time ran out?

Chapter Twenty-Nine

Sam was silent beside her, both of them lost in thought, as the house they were heading toward came into view. As they pulled into the gravel driveway of Shelly's house, Taylor saw a man standing near the front, swinging a weed whacker in a half-hearted attempt to clear the high weeds that had overtaken the yard. When he noticed their car pulling up, he paused and looked at them, his expression guarded.

Sam rolled down his window and spoke first, his tone calm but direct. "We're looking for Shelly. Is she around?"

The man stopped his work, wiping sweat from his brow with the back of his hand before speaking. "She took off. Owes me two months' rent. Left in a hurry this time, though. Took all her stuff, so I'd say it's probably for good." He scratched his chin.

"Do you know where she went?" Taylor asked, her voice steady despite the disappointment creeping in.

The man shrugged. "Nope."

"What about where she works?"

He wiped his arm across his brow, then shook it off. "Last I heard, she was working lates at the Waffle House over by the highway." He gave them a once-over, his eyes flicking between them. "Don't know if she's still there. She's done this before—packed up and left. Never stays in one place too long, you know? Life's been tough on her. Bad luck, bad choices ... I don't know."

Taylor glanced at Sam, who nodded in acknowledgment. They had no other leads right now, and this was the best chance to find Shelly.

"Can we ask you some questions about an incident that happened where Shelly used to live some years ago?" Taylor said.

"Oh, you mean the murder of that Jennings woman?"

"Yes, do you remember when the incident happened?" Sam asked, leaning forward slightly.

The man nodded slowly, his face growing more somber. "Yeah, I remember. That's something you don't forget, what happened to them over there. It was in the news, including Shelly's involvement, so, when she moved to my property, we got to talking. That was right around the time Shelly really started ... well, she was struggling. I remember her saying something about needing help with the kids after all that happened. But, like I said, she kept things close to the vest. Didn't want anyone knowing too much about what was going on behind closed doors."

"And do you remember who was living with her then?" Taylor pressed. "Other than her kids. Maybe a man, in particular?"

He hesitated, eyes darting to the side as if considering the best way to answer. "Not sure about then, but she wasn't supposed to have anyone living here with her, except her kids. Not unless they passed a background check. She kept her love life real quiet. If I tried to push her on it, she'd move them out quick. I've seen her with a few different guys over the years, but they never stayed long. Her luck wasn't great with men."

Taylor nodded, her mind already working through the possibilities. "Thank you for your time," she said, giving the man a polite smile as she shifted the car into drive.

They left the house, the tires crunching over the gravel as they pulled back onto the street. Taylor didn't speak as they drove to the Waffle House. It was just after 3:00 p.m. when they arrived, the neon lights from the diner casting an eerie glow over the parking lot.

Inside, the place was nearly empty, save for a few late-night diners who were finishing their meals. Taylor and Sam sat down at a booth, their eyes scanning the room for any sign of Shelly.

No sign of her. Sam flagged down a waitress, asking about Shelly. She frowned slightly, shaking her head. "She quit," she said flatly, no trace of sympathy in her voice. "Left last week. Didn't say much."

A feeling of frustration surged within Taylor, but she kept her composure. She looked at Sam, and he gave a short nod, understanding the unspoken plan.

"Is there a manager on duty?" Sam asked, his tone polite but firm.

The waitress gestured toward the back of the diner. "Yeah, the manager's back there."

They stood and walked to the back, where a man in a soiled Waffle House apron was wiping down dishes. He looked up as they approached.

"Whatcha need?" he asked before they could even speak.

"We were hoping to get some information about an employee of yours," Taylor said. "Shelly Sexton?"

The manager leaned against the counter, looking tired. "Shelly's gone. She in trouble?"

"No. Not at all, but did she say where she was going?" Sam asked.

He shook his head. "Nope. Just said her mother would be here Friday for her last check. That's all I know."

"What's her mother's name?" Taylor asked.

"Vernelle Sexton. Don't ask me how to spell it."

"Thank you for your time," Sam said.

They left the Waffle House, the stale air of the diner still hanging around them as they walked back to the car.

"Well, guess I know where we'll be doing my first stakeout," Sam said, his voice dry.

"Yeah," Taylor replied, her thoughts turning inward as she stared at the steering wheel. "We need to find out what Shelly's mother looks like before then."

"Facebook, here we come," Sam said, chuckling. "I bet investigations got a lot easier when Zuckerberg stumbled on his bright idea. Next thing you know, we'll be able to pull up a satellite image of exactly where any person is at any given time."

"That's called sharing locations," Taylor said, laughing. "Right now, it requires permission but, who knows? Soon it might be. Complete invasion of privacy, but, on the other hand, it might help keep the criminal count down," Taylor said. "I vote yes."

On that note, she pulled out her phone and opened the app. Before searching for Vernelle, she took a peek at Anna and Cate's pages, looking to see if they'd posted any new pictures of Lennon. She missed her baby girl, and hoped they could get a breakthrough on this case so they could get back to her.

Chapter Thirty

They turned onto the winding gravel driveway that led down to Jack Hartley's house, and Anna shifted the food basket on her lap and glanced over at her son.

"You sure you didn't exaggerate?" she asked Teague, a teasing tone in her voice.

He didn't look up from his phone. "What?"

"You told me his pantry was bare. I just don't want to show up feeding a man who has a freezer full of steaks and thinks I'm crazy."

Teague shrugged. "I dunno. I saw ramen and three jars of peanut butter. That counts as bare."

Anna sighed, a reluctant smile on her lips. It wasn't unusual for the doctors at the hospital to cut corners on meals. Unfortunate, but normal. "Still. This is a little extra. I shouldn't have done this."

"No worries. I told him you were extra," Teague said. "I also said your potato salad is better than anyone's on Earth."

"That's a fact," Bronwyn said from the back seat.

"Flattery will get you more dessert," Anna murmured, pulling into the shaded clearing where Jack's house sat.

The house itself was ... tired. The roof looked sound, and the bones were good, but the siding needed paint, and the flower beds were empty but for a few weeds trying their best to thrive. Still, it had charm, the kind of charm that came from intention, not money. And beyond it, sloping gently downhill, was the lake —serene and glassy—and a weathered dock stretching like an arm into the water. A small, gutted boat was cradled on a trailer near the side of the house, half-sanded and spotted with patches.

Jack emerged from the side yard wearing a ball cap, an old T-shirt, and paint-smeared jeans. His brown eyes lit up when he saw them.

"Evening," he called out. "Smells like someone came to bribe me into finishing the boat faster."

Anna stepped out, holding the basket like an offering. "Teague mentioned your pantry was a little ... uninspired."

Jack laughed. "That kid doesn't miss a thing. I thought the microwave popcorn would hold him over at our break last night. Little traitor."

She smiled. "You're being so kind to him. I just wanted to give you a good meal."

His eyes twinkled. "I can't tell you how much I'm looking forward to it, but you and Bronwyn come on in. You're not getting out of here without eating with us now."

"Yes, Mama!" Bronwyn said, but Teague looked disappointed. He had become a bit possessive with his and Jack's friendship.

Anna hesitated. "We don't want to intrude—"

"Wouldn't be intruding," he said warmly. "Besides, it smells like you brought better food than I've cooked in weeks. Let me pretend I have guests and good taste."

Teague was already bounding toward the boat like he'd

been holding his breath all day to get back to it, and Bronwyn stuck close to Anna's side, eyes wide as they stepped into Jack's house.

The interior was like the outside—worn, a little chaotic, but full of quiet potential. The hardwood floors were scuffed but real. The fireplace—red brick and sprawling—would have looked stunning painted a soft gray or white, Anna thought. The kitchen was dated but solid, the cabinets real wood and the granite countertops still beautiful if you looked past the dishes piled over their top and in the sink. The drawer pulls were the same brass style from the nineties, and her fingers itched to replace them. She could just see how well a flat black would make them pop.

Jack motioned toward the kitchen table. "I'll go grab Teague. Make yourselves at home."

Anna unpacked the food, arranging it quickly—fried chicken, still warm, fluffy rolls wrapped in a cloth towel, a mason jar of sweet tea, and her famous potato salad. It felt oddly intimate, laying it all out like a little family gathering, in a house that clearly hadn't had one in a long time.

By the time Jack returned with Teague, Bronwyn had set out paper plates and even arranged napkins, beaming with hostess pride.

Over dinner, conversation flowed like it had always existed between them. Jack ate like a man who hadn't had real food in a while and murmured "wow" more than once.

"Your wife let you live like this?" Bronwyn asked, grinning around a bite of roll.

Anna cringed inwardly. They hadn't discussed if he'd been married or not.

Jack paused, his smile softening. "She passed away a few years ago," he said gently. "Since then, it's just been me—along with Diablo, my cat—and I'm not very good at keeping things tidy."

"I'm sorry," Anna said quietly.

He nodded. "Thanks. She was brilliant. A trauma nurse. We were both always on opposite shifts, passing like ships. We never got around to starting a family. Biggest regret of my life."

Anna's heart pinched, not just at the loss, but the way he spoke of it—with tenderness and honesty. Most men wouldn't admit regrets. Their alpha energy wouldn't allow them to. She loved that Jack was secure enough in himself to do so.

Teague excused himself from the table and dumped his plate in the trash, then grabbed a brownie and stuffed it whole into his mouth.

"Anyway," Jack said, standing and stretching, "before Teague starts tapping his foot, come see what we've done with the boat in just a week's time."

Outside, the evening air was cooler now, and the little boat gleamed with a new coat of primer and plenty of elbow grease.

"She's an old girl," Jack said, patting the hull, "but she's coming along. We decided on a name. She'll be called the Second Wind."

Teague beamed. "I helped sand the back half. And patch the hull. And next week we do the final coat of paint. I picked the finishing color."

"You're forgetting the most important part," Jack added. "You also handed me the wrong size wrench three times and got paint on Diablo."

"It's his fault! What kind of cat keeps climbing into a boat like he wants to go on the water?" Teague said. "I ain't never seen nothing like it."

They all laughed, and Anna felt the warmth bloom in her chest. She wouldn't correct his grammar this time. He was so proud of the work he'd done with Jack. His chest puffed slightly, and his eyes shone. She hadn't seen that in ages.

He boosted Bronwyn into the boat, and was pointing out his work.

"You've been good for him," she said to Jack, quieter now.

He looked at her. "Ahh. he's a good kid. Just needed something to be proud of."

They talked for a bit more before Jack checked his watch and said they better get started if they wanted to finish before dark. Anna offered to clean up the food and pick up her basket.

"Nah, I can get it later," he said. "But you can go through and grab your basket. You're also welcome to leave me the leftovers, unless you think Teague will want to fight me for them."

"You can have them," Teague called out.

It was clear he'd do anything for his new mentor.

Inside, Anna couldn't help herself. The pile of dishes called to her. She washed them with practiced rhythm, scrubbing the sink until it shone. She resisted the urge to go find a toothbrush to get down into the drain. Instead she wiped the counters, rearranged a few stray items, and then, impulsively, opened the fridge.

She grimaced. Expired yogurt. Five jars of mustard. A dubious container of something green. Why did men want to live like this?

No, she couldn't walk away.

It only took a few minutes to clear it out, tie up a trash bag, and wipe the shelves clean.

Meanwhile, Bronwyn had made it her personal mission to "rescue the living room." She fluffed pillows, folded a blanket across the couch, and even found a lonely-looking plant on the windowsill to water. She even offered to scoop the litter box.

Anna watched her daughter, both proud and amused, as she

held open another trash bag and let Bronwyn drop black clumps into it.

"You still here?" Jack's voice called from the front door.

She startled and pulled the trash bag closed. "Uh—yep!"

When he saw the kitchen, he stopped short. "Wow."

"I—I'm sorry," Anna said quickly, pulling off the cleaning gloves she'd found under the sink. "I shouldn't have done this. I hope you aren't ... I just ... couldn't help it."

Jack smiled slowly when he saw an empty mayonnaise jar peeking out of the top of one of the trash bags. "You cleaned my fridge."

"And your sink," Bronwyn piped up.

"It just needed some baking soda to make it shine again," Anna said, feeling guilty. What if he thought she was implying that he was a pig? That his house was disgusting?

What had she done?

Heat traveled up her neck, filling her face.

He looked between them, something unreadable in his gaze. "I've had a lot of people offer to help in my life," he said. "But not many who actually did."

Anna blushed again, relieved he wasn't mad. "It was just a thank-you. For giving Teague something to do. Something to make him feel needed."

"Well," Jack said, walking them out to the car and holding the door open, "thank you for the thank-you. It smells heavenly in there. Wow—I have a clean house and a full belly. My boat is coming along, too. To be honest, I haven't felt this human in a while. You have my deepest gratitude, Anna."

She blushed. The way he said her name made her feel tingly. And she wasn't ready for tingly again so soon. "You're welcome. I'll come back in an hour for Teague. Tell him to listen for my car so I don't have to get out, please."

He nodded and held the door for them.

As they drove away, Anna watched his figure shrink in the rearview mirror.

She wasn't sure what this was, or if it would ever be more than shared food and sanding jobs. But tonight, it had been simple. And real.

And just ... well, it was nice.

Chapter Thirty-One

Friday arrived sooner than expected. Taylor and Sam sat in his truck, parked in the Waffle House parking lot. It was buzzing with activity—truckers stopping for coffee, tired workers grabbing a bite, and a few afternoon stragglers looking for a midday meal.

But, today, it was just the two of them, waiting.

They'd been doing a lot of waiting lately.

This time, though, the wait felt different. They were waiting for Vernelle Sexton, Shelly's mother, who was a new piece to the puzzle.

Taylor glanced at her phone, watching the minutes tick by. They'd done their homework. Thanks to Detective Harrison, they knew exactly what car Vernelle drove—a red Kia Sedona, older model.

"Here she comes," Sam said, his eyes scanning the parking lot.

Taylor turned her head to follow his gaze. A woman limped slowly toward the Waffle House entrance. She moved with a hesitant shuffle, her shoulders hunched, and Taylor could see years of stress and hardship in her posture. The woman's red

Kia was parked a few spaces away, and, as she got closer to the door, Taylor knew they had their chance.

"She looks just like Shelly, but older," Sam murmured. "If Shelly's been hiding something, maybe Mom is the key."

Taylor's heart thudded in her chest. Shelly's disappearance was suspicious.

They waited for Vernelle to enter the Waffle House, and, as soon as the door closed behind her, they got out of the car.

Their footsteps were quiet, deliberate, as they approached the red Kia. Sam stayed close, his eyes darting back to the Waffle House entrance, watching for Vernelle's return. She didn't take long. As she exited the restaurant and neared her car, Taylor and Sam blocked her path.

"Excuse me, Mrs. Sexton?" Taylor called out, her voice calm and cheery, to put her at ease.

Vernelle froze, eyes widening. Her hands shook slightly as she held onto the door of the car. She hesitated, glancing from one to the other, before she finally spoke. "What do you want?"

"We're private investigators looking into the case of Alma Jennings," Sam said, his voice low and nonthreatening. "We need to ask you a few questions about Shelly. It's important."

Vernelle's expression faltered for a moment, and her gaze shifted nervously. Her voice quivered when she spoke again. "I don't know what you want from me. I haven't seen Shelly in months ... She's ... she's been through enough already. Please, leave her alone."

Taylor stepped closer, her voice quieter now, trying to coax out more information. "If Shelly has any other information—anything at all, that could help us, it might do her some good to be the one to come forward. Don't you want to make sure the right man is sitting in jail? I'm sure she does, wouldn't you think?"

Vernelle's eyes darted to the side, her breath quickening.

She shook her head in denial. "You don't know what it's been like for her. She's suffered. She's never recovered from what happened."

Taylor's gut twisted. Why would the murder have affected Shelly so badly? She barely knew Alma, and had never had interactions with Amy until that morning. Now Taylor was getting the feeling that Vernelle knew more than she was letting on, but the older woman wasn't ready to speak yet.

"I understand, and we appreciate your time. We just want to ask you about a man Shelly had living with her during the incident, a man named Ed," Taylor said. "Do you remember him?"

Vernelle stiffened. Her face immediately hardened, a clear sign she was shutting down. She crossed her arms over her chest. "Ed? I don't know anyone named Ed. I've never heard of him."

Taylor's instincts were screaming. Vernelle was hiding something, but she wasn't going to give it up that easily. Taylor and Sam exchanged a look before she decided to push further.

"Are you sure?" Sam asked, keeping his tone level, but there was a quiet force behind his words. "This man could be important to the case. He might be connected to Alma's death."

Vernelle's eyes darted around, and she shifted uneasily. "I told you I don't know anyone named Ed. Please, just leave me alone," she snapped, her voice rising in frustration.

"Please, just take my card," Taylor said, pushing it into Vernelle's hand.

Without another word, she jumped into her car and slammed the door shut, speeding off before Taylor and Sam could ask another question.

Sam muttered under his breath. "That went well."

Taylor sighed and shook her head, a mixture of disappointment and frustration washing over her. "No surprise there. But we're not done yet."

They headed back to Janelle's house, where she was sitting on the porch when they arrived. As soon as she saw them, she stood up excitedly, her face lighting up with hope.

"You're back!" she exclaimed. "Did you find anything? Did you talk to her?"

Taylor gave a weary smile, shaking her head. "We talked to her, but didn't get anything new."

"I have something," Janelle said, smiling ear to ear. "I found out that Ed Mannopi has been transferred to the same prison Clem's in. We need to get his DNA."

Taylor nodded. "I agree. We can't ignore these coincidences anymore. If Mannopi was in the area during the time of the crime, it's a lead we can't pass up."

Janelle looked from Taylor to Sam. "What does that mean for now?"

"We need to talk to Clem," Taylor said.

Without wasting another moment, Taylor, Sam, and Janelle made their way to the prison, the long, tense drive ahead of them feeling like an eternity. As they arrived at the security gates, the process was familiar, but it never got less stressful. They passed through the usual checks—bag searches, metal detectors, body scans—and, finally, they were ushered into the interview room.

The door creaked open, and Clem stepped in, his hands cuffed and his posture guarded. When he saw them, his face lit up, though there was a trace of skepticism in his eyes.

Taylor let Janelle explain why they were there.

Clem hesitated, looking from one to the other. "You really think this Ed guy is the answer?"

Taylor nodded. "We do. We need to rule him out, and we need to know everything you can tell us about him."

Clem was quiet for a long moment. "I don't know anything about him," he said finally, his voice distant. "Other than there's no evidence to link him to the crime, either. I sure don't want to go around accusing an innocent man. Like they did to me."

"Clem, he's far from innocent," Janelle said, leaning in to whisper. "He was convicted of molesting his own daughters."

Clem looked disgusted. "That's horrible, but it doesn't mean he was Alma and Amy's assailant. I'm going to need more than that, Janelle. I have no plans of framing someone for what happened. I know how it feels to be convicted of something you didn't do, and I won't be a part of it. I want to be free, but not at the expense of someone else. Unless of course, they're guilty."

Sam leaned forward, his voice softening. "Think of it this way. If he's innocent, we can eliminate him and move on. But if he's guilty, we focus on him."

Clem looked between them, considering.

Finally, he gave a small nod. "I'll think about it."

The conversation seemed to stall, and Taylor could feel the unanswered questions hanging in the air. They were close, so close to something, but the path ahead still felt uncertain. And with every step they took toward the truth, more obstacles seemed to rise to block their way.

But they couldn't stop now. Not after all they had done.

They just had to keep pushing forward.

Chapter Thirty-Two

It had been a relatively quiet Friday night—by ER standards—when the call came in. Vehicle rollover on County Road 82. Single car. Teenage driver.

And damn it, no seatbelt.

Anna glanced at the board, already updating with trauma protocol notes, then pulled on gloves and tied back her hair as the trauma room filled with brisk energy. The sound of gurney wheels squeaking down the corridor followed seconds later, and she was already in position when the paramedics burst through the double doors.

"Seventeen-year-old female. Ejected halfway. GCS of 9 on the scene, responsive to pain, but fading. Lacerations to scalp, chest contusion, likely broken femur. BP 84/60 and dropping."

Anna stepped in quickly, helping guide the stretcher into place. The girl's face was covered in blood, a jagged cut across her forehead still weeping. Her shirt had been cut away, revealing bruises darkening fast across her ribs. Anna took over vitals as someone else worked on stabilizing the airway.

"Stay with us, sweetheart," she murmured, brushing a

strand of blood-matted hair from the girl's eyes. "You're going to be okay."

Then Jack appeared.

His presence was like a steadying force in the middle of chaos. His brown eyes scanned the vitals screen, then locked briefly with Anna's, and, without a word, they moved as a unit—him ordering fluids and imaging, her prepping IVs and calling out stats. It was the first time they'd worked together, and something about this girl—so young, so fragile—made it feel heavier.

"Collapsed lung. Probably broken femur," he muttered under his breath as he pressed his stethoscope to her chest. "We need to get her stabilized."

Anna helped apply pressure to her abdomen while they worked to insert a chest tube.

He paused to examine the girl's leg more closely and grimaced. "Compound femur fracture. She's going to need pins and a long recovery, but she's young. She can bounce back if we don't lose her to infection or shock first."

"You doing the surgery?"

Jack shook his head. "Not my specialty. I'll call Grady—my colleague who specializes in trauma ortho. He's good. And fast. I'll make sure she's on the schedule first thing."

Twenty focused minutes later, they had her stabilized and wheeled toward imaging. Anna peeled off her gloves and exhaled hard.

In the washroom, she stood beside Jack at the sink, scrubbing quietly. Her hands ached, and her shoulders felt like she'd been holding up the ceiling.

"She'll make it," Jack finally said, drying his hands. "She's lucky she got here when she did."

Anna nodded. "Lucky. And unlucky."

Jack gave her a tired smile, then added, "I'm going to go talk to the parents."

Now and Then

"I'll hang back," Anna said, watching him go.

She lingered near the nurses' station, just close enough to hear his calm, even voice as he spoke with the girl's mother and father. He didn't sugarcoat. Didn't overpromise. But he somehow gave them hope without saying the word miracle.

Anna felt something stir in her chest that wasn't strictly professional.

Later, Jack stepped outside, and she followed, the sunlight warm on her face. The courtyard was quiet, just birdsong and the hum of traffic on the edge of town.

"You ever wonder," Jack asked, "why we let sixteen-year-olds drive?"

Anna raised an eyebrow.

"They can't enlist. Can't vote. Can't get a tattoo without permission. But we hand them the keys to two-ton death machines."

Anna laughed. "Because someone decided curfews were more dangerous than car keys."

"They can barely tie their shoes some days. But, sure, let them barrel down the highway while scrolling TikTok."

Anna exhaled. "She had her whole life in front of her. But at least she'll get another shot at it. Thanks to you."

He brushed it off with a slight shrug. "Thanks to all of us. But now that we have a minute, how are things going for you?"

She tucked her hands into her pockets. "Things have been ... quiet lately. No surprise locker searches. No meetings. But I haven't heard from HR, either. Not since they reinstated me."

"Still waiting to see if the board closes the investigation?"

"Yep." Her voice was flat. "I assume if Thatcher Chambers had moved on, they would've told me."

Jack's face darkened slightly. "Want me to look into it? Quietly?"

Anna hesitated. "I do. But be careful. If Thatcher's still fuming, I don't want you caught in the fallout."

"I can handle myself," he said, and there was something solid behind the words. "I had a lot of practice with my own father."

Anna's eyebrows rose. "You had mentioned that. Bad?"

Jack gave a short nod. "Real estate shark. Built half of Savannah's luxury market by stepping over everyone in his way. When I left law school, he couldn't be satisfied with having a doctor for a son. Wanted me to handle all the family legal woes and didn't want to take no for an answer. He told me I'd regret disappointing the family name."

Thinking of him as anything but disappointing, Anna turned to him. "Do you regret it?"

"No." He gave her a half-smile. "Not for a second. But I do regret not standing up to him sooner."

Anna studied him. "You and I have more in common than I thought."

He looked at her. "We really do."

They were quiet for a moment before Jack added, "Oh, we're probably finishing the boat this weekend. Teague's been a machine. I think he's memorized every inch of that hull."

"He's obsessed," Anna said, smiling. "It's been good for him."

Jack hesitated. "Any chance you and Bronwyn want to join us for the maiden voyage?"

She blinked. "Oh ... I mean ..."

"I figured Teague would want the first-round solo. I'll take him out, make sure it floats. Then come back for you and Bronwyn for the real cruise."

Her instincts told her to decline. To keep boundaries clear. But the truth was, she liked being around Jack. Liked how he treated her kids. Liked how safe she felt near him.

"Okay," she said quietly. "We'll be there."

He grinned. "And, hey—don't forget the chicken."

Before she could answer, sirens wailed in the distance.

They both turned toward the ER doors.

"Break's over," Anna said.

They were running before she could second-guess anything else.

Chapter Thirty-Three

The lake shimmered beneath a morning sun that felt warmer than usual, as if the weather itself had signed off on their little adventure. Jack's old boat, newly restored with Teague's help, bobbed gently at the dock. It wasn't fancy—just weathered wood, a new coat of navy paint, and a modest outboard motor—but it had heart. Anna admired the work they'd done on it. The pride in her son's face alone had made it all worth it.

The first leg of the ride was just for Teague and Jack, as promised. Anna and Bronwyn had sat on the dock, legs dangling, watching them motor around the lake. The boat cut through the water cleanly, Jack's laughter carrying back toward shore.

Teague's voice was louder than she'd heard it in a while, full of joy.

Now they were back, and Jack helped Bronwyn into the boat with a steady hand and a smile. She had a bright pink life vest snug around her chest, and her arms were wrapped tightly around a plastic tote filled with snacks and juice boxes. They had chicken for later, when they were ready to come in.

Teague climbed in next, his whole demeanor light and playful, like he was a kid again instead of the teenager who too often shouldered too much.

Anna hesitated for a second on the dock. Something twisted in her gut—mother's intuition or residual anxiety, she couldn't be sure. But when Jack offered his hand, she took it. His brown eyes were warm and confident, and, today, that was enough.

They settled in for a longer ride, coasting along the tree-lined edge of the lake, pointing out birds and coves. Jack told stories about fishing as a kid, about the one that got away, and Bronwyn sat at the bow like the queen of the lake, hair tangled in the breeze.

Anna let herself exhale for the first time in weeks.

Then, in an instant, everything changed.

Bronwyn leaned forward a little too far, trying to grab a floating leaf. She rocked the boat, and, with a small yelp and a splash, she was in the water and they were quickly past her.

"Bronwyn!" Anna screamed, scrambling up, panic constricting her throat.

Before she could move, Teague was over the side in one smooth motion, followed a split second later by Jack. The boat rocked wildly behind them as they swam fast and hard toward the flailing child.

Anna sat frozen, her knees weak, heart pounding in her chest like a drum.

"Bronwyn!" Jack called, reaching her first. "I've got you, sweetheart."

Bronwyn was sputtering and gasping, arms flailing wildly.

Anna's thoughts racing. *She knows how to swim! Why is she panicking?*

"Bronwyn! Stop it and, and ..." Anna called out, fear making her words impossible to find.

"It's okay, Bron!" Teague said, reaching Bronwyn's other side. "Just hold on."

They supported her together, Jack keeping her head out of the water as Teague stayed close. Bronwyn's eyes were wide with shock, but she was breathing. Crying.

Afraid. But okay.

Anna dropped to her knees, shaking, hands gripping the edge of the boat. She needed to feel her child in her arms. Stat.

Jack guided Bronwyn toward the side while Teague boosted her from behind. Jack followed, climbing up dripping wet, and Teague scrambled back in last, panting but triumphant.

"I'm okay," Bronwyn sobbed, clinging to Anna. "I didn't mean to, I just slipped—"

"Oh, baby girl," Anna whispered, wrapping her in a towel. "You're safe now."

Jack crouched beside them, dripping, his smile gentle. "That was a good save, Teague. Proud of you for not hesitating to jump in."

Teague was shivering slightly, cheeks flushed, but he grinned. "She's my sister."

Anna looked at both of them, her chest aching. "Thank you. Both of you."

Jack reached over and touched her shoulder. "She's okay, Mama Bear. You can relax."

Anna blinked fast, trying to hold back tears. "I'm just ... so grateful she's okay."

"I think we should pack it in and go eat some chicken," Jack said.

He turned the boat back toward shore. Bronwyn stayed nestled beside Anna the whole ride, quiet and subdued, but safe. Jack steered with one hand, the other wiping water from his brow. Teague sat beside him like a copilot, more grown-up in Anna's eyes than ever before.

By the time they docked, the sun was higher, the lake glittering as if the whole world had taken a breath.

Anna wasn't sure what had changed between her and Jack out there on the water.

But something had.

And, for once, instead of bracing herself for what might go wrong, she let herself feel what was going right.

The sky above the farm was bathed in hues of amber and indigo as the sun dipped behind the ridgeline. The air had that unmistakable smell of late summer—damp earth, honeysuckle, and the musky warmth of animals settling in for the night.

Anna had barely turned off the car engine when she heard the commotion.

"Mama! Did you hear that?" Bronwyn was already unbuckling, her still-damp curls sticking to her forehead from their boat outing. "Something's going on in the barn!"

Teague, his mood light for once, was already halfway across the yard, following the noise without question. "C'mon!" he called over his shoulder.

Anna stepped out, following her kids across the familiar stretch of gravel and grass, her limbs still tingling from the adrenaline rush of Bronwyn's fall and the emotional come-down afterward. The barn doors were wide open, golden light spilling out onto the dusty path like a scene from an old storybook.

Inside, it was controlled chaos.

Cate was kneeling in a pile of clean hay, her sleeves rolled up and hair pulled back, while Ellis stood over a bleating goat, both arms elbow-deep in the situation at hand. Jo was near the water trough, prepping clean towels. Cecil, bless him, was pacing with a flashlight he clearly didn't need, murmuring about "good goat karma" and "full moon births." A couple of the younger rescue dogs hovered at the barn's edge, their ears perked curiously.

"Oh boy," Anna muttered as she stepped inside, instinctively guiding Bronwyn behind her. "What's going on?"

Alice was there, all eyes, her expression serious and reverent. Quig sat beside her, just as childlike with amazement as the kids.

"Twins," Cate called over her shoulder, not looking up. "Ellis says they're positioned fine, but she needs help."

"I'm just glad I haven't forgotten everything from med school," he added, his voice calm, patient, almost amused. "This little mama's doing most of the work herself. Just needs a bit of guidance."

Bronwyn moved closer to the stall rail. "Can we watch?"

Cate looked up and smiled. "As long as you're quiet and respectful. This is a special moment."

Teague stood beside Jo, hands in his pockets, watching intently but with the kind of detachment only a teenager could pull off.

Ellis leaned back just a bit, his voice soothing. "Okay, girl. Just a bit more. There we go ... You're doing great."

The goat let out another sharp bleat, and then, suddenly, there was a wet little bundle on the straw. Cate swooped in with a towel, clearing its tiny nostrils, and the newborn let out a weak, warbling cry.

Bronwyn gasped. "It's so small!"

"Just wait," Alice murmured. "There's one more."

And, sure enough, moments later, another twin was born—this one slightly bigger and squirming more energetically.

"Healthy and strong," Ellis declared, stepping back as Cate tended to both kids with the same care she once offered her own children.

Anna watched, her heart full. There was something magic about the way her mother and Ellis worked together—like gears in a well-oiled machine. They moved with grace and intention, barely needing words. Their connection was quiet but powerful. Her mother—who'd once swore off love entirely—had found it again. And not just found it, but bloomed in it.

"She glows around him," Anna said softly, mostly to herself.

"Who?" Jo asked, appearing at her side with a fresh bottle of water and a knowing look.

"Mom," Anna replied. "She ... I don't know. She just lights up when he's around."

Jo nodded. "Ellis has been good for her. He listens. He stays. That's all she ever needed."

Soon enough, the barn quieted again. The goat rested with her two babies curled beside her, their fur drying and fluffing up already.

Cate stepped out of the stall, brushing her hands off on a towel.

"Well," she said, "miracle achieved."

"You should just go to veterinary school, Mom," Jo said, only half joking.

Anna agreed. Dr. Terry was their usual vet, but she'd been wonderful about teaching both Cate and Ellis things they needed to know in an emergency. She'd said time and again that Cate was a natural.

"We gonna name 'em?" Bronwyn asked, bouncing excitedly.

"Sure. You guys think of something," Cate replied, wiping her forehead. "Just not anything like Princess Sparkle again, please."

The kids laughed and ran off into the yard, chasing fireflies and arguing over goat names as they disappeared into the growing dusk. Quig got up and followed, saying she'd keep an eye on them.

Anna lingered behind, watching her mother gently fold a towel and set it aside. The barn had that quiet hum now—the kind that follows new life and hard-earned peace.

"You okay?" Cate asked, glancing up.

"Sure," Anna said. "You think they're okay with Quig supervising?"

"Oh, yeah, that girl is a godsend. She's really come out of her shell since she moved in. I really think that sometimes when you have someone who seems to be purposely wrecking their life, all they need is another chance, and someone to believe in them. We're giving that and more to Quig and she'll be grateful forever. She told me recently that we treated her more like family than anyone blood-related ever did.

"That's really nice," Anna said. "Can we sit for a minute?"

Cate didn't hesitate. They settled onto an overturned feed bucket and an old wooden stool near the stall gate.

For a moment, they just listened to the soft sounds around them. A far-off cricket. The kids shouting gleefully. A newborn goat bleating faintly in the straw.

"I think I might be falling for someone," Anna finally said, the words falling out of her mouth unexpectedly.

Cate didn't even blink. "Jack?"

Anna blinked. "How—?"

"Anna, sweetheart. Your kids are sponges on repeat. I've heard that you cooked for him and cleaned his entire kitchen. And you've been smiling more. That typically happens when a man enters the picture—or leaves it."

Anna gave a soft laugh. "It's just ... complicated."

"Everything worthwhile is."

Anna exhaled. "He's kind. Gentle. He listens. And he's good with the kids—especially Teague. That means everything to me right now. But what if I'm not 'good enough' again?"

Cate leaned forward, resting her elbows on her knees.

"Listen to me, Anna. You're good enough for anyone who has the privilege of loving you. I think that your inner narrative has been shaped by someone who didn't want you to be you. It's time to let go of those narratives and start building your own based on who you are now, and who you want to be. Don't give up any more real estate in your head to people who shouldn't be there."

Anna's eyes stung. "Thanks, but I come with a lot of baggage. Pete. The Chambers. The accusations. My whole past. I doubt a good man would be able to put up with it all."

Cate reached over and took her daughter's hand. "We all come with something. And if Jack has any sense at all, he won't care about your past. He'll care about your heart. And from what I've heard, his heart's pretty scarred, too. Maybe that's the best kind of love—two people who understand what it means to be broken, and choose to be gentle with each other."

"Like you and Ellis."

"Exactly. We're lucky to have found each other."

Anna swallowed. If only she could find something like what they had, life would be perfect. That kind of luck had never been her friend. "He said he doesn't talk to his parents anymore. That they're manipulative, and powerful, and that he had to walk away from all of that. But what if someday he wants that connection again? They're a lot like Thatcher and Elizabeth Chambers. What if they come back and hate me because I wasn't born into a world like his?"

Cate smiled. "You remember, Ellis's kids didn't approve of me at first."

Anna looked at her. "Yes, I remember. And I still don't like the way you were treated at the wedding."

She shrugged. "It's fine. I think they thought I was planning to steal their inheritance. That I wasn't 'worthy' of their daddy.

Things are getting better now. Time and love have a way of softening edges. Especially when they can see that the love is real."

Anna's throat tightened. "I want to believe it could work with someone new. But I'm scared."

"You're allowed to be scared. And maybe Jack isn't the one. Or maybe he is. Just don't let fear stop you from living a full life. You've already done the hard part—raising two amazing kids mostly on your own. And now you might be getting a second chance at happiness. Take it slow. Listen to your instincts. But don't slam the door just because you're scared of what might be on the other side."

Anna let out a shaky breath. "I have a question."

"Shoot."

"Do you think God really gives us the desires of our hearts?"

Cate's eyes sparkled. "Yeah, I do. But I also think He expects us to stop throwing up roadblocks every time He tries to hand us a gift."

They sat in silence after that, watching the moon rise over the trees, the laughter of children echoing from the farm like a lullaby.

Chapter Thirty-Four

The soft notes of a string quartet rendition of "Someone Like You" still echoed in Anna's mind as she and Jack stepped out into the warm night air. The candlelight concert had been breathtaking—hundreds of flickering flames casting golden light across the velvet-curtained stage, music swirling through the grand church-turned-concert venue in haunting, beautiful waves.

"Was it everything you hoped it would be?" Jack asked, his hands casually tucked into the pockets of his dark blazer as he walked beside her.

Anna nodded, her heels clicking on the cobblestone sidewalk. "It was ... more. I didn't know Adele songs could make me cry all over again when played by violins."

Jack laughed softly. "Yeah. Something about that much music and the soft candlelight—it gets into your bones."

It had gotten into her bones. So had the nerves.

Anna felt like a fraud in her carefully chosen dress, her hair pinned up with more effort than she'd given it in a few years. Her heels were pinching, her mind was racing, and every time Jack's warm brown eyes landed on her, she felt like she'd been dropped into someone else's skin. Someone more glamorous. More confident. Not Anna Gray, single mom of two, recovering from an emotionally manipulative marriage and barely holding her life together.

Pete had had a way of making her feel small in every room. Even now, years later, those feelings clung to her like static electricity. Jack wasn't like him—not even close—but the fear whispered anyway. That she wasn't enough. That someone like him would eventually figure that out.

"You okay?" Jack asked, glancing sideways at her as they reached the corner.

She pasted on a smile. "Just soaking it all in."

"It's still early," he said. "Want to grab a drink? There's that new wine bar up the street. Supposed to have live acoustic music on Fridays."

"Sure," she said, though her stomach twisted.

Inside the wine bar, low lighting and exposed brick gave the place a rustic charm. Couples dotted the room at small, intimate tables, candles flickering between glasses of rosé and merlot. A young woman was tuning her guitar on the small stage in the back.

They slid into a booth, and the server arrived moments later with menus.

"I'll just have a sparkling water," Anna said after a quick glance.

Jack raised an eyebrow. "No wine?"

She shook her head, folding her hands in her lap. "Not really my thing anymore."

"Fair enough."

"It's not a big deal," she added quickly, not wanting him to think she was judging him if he ordered a drink. "I used to have a glass—or three—every night to wind down. Especially during my marriage."

Jack's face softened. "Ah."

"I haven't had a drink since the divorce," she said. "I just didn't like the way it made me feel anymore. And with my dad's history of addiction ... I guess I wanted to make sure I didn't go down the same road."

He nodded, slowly. "That's really admirable, actually."

She shrugged. "You can order alcohol if you want. I don't mind."

"I'll have what you're having," he said, signaling the server.

She smiled faintly. "Solidarity?"

"Something like that."

They sipped their drinks in comfortable silence for a moment, the soft hum of conversation and guitar tuning creating a relaxed backdrop.

Then Jack leaned forward. "I hate to bring up something heavy on a date, but ... any word on your side about the bracelet situation?"

Anna's spine stiffened. "Not really. HR hasn't called me back in since they told me I was reinstated. I was hoping it was done."

"It's not," he said quietly. "I overheard something yesterday—Thatcher Chambers is still trying to make noise behind the scenes. Calling in favors. Pushing for you to be removed quietly. I'm so sorry."

Anna's heart sank. "Still?"

Jack's expression was grim. "His deep pockets give him a lot of pull. But it sounds like most of the board is tired of the drama. He's got one hold out, but hopefully the majority will sway him to let it go."

She exhaled slowly. Her pulse had begun racing, and not in a good way. "Thanks for telling me."

He reached across the table and gently touched her hand.

"You shouldn't have to keep looking over your shoulder. It's exhausting."

"It is," she admitted. "I keep telling myself to stop letting Pete—or his father—control how I feel. But every time I think I'm clear, they find a way to hurt me again."

"Do you regret going back to nursing?"

"Not even for a second," she said without hesitation. "I just wish they didn't have so much power to make it harder."

They sat in silence for a beat, then Jack tilted his head slightly. "Can I ask you something a little more personal?"

"Sure."

"Have you dated anyone seriously since the divorce?"

Her first thought was Hazard—the whirlwind that had been Mexico, the escape, the reckless spark of it all. He had given her back her smile, and made her feel pretty again. But that hadn't been real. It had been survival. A fling with a younger man who made her laugh and dance, when she didn't think she could again. It was never meant to last.

"No," she said honestly. "I've been too busy. Kids. Work. And I think I needed time to figure out who I was again. I'm sort of still working on that part."

Jack nodded thoughtfully. "I've been in a couple of relationships since—well, since my wife passed. Nothing serious. I work a lot. I also ... have trouble trusting people."

"Yeah," she said softly. "Same."

His eyes met hers. "I can tell you're cautious. I am, too. But I'm wondering if you might be open to seeing where this goes. A few more dates?"

Anna stared into her glass for a long moment.

Was she ready?

Could she let someone in without constantly waiting for the rug to be pulled?

She wasn't sure. But she also wasn't sure she wanted to go

back to the kind of life where she never said yes. Never took a chance.

So she looked up and said, "Maybe."

Jack smiled. Not disappointed. Not smug. Just ... patient.

"I'll take a maybe," he said, raising his glass.

"To maybe," she echoed, clinking gently with his. The word made her nervous, but the thought of never seeing Jack again outside the hospital was worse.

Chapter Thirty-Five

The visit to the prison was as suffocating as usual. Janelle hated it so much, but she always hid her disdain from Clem. He already didn't like her coming there. Today the walls of the small visiting room seemed to close in around her as she sat across from Clem, her heart pounding in her chest. The fluorescent light buzzed overhead, casting harsh shadows and making his face appear a sickly grayish color.

He sat before her with his usual calm, though it seemed deeper now, almost unnervingly so. He was no longer the angry, desperate man he had once been when he'd first entered prison. This Clem, this man sitting across from her, had a quiet serenity to him—a resignation that both disturbed and comforted her. He had been inside for so long, but his eyes, still sharp and calculating, betrayed a subtle edge of urgency today.

He greeted her, then opened a worn Bible slowly, the pages yellowed from years of use. His fingers traced the edges with a tenderness that made Janelle's chest tighten. She watched him, the way his thumb ran over the text as if it were the only thing keeping him tethered to the world outside those bars. He looked up at her, his eyes a mix of hope and something else—something she couldn't quite place.

"I've been reading this. A lot," Clem said softly, his voice almost a whisper, but it was a whisper filled with emotion. "It helps me get through. Helps me keep my mind sharp, you know? This chapter ... it means a lot to me. You'll understand why." His lips curled into a faint, almost imperceptible smile, one that was not quite of joy, but of something deeper—of acceptance, of faith. He read aloud the scripture he followed with his finger.

"'For the Lord loves the just and will not forsake his faithful ones. Wrongdoers will be completely destroyed; the offspring of the wicked will perish.'"

Janelle nodded, though she didn't quite know what to say. Her thoughts were elsewhere, distracted by the sight of his hands, so steady as he turned the pages. Her eyes followed his movements with a kind of trepidation. His calmness was unsettling, and the way he touched the Bible was almost reverent, but, also, Janelle couldn't shake the feeling that he was hiding something from her. It wasn't just in the words he spoke, but in the way he avoided her gaze sometimes, in the occasional flicker of unease that danced behind his eyes.

And then—there it was.

As Clem continued to read, her gaze dropped to the page in front of him. Among the well-worn lines of scripture, something caught her eye. Something that didn't belong. There, nestled between the thick pages of the Bible, was the unmistakable tip of a cigarette butt—its dark edge sticking out slightly, as if it had been carefully tucked away.

Her heart skipped a beat. Her breath hitched in her throat.

He'd done it. Despite his reluctance to blame another man without proof, he was trusting her and had provided the next step.

She didn't dare look up, didn't dare make a move. She knew the guard was watching from the corner of the room, his eyes trained on the visitors. Her pulse raced as the moment pressed down on her chest. The cigarette wasn't just a cigarette. She had to be careful—any wrong move, any sudden action, and the guard would notice. They were both in the same room, but it was a world of difference between them. Clem had been trained in subtlety, in secrecy, and, now, so had she.

Slowly, cautiously, Janelle leaned forward, her movements as quiet as the breath that escaped her lips. She could feel the sweat forming on the back of her neck as her fingers brushed against the Bible, lightly grazing the edge of the cigarette butt. She closed her fingers around it, gently lifting it without disturbing the rest of the pages. As if the universe itself were watching, the moment felt fragile, like the smallest sound could shatter everything. Her heartbeat echoed in her ears, drowning out everything else as she slid the object into her sleeve, her fingers trembling.

Clem didn't seem to notice. He continued reading, his voice steady but increasingly hollow. "... and I will bless those who bless you, and whoever curses you, I will curse." He paused and looked up at Janelle, as though searching for her reaction to something he had just said. But Janelle's mind was elsewhere, her focus entirely on what was hidden in her sleeve, on the cigarette that could change everything.

She forced a smile, nodding at the right moments, pretending to listen as Clem recited more verses. She hadn't clung to her faith during the last ten years. If anything, she'd abandoned it as God had abandoned them in their time of need.

Clem's voice was soothing, a quiet lull, but Janelle felt like she was being pulled in two directions at once. She had to stay in the moment, had to play along. She had to make the guard believe that she was listening, that this was just another visit, just another conversation. But inside, her mind raced.

Finally, the guard signaled for the visit to end. Janelle stood up, her hands shaking ever so slightly. Clem rose as well, meeting her with that same steady gaze, that same unsettling calm. He didn't say much, just gave her a tight hug, his arms—as well as possible with handcuffs—encircling her in a way that made her feel both protected and like a prisoner at the same time.

"Be careful," Clem whispered as he pulled away. "Don't let them see it. If this doesn't match the scene, we leave Mannopi alone."

Janelle nodded, her throat tight with emotion. She didn't want to let go, didn't want to leave him again. But she had to. She had to take this step, and Clem had trusted her with something—something that could change everything.

She walked out of the meeting room, the guard's eyes still following her, and then, finally, after a stressful walk through the halls, she was outside. Taylor and Sam were waiting for her, their eyes searching her face for any sign of what had happened inside. She walked toward them, clutching the end of her sleeve with her fingers, willing the cigarette butt to not fall out.

Her heart raced, but she couldn't decide if she felt exhilarated or terrified.

"We have something," she said, her voice shaking slightly as she reached them and climbed into the back seat of the truck. She pulled the cigarette from her sleeve and handed it over to Taylor. "It's from Clem. He hid it in his Bible. It could be the proof we need."

Taylor's eyes widened, and Sam leaned in closer, taking a deep breath as he examined it. "We need to get this tested," he said, his voice firm. "This could be the breakthrough we've been waiting for."

"I'll call Thompson," Taylor said, already pulling her phone from her pocket so they could try to reach the attorney before he left for the afternoon.

Sam started the car, and they were off.

Back in town, they drove straight to John Thompson's office. He was already waiting for them when they arrived, his usual serious expression softened by the hint of something approaching optimism.

"I've seen it all, but this ... this is interesting," John said, carefully examining the cigarette butt. He was quick to set up an official forensics test, the next step being to have a qualified forensics team pick it up for analysis. "If this checks out, Clem just might have a solid chance."

"And if it matches DNA from the crime scene?" Janelle asked.

John leaned back in his chair, his fingers interlaced thoughtfully. "We'll know soon enough. But if this works ... you can't just go after anyone without real evidence. It'll take time."

She looked like the air was sucked out of her suddenly.

Taylor reached over and squeezed her hand.

"I get it," Sam said, running a hand through his hair. "But, until now, we've been chasing shadows. But this ... this could be it."

Back at Janelle's house that evening, Taylor watched Sam pace the living room, his mind clearly working through the details of the case. She went back to staring at her phone, reviewing the last batch of information they'd gathered. But it wasn't the case that was occupying her mind; it was the sensation of something slipping just out of reach.

"I really need to check in on Anna. Find out what's going on with her at the hospital. I feel like I haven't been there for her like I should."

Sam stopped in front of her. "You can't be everywhere and everything to everyone, Taylor. Listen, I've been doing some more digging," he said. "I found out something interesting about Ed Mannopi. Something I didn't catch earlier."

Taylor turned her head toward him, curiosity sparking. "What's that?"

Sam pulled up a website on his phone and handed it to her. "Mannopi's from Ohio, and, while I was looking through his background, I found something peculiar. The Ohio Bobcats ... their mascot is a bobcat. And the school colors? Red and white. Just like the shirt the man in Amy's hypnosis session was wearing."

Taylor froze. It clicked in an instant. The shirt, the angry cat. Ed Mannopi. It was coming together.

"I think we've got our man," Taylor said quietly.

"Maybe," Sam agreed. "But we need the DNA to confirm it. And I think the universe just handed us the golden ticket in the form of a nasty cigarette butt."

Taylor felt the tension in the room lift, but she knew better than to assume anything. They still had a long way to go. But they were closer. So much closer. Sam was hopeful, no longer suspicious that his uncle had indeed committed the murder. She finally felt like they were a true team, on the same side and fighting for the same justice.

Chapter Thirty-Six

Once Janelle had gone to bed, and Taylor was showered and in pajamas, she sat cross-legged on the edge of the bed, her laptop open, the cold case file she'd put together blinking back at her in silent judgment. She'd read the same paragraph three times and still couldn't absorb a word.

Across the room, Sam sipped on a bottle of water. "You're chewing the inside of your cheek again," he said.

She exhaled, letting the laptop lid fall shut. "I can't stop thinking about what happens if Mannopi's DNA matches that found on the scene. Don't you need to go get your shower?"

"Try to relax," Sam said simply. "There's nothing we can do about that until the lab clears the backlog and they get to ours."

She nodded but didn't respond. She hated waiting for something out of her control. Hated it more than almost anything else.

A list.

That's what she needed. She probably already had a hundred of them pertaining to the case, but lists were what made her feel more in control, and it was a habit she couldn't stop. She grabbed her list notebook and got to work.

Her phone buzzed on the nightstand, pulling her attention away. She saw Cate's name flashing across the screen and instinctively sat up straighter.

"Hey, Mama," she answered, already sensing something was off. It was much too late for Cate to be up and around.

"Taylor," Cate said, her voice steady but tight. "Don't panic. Lennon's okay—but she's running a fever. It spiked kind of suddenly this afternoon. She's been fussy, not eating much. I called the pediatrician and we're on our way to the emergency department now."

Taylor's heart dropped into her stomach. "How high?"

"103.6. I gave her Tylenol, and it's come down a little, but they still want her seen. They think it's probably viral, but I didn't want to wait it out just in case."

Taylor was already standing. Sam had crossed the room toward her, eyes alert, trying to read the expression on her face.

"We're on our way," Taylor said.

"Taylor," Cate interrupted, "you don't have to come all the way home. We'll be home in a few hours, and you'll still be on the road."

But Taylor was already shaking her head. "I know. But I need to see her. I need to—" She cleared her throat. "I have to pack. We'll call when we're on the road." After hanging up, she turned to Sam. "It's Lennon. Cate's taking her to the emergency room."

Sam didn't hesitate. "Let's get going."

She nodded, grabbing her jacket and slipping her feet into sneakers. She and Sam simultaneously threw all their things into their suitcase.

"We're not going to get anything done here anyway," she

said. "That DNA is stuck in line behind a hundred other cases, and the lab already said it could be another ten days."

He grabbed the keys from the table. "So we make our daughter the priority. Like we always said we would."

It was a relief to hear it from him, to have the unspoken burden of decision lifted. As much as they both lived and breathed their work, family still came first.

As they packed up the last of their things, Taylor glanced around the room. The corkboard covered in notes. The folders stacked on the desk.

They weren't quitting. Just pausing.

"I hate leaving when it feels like we're so close," she admitted, her voice quiet as she zipped her bag.

"We are close," Sam said, "but it won't matter if we burn out or miss what's happening at home. Lennon needs us now. That's not negotiable."

Taylor nodded, her throat tightening. "What if we get home and she's worse?"

"Then we'll be there to deal with it. Together."

They stepped into the hallway, the door clicking shut behind them. Outside, Taylor took a deep breath of the crisp air and tried to center herself.

She hadn't seen Lennon and Alice in two weeks.

This wasn't how she imagined their reunion. She'd hoped to arrive back home with Janelle's case wrapped up in a shiny bow, everything straightened out and Clem on his way out from behind bars.

"Do you think this is our new normal?" she asked as they climbed into the car. "Chasing justice in one hand and balancing parenthood in the other?"

Sam gave her a sideways smile. "I think this is the version of normal we signed up for."

She leaned back in her seat and watched the map app route them back toward Hart's Ridge.

"We'll check on Lennon," she said. "Get her over this and then finish what we started here"

Sam reached over and squeezed her hand. "Exactly. We're just shifting gears. Not giving up. I'll send Janelle a text so she's not worried when she gets up to find us gone."

And as they pulled out of Kokomo, Taylor let her focus drift to the tiny girl with a fever back home.

Justice could wait.

Their daughter couldn't.

Chapter Thirty-Seven

Anna was halfway through her twelve-hour shift, and, while her feet ached and her stomach reminded her that she hadn't eaten more than a protein bar since sunrise, her mind was focused elsewhere.

The board.

They held all the power in her life right now. The board could suspend or even revoke her nursing license, if they felt like she'd violated norms of conduct.

She hadn't, but sometimes the truth didn't matter.

What would she do if she lost her job? She'd have to depend on what she made from the family boarding business, which was already split so many ways that none of them were getting rich from it. A big part of their profits also went into running the rescue. Donations were hard to come by with so many animals in need around the county.

For Cate and Jo, they loved what they did at the farm. But Anna had another hunger, and it was nursing. Just like Taylor felt about the justice she was always searching for.

Every person was built differently and, while Anna respected those in love with animal care and rescue, she didn't mind it in small doses but also didn't want it to monopolize her life.

Could she forget her own passion and just leave it?

She really didn't think so. After everything it had taken for her to get where she was now with her life, losing her career would gut her.

No one had said anything yet, and maybe that was a good thing. Maybe no news really was good news. But Thatcher Chambers had never struck her as the kind of man who let things go, and the silence was making her skin crawl. Every time the phone at the nurses' station rang, her stomach twisted.

Keep your head in the game, Anna.

Luckily, she was doing just that. After she'd finished charting her assessments, she helped her CNA clean up a surprisingly violent fecal case, changed out IVs, and was now working on handing out as-needed meds.

She was walking briskly through the hallway with a chart in hand when she caught sight of Jack coming from the opposite direction. He was wearing scrubs, clipboard under one arm, his brown eyes warm when they landed on her. He slowed as they neared, and, with a quick glance around to make sure the coast was clear, he leaned in and pressed a soft kiss to her temple.

"Hey," he murmured with a crooked smile.

The heat rushed to her cheeks like she was back in high school. "Hey."

And then he was gone, back to his rounds, leaving her blinking and flustered with a dumb smile on her face as a CNA passed her and smirked.

They'd gone on a few more outings—she wasn't yet ready to call them dates—after the first one. It had gone well, but she was still wary to put a label on what they were doing. She loved that he was including the kids on their outings now, though he was probably using them to win her over.

Not that she minded.

He either put on a good show or he was just a wonderful human being. She was shocked no one else had snatched him up yet.

And still a bit surprised that he was interested in her.

She was no longer the perfectly dressed and coifed Anna Chambers with expensive nails, clothes, and jewelry. She'd turned a lot of heads as that Anna.

Thankfully, Jack seemed to find her attractive without all the armor.

She ducked into the next bay to collect herself and stepped up to the bedside of her next patient, a middle-aged woman with a twisted ankle and an anxiety disorder that was making the visit twice as stressful—for everyone.

"Hi, Mrs. Langston," Anna said, smoothing down the sheet. "Let's see if we can make you a little more comfortable while we wait on radiology."

"I don't like small spaces," the woman said immediately. "I can't go in that tube."

"We'll do our best to keep you calm. You're not alone."

She was adjusting the woman's IV when the overhead speakers crackled.

"Code Blue. Room 208."

Anna didn't even pause to think. She was the closest.

She darted into the hallway and ran down the corridor, adrenaline spiking. Room 208. Her sneakers squeaked against the linoleum. A small crowd of staff was beginning to form as she pushed through the door.

And then her heart dropped.

Kelsey.

The woman was pale, her skin almost translucent, her eyes wide and glassy with terror. She was clutching at her chest, gasping, her words coming out in broken sobs.

"It hurts—can't—breathe ..."

Anna didn't even think. She moved to the side of the bed, grabbing the oxygen mask and sliding it over Kelsey's face. Another nurse was already checking vitals.

"It's okay, just breathe with me. In. Out. Good, again," Anna said, keeping her tone calm and reassuring. Pretending it was just a patient, not the woman who was involved in trying to bring her down.

This was her job. She'd promised to do no harm and to help keep people alive.

No matter who they were.

The door opened behind her, and in came Dr. Fletcher Bane, or as the staff affectionately called him—Fletch. He was sharp, fast with a diagnosis, and had a bedside manner like a brick wall. He made everyone nervous.

Anna briefed him quickly. "Patient's name is Kelsey Marshall. Recently discharged after a case of pneumonia, about ten days ago. She came in through intake an hour ago complaining of chest pain and shortness of breath."

Fletch barely glanced at Kelsey. "It's anxiety," he said, pulling out her chart. "Probably panicking. Give her a sedative and monitor. Call respiratory to rule out anything obstructive."

Anna was terrified, but she had to speak up. "Doctor, her pulse ox is dropping, and her coloring is off. I think we should get a stat EKG and run bloodwork to check for—"

"I said it's anxiety," he snapped, voice sharp. "You've been back on the floor five minutes and already playing doctor again?"

Anna flushed. "I'm not trying to overstep—"

"Then don't." He scribbled in her chart. "I'll sign off. She's stable."

And then he was gone, just like that. The room cleared with him.

Anna turned back to Kelsey, whose lips were a light blue. "I'm going to get you another nurse," she whispered. "I'm sorry."

Kelsey's breath came in ragged gasps. "I called Pete. He said he couldn't come. Bourbon night with the guys ..."

Anna's chest twisted. "Is anyone else with you?"

Kelsey shook her head. She looked more scared than Anna had ever seen her. And in that moment, Anna didn't see the woman who'd stood by while Pete tried to ruin her life. She saw a patient in pain. And she saw herself—alone, afraid, dismissed.

She looked at the vitals again.

Something was wrong. She'd bet on it.

Anna left the room and tracked down Fletch in the hallway, catching him just before he turned the corner.

"Doctor," she said firmly, blocking his path. "I'm telling you—her vitals are wrong. That girl is not panicking. Please, we need to rule out a PE."

He gave her a look of pure irritation. "I already said no. What part of that do you not understand? You don't have the authority to override me. As a matter of fact, I'll have you written up for insubordination."

And, with that, he stomped off.

Anna stood frozen, chest heaving.

"Anna?"

She turned to find Jack approaching, concern etched in his face. "What's going on?"

"It's Kelsey Marshall," Anna said. "She was brought in with chest pains and shortness of breath. They put her in 208. Fletch is dismissing her symptoms as anxiety, but she just got over pneumonia, and I've got a gut feeling—her vitals are off, she's pale, her breathing's labored—I think it could be a pulmonary embolism."

Jack didn't hesitate.

"Okay," he said. "Let's go."

Together they hurried into Kelsey's room. Jack examined her quietly and carefully while Anna assisted. When he stood, he didn't look pleased.

"You were right to trust your gut," he said. "Just to be safe, let's run a D-dimer and an EKG. I'll put in the orders. Call for transport just in case."

Anna breathed out shakily. "Thank you. I hope this doesn't cause trouble between you and Fletch."

He scowled. "I'll handle him."

An hour later, the results were in.

Pulmonary embolism.

Massive, but caught just in time.

When Anna returned to the hall outside Kelsey's room, she was being stabilized and prepped for transfer to the ICU at a facility twenty miles away, and Jack stepped into the nurses' station where Anna stood, still reeling.

"I want you to ride with her," he said.

Anna blinked. "I—I can't. HR said I wasn't supposed to be near her. After everything that happened with Pete—"

Jack's expression softened, but he held her gaze. "You just saved this woman's life. She's not going to care about a suspension or petty politics. She needs someone she trusts."

"She doesn't trust me."

"She just asked for you," he said gently. "Don't make her face that ambulance ride alone."

Anna hesitated. Then nodded.

When she entered the room, Kelsey looked up at her with eyes that were no longer angry or guarded. Just tired. Grateful.

"You'll come?" she asked, voice raspy.

Anna nodded and took her hand. "Yeah. I'll come."

The ride was silent, broken only by the soft hum of the engine and the beeping of machines.

Anna didn't know what would happen when she got back.

If the board would come down on her again. If Pete would stir up more trouble.

But, for now, in this moment, she was just a nurse again.

Doing her job.

Saving a life.

And that had to mean something.

Chapter Thirty-Eight

Taylor inhaled deeply and realized that Cate's kitchen smelled like home. She marveled that, though it was a beautifully-constructed house, that didn't matter. Because you don't build a home with walls alone. You built it with forgiveness, laughter, and the stories that were told there.

Cate and Ellis made everything they touched feel like love.

Bacon sizzled on the stove, biscuits steamed in a basket lined with a faded checkered dishtowel, and Sam had already set out the jam and honey. Jo put out paper plates, plasticware, and napkins. She'd brought over a platter of fruit, all washed, chopped and ready.

Taylor balanced Lennon in the soft carrier strapped to her chest while stirring the gravy with her right hand and sipping coffee with her left. Diesel stood at her feet, not wanting to leave her side since they'd driven through the gates just a few hours before.

The other dogs meandered in and out, hoping for a crumb to fall.

Sam manned the bacon, the tongs clicking rhythmically as he hummed under his breath. Every now and then, he'd lean over to peek at Lennon and make a ridiculous face just to see if she was awake. He was surprisingly chipper for a man who hadn't had much sleep.

Taylor smiled, her body still warm from his snuggles beneath the organic sheets she'd splurged for, on their own bed. They'd grabbed a few winks before giving up and giving in to their anticipation of waking Lennon from the porta crib at Cate's house.

Now she felt relaxed.

It was the first time in what felt like forever that they weren't racing to solve someone else's tragedy. And even though unfinished business still waited for them in Indiana, she'd promised herself she'd be fully present this morning.

For Alice. For the rest of her family. And especially for Lennon.

Quig hadn't made it. She was spending a day with her mother, doing her best in little spurts to try to bridge the gap all her past behavior had created. Taylor was so proud of how far Quig had come in the last year, nearly completely turning her life around. She'd also turned into a priceless employee at the farm and boarding. She was doing well with her kids, starting to date a bit, and had even paid to have the tattoo next to her eye removed.

Yes, Taylor was determined. Quig was going to be a happily-ever-after story.

Cate and Ellis came down the stairs, looking a little ragged but still upright after their long night at the hospital. They paused at the kitchen doorway, taking in the sight of the full table and all the food.

"Well," Cate said, surprised, "this is either a bribe or an ambush."

"Neither," Sam said, setting the last of the bacon down and pulling out a chair for her. "Just a thank-you."

"You were up half the night with Lennon," Taylor added, shifting her weight so her daughter could stay nestled and asleep. "It means everything that you didn't second-guess yourself when you knew she was sick. You trusted your gut."

Cate brushed it off, but Taylor could see how her shoulders relaxed. Maybe it had meant something to hear it said aloud. Maybe it gave her a bit more confidence that she could still be counted on—not just as a mother, but now as a grandmother, too.

Ellis filled his coffee mug. "I was just there for moral support. Cate ran that visit like a pro." Ironically, when it came to family members, especially the children, Ellis didn't step into his doctorly role unless it was an emergency.

"Of course she did," Taylor said. "Mama mode never really shuts off."

Anna arrived next, cheeks flushed from the morning sun and a to-go coffee in hand. She slid into the chair next to Taylor and accepted a biscuit from the basket Sam passed her.

"You look better than the last time I saw you," Taylor said softly.

"I feel better." Anna took a sip of her coffee, then exhaled. "It's been ... a week. But I think things are finally settling."

Cate leaned forward. "So? Are you going to tell us what happened or are we going to have to dig it out one comment at a time?"

By now everyone had gotten wind of Anna's work dilemma.

Anna smiled slightly, though it didn't quite reach her eyes yet. "I got called into a meeting. HR, Monica, Fletch ... and Jack."

Taylor raised a brow. "Dr. Fletcher? What now?"

Everyone knew Fletch—and his reputation.

Anna nodded. "It was about Kelsey Marshall. She came into the ED again. A pulmonary embolism, caught just in time. Jack was the one who listened to me and ordered the tests."

"You were right again," Sam said.

Anna gave a small nod. "She was scared. Shaking. Told me before the ambulance ride that Pete had refused to come with her. Said it was bourbon and cigar night with the boys, and he wasn't canceling it for what he called another one of her 'overreactions.'" Anna looked down at her hands. "She said she knew what it felt like to be treated like she didn't matter. Said she was done with it. Pete's in her rearview mirror now."

Taylor let out a breath. "Good for her."

"She wrote a letter to HR. Told them everything. About the bracelet. About Pete admitting he planted it in my flask." Anna's eyes glistened, but she blinked it back. "Said she owed it to me after I helped save her life."

Cate reached across the table, placed a hand over Anna's. "I'm so proud of you."

"She said Pete was controlling. Demanding. That he made her feel like she was crazy half the time," Anna continued. "Sound familiar?"

"Oh, yeah," Taylor said. "He's always been a manipulative jerk."

"But I'm not afraid of him anymore," Anna said, a quiet strength behind her words. "Not for myself. And not for my kids."

That earned a round of quiet nods around the table.

Before Taylor could say more, Cecil burst through the screen door, nearly tripping over a video game controller left near the rug. His overalls looked fresh and clean, ready for a new day of work.

"Biscuit and Nibbles are thriving," he announced. "Levi says Biscuit is the daredevil, and Nibbles is the sensitive artist of the pair."

"Sensitive artist?" Sam repeated, amused.

"They finally named the baby goats?" Cate asked, already laughing.

Anna nodded. "Apparently Bronwyn came up with the names and Teague didn't object. Which is a miracle in itself."

Speaking of—Taylor heard the clatter of game controllers from the living room and peeked around the corner. Sure enough, Teague and Levi were deep into some kind of digital battle while Bronwyn sat nearby, coaching them from the couch.

"Jack says I could probably get the motor running myself next time," Teague said as Taylor stepped closer. "He let me steer for a while yesterday. Not, like, fast or anything. Just around the dock."

"Who's Jack?" Levi asked.

"Mom's new friend," Teague answered, a little shy, but proud. "He's cool. He's a doctor. But not a snob or anything."

Taylor made a mental note to circle back on that detail later.

Back in the kitchen, Alice was showing Ellis and Cate something on her tablet. "So we're using solar panels to collect power during the day and then routing the energy through a low-voltage circuit that controls the irrigation timing."

Taylor arched a brow. "Is this for school?"

Alice grinned. "STEM fair. If it works, we're going to try to install it at the senior center."

"Looks like the next generation of Stone masterminds is stepping up," Sam said proudly.

Taylor laughed and sank back into her seat, looking around at the kitchen full of conversation, clinking coffee mugs, and overlapping stories. Lennon stirred against her chest and she gently rocked her, taking in every tiny sound and moment.

She was home.

And as much as part of her was itching to get back to the

case in Indiana—to Janelle, to the man still sitting in a cell—she knew she'd made the right choice.

Lennon had needed her.

And so had the rest of them.

They would return to the case soon enough. But, for now, she was where she was meant to be. Home, amidst the noise and the love and the goats named Biscuit and Nibbles.

Chapter Thirty-Nine

Anna sat at the polished conference table, hands clasped tightly in her lap, her stomach a riot of nerves. Across from her, the faces were still—measured and unreadable. Monica, her direct supervisor, offered a tight-lipped smile that didn't quite reach her eyes. Beside her sat two HR representatives with laptops open, fingers poised, as if ready to document every syllable spoken. Monica and Patricia were like bookends, their stoic expressions identical.

At the end of the table, slouched back with his arms folded and expression sour, sat Dr. Fletch.

And at the head of the table, presiding over it all like a judge, was Dr. Sanderlin, the Director of Emergency Medicine. Silver-haired, sharp-eyed, and notoriously intolerant of anything that risked the hospital's reputation, he radiated quiet authority. Anna had barely spoken to him directly in her tenure at the hospital—but she knew enough to be intimidated.

"Thank you for coming in, Nurse Gray," Sanderlin said without preamble. "We'd like to start by hearing your account of the events that took place last week with patient Kelsey Marshall."

Anna nodded, her voice caught somewhere between dry nerves and residual trauma. "Yes, sir."

She took a breath and started at the beginning—how Kelsey had come into the ED pale, short of breath, clutching her chest. How she'd remembered that Kelsey had just been discharged following pneumonia and knew something wasn't right. How she'd tried to speak to Dr. Fletch about her concerns and had been dismissed.

She turned slightly toward Fletch, her tone cautious but sincere. "I want to formally apologize, Doctor. I know it was not my place to question your decision, and I did not mean to overstep. But I truly believed the patient's life was at risk, and I acted on instinct. My only goal was to get her the care she needed."

Fletch's jaw tightened. He didn't say a word. Just glared.

The silence stretched for one painful beat too long.

Then the door opened, and in walked Dr. Jack Hartley.

"Sorry I'm late," he said with a breezy smile, setting his tablet down and sliding into the seat beside Anna. "We're short on imaging techs again."

Even Monica gave a half-smile at his presence. The HR reps straightened in their seats.

Jack turned to Anna, gave her a subtle nod of encouragement, and then looked to Dr. Sanderlin.

"I believe you wanted my input as well?"

"Yes," the director said. "Please share your version of events."

Jack leaned back slightly, hands folded in front of him. "I came around the corner and saw Anna—Nurse Gray—standing outside a patient room. She looked upset. I asked her what was going on, and she explained that the patient, Kelsey Marshall, had come in with chest pain and a recent history of pneumonia.

She suspected something serious and said she'd already spoken to the attending, who had dismissed the symptoms."

He glanced briefly at Fletch before continuing. "I decided to assess the patient myself. She was in distress—her vitals were off, and her coloring was concerning. I ordered an EKG and D-dimer panel. The results confirmed it—a pulmonary embolism. Had we not acted, she could've gone into cardiac arrest or worse."

He paused, his gaze steady. "I know there was some concern about chain of command here. But, respectfully, I think we're focusing on the wrong issue. The truth is, Nurse Gray saved that patient's life. That alone deserves recognition."

He turned, then, toward the HR reps. "And I'd like to point out something else—if Nurse Gray hadn't stepped in, and the PE had been missed or misdiagnosed? That could've led to a wrongful death. A lawsuit. A malpractice claim. She didn't just save Kelsey's life—she likely saved this hospital from a major legal disaster."

That statement seemed to land hard. Dr. Sanderlin blinked, clearly calculating what a lawsuit would've cost in both dollars and reputation. Patricia tapped rapidly at her laptop, making notes.

Monica cleared her throat, then glanced toward Patricia. "We did receive a statement this morning," she said. "From Kelsey Marshall herself."

Anna's breath hitched. Her stomach turned cold. She braced herself for whatever fresh accusation might be waiting in that message.

Patricia opened a document on the screen and began reading aloud:

"To Whom It May Concern,

I am writing to commend Nurse Anna Gray for her care during my recent emergency room visit. Though I was frightened and overwhelmed, it was her attention and persistence that led to my diagnosis and likely saved my life. I also want to share something I should have disclosed sooner. My ex-boyfriend, Pete Chambers, admitted to me that he planted my bracelet in Nurse Gray's water flask. He was angry at her, and at me, and acted out of cruelty and spite. I was scared to come forward, afraid of what he might do. Nurse Gray chose to save me despite everything, and it showed me what real courage looks like. I owe her the same. Please clear her name and recognize the extraordinary care she gave me. With deep gratitude, Kelsey Marshall."

The room fell silent.

Anna's hands trembled. She couldn't lift her gaze from the table. Her chest was tight, as though she were holding back not just tears, but every moment of humiliation, fear, and stress from the last few weeks. It was all laid bare now—and, for once, the truth had spoken louder than the lies.

Dr. Sanderlin stood. His chair creaked back behind him. He looked around the room, then landed his gaze squarely on Anna.

"Well," he said. "That about wraps it up. Nurse Gray, you did the job you were trained to do. Better than most, in fact. It takes guts to follow your instinct. And it takes grace to do it under fire. You've got both."

He turned toward the others. "I'd say she's owed more than just an apology."

Then, in his usual brisk fashion, he gathered his papers, nodded once at Anna, and said as he walked out, "And I'll have a few words with Thatcher Chambers next weekend. On the golf course."

When the door shut behind him, silence lingered for a moment.

Then Monica turned to Anna, her expression softening. "I'm so sorry, Anna. Truly. I failed you. We all did. You were put in an impossible position, and you didn't just survive it—you rose above it."

The HR representative spoke next. "Your file will reflect a commendation for exceptional performance under pressure. All prior notes from the original accusation with the jewelry have been removed. As far as we're concerned, you're owed a clean slate—and our gratitude."

Fletch remained stone-faced, but he didn't speak. Jack, beside her, gave Anna a wink and reached out to squeeze her hand under the table.

It was over.

Not just the accusation, and not just the smear campaign. But the long, slow war Anna had been waging with herself—over whether she was capable, whether she belonged, whether she could stand tall after so many years of being made to feel small.

The meeting concluded with formal apologies, a few polite nods, and murmurs of dismissal. But Anna couldn't move just yet.

She sat in her chair, the rush of emotion finally catching up. There was relief. There was gratitude. But, most of all ... there was pride.

She had stood her ground. And she had won.

That night at home, Bronwyn curled up beside her on the couch.

"Did you fix it, Mom?"

Anna kissed her daughter's forehead. "I think so, baby.

Remember, though, sometimes we don't get to fix everything. But we can tell the truth. We can stand up for ourselves. All that together will help set things right."

She looked at her daughter's eyes—wide, strong, brave.

"And now and then, that matters more than anything," she said, finishing the subject for what she hoped was the last time.

Chapter Forty

Suspense can sharpen the world, making a ticking clock sound bolder, the breath tighter, and the mind louder than reason. Taylor and Sam sat across from defense attorney John Thompson and Prosecutor Rosana Calloway in the gray-green conference room of the Kokomo courthouse. Lennon was tucked into Sam's chest, sleeping contentedly in the military-green cloth papoose he wore. Rosana looked a bit surprised when she'd first seen the baby, but quickly recovered and went back to her usual ice queen expression.

Beside them, Janelle perched on the edge of her seat, her hands tightly clasped in her lap like she was bracing for a crash she wasn't sure would come.

Silence lingered until John Thompson cleared his throat and opened the manila envelope in front of him. He slid a printed document across the table toward Rosana. "Here's a copy of what I emailed you this morning. It's the same lab's report—DNA analysis results." His voice carried the practiced calm of someone who had done this too many times, but the flicker of hope in his eyes gave him away. "The sample came from a fellow inmate currently incarcerated at the same facility as Clem Tiffin. We obtained it quietly.

No press, no notice. The match to the DNA found on and in Alma Jennings' person at the crime scene is solid. Very solid. And, as you now know, does not belong to Clem Tiffin."

Rosana adjusted her reading glasses and scanned the top of the report, flipping the first page with a quick flick of her manicured nails. "Edward Mannopi." Her eyes narrowed. "My first question is, how exactly was his name brought into question?"

"I'll let Janelle tell you that," Thompson said.

Janelle, who had barely moved until now, straightened. "I saw his photo online." Her voice trembled slightly at first, but steadied as she continued. "I was digging—again. I came across a news article about him and ... I don't know. He looked like Clem. The resemblance was eerie. Something about his eyes, his build. It got under my skin. And when I read what he was in prison for—sexual violence, a long string of offenses ..." She hesitated. "I don't know how or why the article landed in front of me that night. Call it divine intervention if you will."

Rosana arched a brow, not quite skeptical, but cautious. "That's not an evidentiary path I can follow in court. But—" she tapped the report "—there are other details that have made us look at Mr. Mannopi more seriously."

Taylor's pulse thrummed beneath her skin.

Rosana looked at her then, her eyes clear and serious. "I'm not going to avoid what's obvious. This man fits the profile of Alma Jennings' killer far more convincingly than Clem Tiffin ever did. The crime scene, the pattern, the method ... but we need to tread carefully. We need to verify his whereabouts the night of the crime. We can't spook him before we get the truth."

Taylor nodded slowly, trying not to show her excitement. Janelle had fought so long and so hard—file after file, interview after interview, years of doubt and hope and heartbreak.

Rosana set down the report and folded her hands. "Your

email, John," she said, nodding toward him, "prompted me to review the entirety of Edward Mannopi's file. I read through his history, his prior offenses, the pathology reports. And I have to tell you ... my jaw dropped." She turned toward Janelle. "I see why you're fighting. And I'm here now, officially, because I believe it's worth pursuing. I'm never too proud to admit when I might be wrong."

Janelle's lips parted, but no words came. Her throat bobbed with a swallow. For a long moment, she simply blinked, overwhelmed.

"But," Rosana continued, her tone gentle but firm, "what we are discussing today is not certitude. Not yet. The match is strong, but it's not enough to charge Mannopi with aggravated murder—not yet. Still, it's disconcerting, and we believe it's enough to move forward. To dig. To question. To press where it hurts."

She turned her full attention to Janelle. "We've already requested clearance to interview Mannopi. My investigators will speak with him directly in the coming days. Quietly. Thoroughly. We won't tip our hand."

Janelle exhaled, a sound of both release and disbelief. "Then ... this might really clear Clem?"

"Don't jump too far ahead. We're not there yet," Rosana cautioned, "but it's the strongest step in that direction I've seen in years. Our goal was never to put away your husband, Mrs. Tiffin. It's justice—for Alma, for Amy, for the truth. And maybe," she added with a softer note, "for Clem."

Thompson leaned forward. "We'll need to have the rest of the evidence retested. Anything that's still available. Every scrap, every swab. We have a real shot at getting this right, and I don't want anything to go wrong."

Sam reached under the table and took Taylor's hand,

squeezing it gently. She glanced over at him, seeing the same fire in his eyes that had pulled her to him in the first place.

"We've already set that in motion," Rosana assured them. "Labs are slow, but we'll push. Time matters."

Janelle's gaze met Taylor's then, and, this time, her voice found the strength it needed. "Thank you. I know you probably think you're just doing your job, but ... we wouldn't have gotten this far without you and Sam. Without Graystone."

Taylor smiled, small and sincere. "You did the work. We just helped get the wheels turning."

Rosana stood, tucking the report back into the folder. "We'll keep you in the loop as this unfolds. I give you my word."

The late morning sun felt oddly celebratory as they stepped outside the courthouse.

Taylor's shoes clicked softly against the pavement, her shoulders looser than they'd been in weeks. "It feels ... strange," she murmured, eyes squinting against the brightness. "Lighter."

"Like closing one door and opening another," Sam said, still holding her hand.

Janelle walked a few steps ahead of them, her head high, but her shoulders trembling with quiet emotion. She looked back. "You two are the real deal, you know that? No one else even answered my emails. You gave me the chance to breathe again."

Taylor didn't know what to say to that. So she just nodded.

That evening, back at Janelle's house, the atmosphere had shifted. Lennon slept upstairs in a crib that Janelle had picked up at a thrift store. The house smelled of lemon and rosemary from the chicken Sam had roasted while Taylor chopped vegetables. It was a simple dinner, quiet and nourishing.

They didn't talk much—just sat around the table, the clink

Now and Then

of silverware against plates the only soundtrack. Janelle looked dazed but present, as if her mind kept returning to the words spoken in the conference room earlier that day.

After the dishes were done and Janelle went on to her room, Sam poured two glasses of iced tea and joined Taylor on the back porch. The sun was just dipping behind the trees, painting the sky with strokes of coral and lavender.

Taylor's phone buzzed with a text message. She read it once, mouth agape. Then again to be sure.

"What is it?" Sam asked.

"It's Vernelle. You are never going to believe this."

"Read it to me."

> After speaking to Shelly, we've decided the best course of action is to be transparent about the morning that Alma Jenning's granddaughter knocked on her door. The reason she made the girl sit outside for some time was because her boyfriend at the time, Ed Mannopi, was inside the home. Shelly does not know anything other than he was in close proximity to the crime scene when things happened, and that made her wary to let him know that Alma's granddaughter was standing outside their door.

"Well, that ties it up into a neat little bow," Sam said, shaking his head. "You're kidding me," Sam said.

"There's one more." She read the next one to him.

> She wants immunity but will testify.

"She knew it all the time. I don't care how much she denies it," Taylor said. "But at least it sounds like she'll be a witness on our side. That, along with the DNA, is enough to at least get Mannopi into the hot seat. I think we did it, babe."

He smiled as he raised his glass. "To the pursuit of justice."

Taylor tipped hers toward his. "To justice, the truth, and us."

As they sat together in the silence, a gentle nighttime breeze rolling in from the yard, Taylor allowed herself a small moment of peace. The fight wasn't over. Not even close. But for the first time in a long time, it felt like they were standing on solid ground.

Chapter Forty-One

Anna never imagined she'd end up at an amusement park with a man like Jack Hartley. Yet here she was, standing beneath the towering roller coasters and fluttering flags of Dollywood, her daughter's sticky hand in one of hers, and Jack's warm palm brushing hers in the other whenever their fingers accidentally met.

Or maybe it wasn't accidental at all.

It was a weekend to be remembered, from the red-and-white kettle corn tents to the patchwork groups of families winding through the entrance. The air smelled like funnel cakes, roasted nuts, and cinnamon—all comfort and joy bundled into scent. Laughter floated from every direction, mingling with the occasional screech of a ride and the old-time country music softly playing from nearby speakers.

Teague, armed with a refillable souvenir cup and a map crumpled in his fist, had already dragged Bronwyn ahead toward the wooden coaster. She chased after him, giggling, her backpack bouncing on her shoulders.

"Think she'll pass the height requirement?" Anna asked, watching her daughter's ponytail whip through the crowd.

Jack chuckled. "If not, she'll probably convince them she should run the ride herself."

Anna smiled, her nerves still tucked in under her ribcage like tightly-folded wings. This was Jack's idea. A victory trip, he'd called it. A celebration for how everything at the hospital had played out. For her name being cleared. For Kelsey's letter. For the board finally seeing her for what she was—capable, dedicated, and good.

He'd even insisted on covering the hotel, the park tickets, and meals. "Don't argue with me, Gray," he'd said when she protested. "You deserve something that's all fun for once. And if the only way you'll let me give that to you is by inviting the kids, then I consider myself lucky."

She'd agreed—but with stipulations. Separate hotel rooms. Clear expectations. She needed time to adjust to the idea of letting someone in again.

But now, walking beside him, watching him joke with Teague about tackling the "Lightning Rod" first thing, Anna felt something begin to shift. The wall she'd built around her heart —stone by stone, layer by layer—wasn't as solid as she thought.

They'd spent the morning moving from ride to ride. Jack had sat beside Bronwyn on the swings and held her hand while she shrieked with joy. He and Teague tackled every roller coaster, arms raised high, their laughter echoing above the crowd.

Anna followed, sometimes in the ride, sometimes watching with her phone in hand, snapping photos. Doling out sips of water, and keeping the sunscreen fresh.

At lunchtime, they sat at a shaded picnic table with pulled pork sandwiches, coleslaw, and lemonade. Bronwyn draped across Anna's lap, sticky and content. Teague sprawled out beside Jack, listing off stats for some NBA player Anna didn't recognize. Jack matched him fact for fact, and her kid beamed.

Anna watched it all with a strange mix of warmth and sadness. This was what she'd always wanted—peace, safety, laughter. A man who made her children feel seen. Not obligated to be perfect, or polite, or silent—but just ... themselves.

Jack noticed her watching him. He smiled over the top of his lemonade, a lopsided grin that made her chest squeeze.

"What?" he said quietly.

"Nothing," she replied, her voice just above a whisper. "Just ... taking it all in."

That evening, after the fireworks show lit up the Smoky Mountains in gold and silver, and after two very sleepy kids stumbled off toward the hotel lobby, Jack offered to take them up to the rooms while Anna grabbed some drinks from the gift shop cooler.

She needed a few minutes to breathe. To think.

They had rooms across the hall from each other. Jack had never pressed for more. Never made her feel rushed or like she owed him something. And, somehow, that made her feel even more drawn to him.

When she stepped off the elevator with the drinks in hand, Jack was just emerging from her room, a hoodie dangling from his hand.

"In case you need this," he said. "I tucked them both in. Teague pretended he didn't want a hug, but I caught him."

Anna smiled softly. "I'm sure he appreciated it."

"I'm sure he did too," Jack said. Then he stepped back, not making a move toward her, giving her space even as every part of him radiated the same quiet question: What now?

She reached for the hoodie and paused. "You know ... this trip ... it's meant more than I expected."

He tilted his head. "Yeah?"

She nodded. "I didn't think I could do this. I've been

walking through life expecting the worst from men. From people. Even from myself. Pete really did a number on me."

"I know he did," Jack said gently. "You wear the armor well. But it doesn't quite fit who you really are."

Anna looked down, the corners of her mouth twitching in a smile. "I used to be spontaneous. Open-hearted. Believed the best in people."

"I think that version of you is still in there," he said, voice low. "I see her. Every time you smile. Every time you fight for your patients, or tease Bronwyn, or go toe-to-toe with Teague. She's still in there. Just waiting to believe it's safe again."

Anna swallowed hard. "I want to trust you, Jack. I want to believe you're not going to turn into someone else when things get complicated."

"I won't," he said. No hesitation. "But I get why you'd need time to be sure."

Anna took a long breath. "Maybe I'm ready to call this something. Not everything. Not yet. But something."

His eyes lit up. "Wow. That's more than I expected tonight."

"Let's not rush it," she added, her voice softer. "But, if you want ... maybe tomorrow, we grab breakfast? Just the two of us. Before the kids wake up."

"I'd like that," Jack said. "A lot."

She stepped forward, lifted onto her toes, and pressed a kiss to his cheek. "Good night, Jack."

"Good night, Anna."

She turned and walked into her hotel room, her heart lighter than it had been in a very long time. She'd seen that happily-ever-afters *did* exist.

Her mother and Ellis.
Taylor and Sam.
Lucy and Jorge.

Now and Then

Anna looked at her bed where Bronwyn was sprawled out, then over at the other bed at Teague, his covers over his head. They'd gone to sleep happy.

Things were looking up. Maybe now and then she could catch a break.

What if she did have a chance at a fairytale ending for herself, after all?

Outside, the last of the fireworks echoed in the distance—and, inside her chest, something new sparked to life.

It wasn't just a victory trip anymore.

It was the beginning of something real.

Epilogue

Taylor settled onto the couch, her legs curled beneath her, a glass of iced tea sweating on the end table beside her. Diesel lay sprawled across the floor, his massive head resting on his paws, his dark eyes following the lazy path of a fly as it buzzed around the room. Every so often, Taylor reached out with her bare foot to scratch his scruff, earning a low, grateful groan in return.

Alice was nearby, down on the floor with Lennon, entertaining her with a stacking ring toy and exaggerated sound effects. The baby's delighted shrieks echoed off the farmhouse walls, and the scent of rosemary and cornbread lingered in the air from dinner.

For the first time in a while, home felt like home—solid and still.

Sam came in from the kitchen, wiping his hands on a dish towel and nodding toward the television. "They're starting."

Taylor grabbed the remote and unmuted the screen.

The image shifted to a press conference outside the Kokomo courthouse. A small crowd had gathered behind the podium, flanked by uniformed officers and courthouse staff. Standing at the microphone, poised and deliberate in her sharp navy blazer, was Prosecutor Rosana Calloway.

Taylor leaned forward. "This is it."

Rosana cleared her throat and began. "Today, after a lengthy and thorough investigation—fueled by new evidence and dedicated advocacy—we are announcing that all charges against Clem Tiffin have been dropped. He will be released from custody before the end of the day."

The camera shifted to show Janelle, standing just off Rosana's right shoulder. Tears shimmered in her eyes, but her chin was lifted high, her hands clasped in front of her like she'd willed them to be steady.

Taylor felt her own chest tighten at the sight. Janelle had done it. She really did it.

Beside her, Sam exhaled slowly. "Damn. That's a good woman right there."

"She never gave up," Taylor said, her voice quiet. "Not when the world told her she should. Not when her husband lost hope. Not when the system kept telling her no."

Rosana continued, thanking various legal teams and partners in the case, but said nothing about Edward Mannopi.

Taylor shot a glance at Sam. "She's being careful."

"She has to be," Sam replied. "They're building something. If they even whisper his name right now, Mannopi could get spooked. His people could find Shelly."

Taylor nodded, reaching for her tea. "Her team played it well. The whole approach—acting like they were just ruling him out, not accusing him."

Sam gave a small smile. "He bought it. Hook, line, and scumbag sinker. They said, 'just a formality,' and he sat down for three polygraphs."

"Failed all three."

"And Shelly?" Sam continued, lowering his voice as if the house might have ears. "The second interview we did with her? She couldn't look me in the eye. But she gave us everything. The timeline, the threats. Even told us Mannopi had come home the night of the murder ... soaked."

Taylor clenched her jaw. "Ten years. Ten years that woman sat on that truth."

"She said it's eaten her alive."

"I hope it haunts him worse."

The screen cut away from the press conference and into a live anchor commentary. Taylor muted it again and leaned back, letting herself feel the moment. Not victory. Not quite justice. But progress. Truth. The real kind.

Alice's laughter broke her thoughts. She was making Lennon giggle now, blowing raspberries against the baby's belly. Taylor smiled, a familiar warmth blooming in her chest. The hard parts of this job—the shadows they walked through—it was moments like this that pulled her back into the light.

"I love being home," she murmured to Sam, who had settled beside her.

"Same. And maybe next case, we don't go twelve hours away."

Taylor chuckled. "Please."

Diesel stirred at her feet, shifting to press his warm body against her toes. She rubbed him absentmindedly, her body finally relaxing.

Then her phone rang.

Taylor glanced down. The screen showed Shane Weaver's name. Her former partner at the sheriff's department.

She grimaced.

"I really don't want to talk to him," she muttered.

"Then don't," Sam said.

But something in her gut told her to pick up.

She swiped to answer. "Hey, Shane. What's up?"

His voice was low, grim. "You're gonna want to come in."

She straightened and felt her stomach drop. Had something happened to Sheriff Dawkins? "What's going on?"

"We got a call early this morning. There was a car—burned out. Still smoldering when the fire department arrived."

Taylor frowned. She didn't know why he thought it should involve her. "And?"

"It's registered to your address out at the farm."

Her stomach dropped. "What kind of car?"

"Before we get to that, Taylor, I have to tell you. There were human remains inside. Too damaged to ID."

Her hand went slack, and the phone slipped from her fingers, clattering to the hardwood floor.

"Taylor?" Sam reached for her immediately.

She couldn't speak. Her breath caught. Her mind refused to process the words.

"Taylor, what is it?"

She stared at the phone. Her heart pounded, her limbs suddenly cold. How could she even say the words? That someone she loved might already be gone, just ashes in the wind.

But who?

When she picked up the phone, she braced herself. Home no longer felt solid and still. Not with her world about to be turned upside down.

A NOTE FROM THE AUTHOR

Hello, readers! I hope you enjoyed **Now and Then**, the thirteenth book in the Hart's Ridge series. The true crime wrapped into the fictional town of Hart's Ridge and its fictional characters was loosely inspired by the case of Clarence Elkins, who was accused and falsely convicted of murdering his mother-in-law and attacking his niece. Elkin's wife refused to give up fighting for Elkin's freedom, and, mostly due to her unrelenting commitment, his case was overturned, and he was released ten years into his life sentence.

If you've enjoyed the thirteen books of Hart's Ridge, you'll be happy to know that I've decided to continue the series. Next up is **Tell Me Why**. In it, you'll find that a past Hart's Ridge character needs Taylor Gray's investigative skills.

If you'd like to be notified when there is a new title and pre-order button, you can sign up for my monthly newsletter at the following link: JOIN KAY'S NEWSLETTER HERE

While you're waiting on the next in this series, I have many more books for you to read! I'd love for you to check out my By the Sea trilogy, starting with True to Me, a mystery with lots of family drama that packs a heck of a twist! I'd also like to invite you to join my private Facebook group, Kay's Krew, where you can be part of my focus group, giving ideas for story details such as names, livelihoods, sneak peeks, etc. in this series. I'm also known to entertain with stories of my life with the Bratt Pack and all the kerfuffles I find myself getting into. Please join my author newsletter to hear of future Hart's Ridge books, as well as giveaways and discounts.

Until then, scatter kindness everywhere.

Kay Bratt

*Learn More about **True to Me** at this link: My Book or keep scrolling to see the book description:

From the bestselling author of *Wish Me Home* comes a breathtaking novel about the secrets that families keep and one woman's illuminating search for the truth.

Quinn Maguire has a stable life, a fiancé and what she thinks is a clear vision for her future. All of that comes undone by her mother's deathbed confession—the absentee father Quinn spent thirty years resenting is not her real father at all. With that one revealing whisper, Quinn embarks on a journey to Maui, her mother's childhood home, a storied paradise that holds the truth about her mother's past and all its secrets Quinn is determined to uncover.

But settling on the island has its complications, and with the fiancé she left behind questioning every choice she makes, Quinn's quest for her truth is even more difficult than she expected. As time passes and she digs deeper into her family history and her own identity, one thing becomes clear: Maui is as beautiful as she'd always imagined, and its magic is helping uncover the woman that Quinn was always meant to be.

Get ***True to Me*** in eBook, Paperback, and Audio here:
TRUE TO ME (Kindle)

About the Author

Photo © 2021 Stephanie Crump Photography

Writer, Rescuer, Wanderer

Kay Bratt is the powerhouse author behind over 40 internationally bestselling books that span genres from mystery and women's fiction to memoir and historical fiction. Her books are renowned for delivering an emotional wallop wrapped in gripping storylines. Her Hart's Ridge small-town mystery series earned her the coveted title of Amazon All Star Author and continues to be one of her most successful projects out of her more than two million books sold around the world.

Kay's literary works have sparked lively book club discussions wide-reaching, with her works translated into multiple languages, including German, Korean, Chinese, Hungarian, Czech, and Estonian.

Beyond her writing, Kay passionately dedicates herself to rescue missions, championing animal welfare as the former Director of Advocacy for Yorkie Rescue of the Carolinas. She considers herself a lifelong advocate for children, having volunteered extensively in a Chinese orphanage and supported nonprofit organizations like An Orphan's Wish (AOW), Pearl River Outreach, and Love Without Boundaries. In the USA, Kay served as a Court Appointed Special Advocate (CASA) for abused and neglected children in Georgia, as well as spearheaded numerous outreach programs for underprivileged kids in South Carolina.

As a wanderlust-driven soul, Kay has called nearly three dozen different homes on two continents her own. Her globe-trotting adventures have taken her to captivating destinations across Mexico, Thailand, Malaysia, China, the Philippines, Central America, the Bahamas, and Australia. Today, she and her soulmate of 30 years find their sanctuary by the serene banks of Lake Hartwell in Georgia, USA.

Described as southern, spicy, and a touch sassy, Kay loves to share her life's antics with the Bratt Pack on social media. Follow her on Facebook, Twitter, and Instagram to join the fun and buckle up for the ride of a lifetime. Explore her popular catalog of published works at Kay Bratt Dot-Com and never miss a new release (or her latest Bratt Pack drama) by signing up for her monthly email newsletter.

For more information, visit www.kaybratt.com.

Made in the USA
Monee, IL
05 October 2025